GET MONEY CHICKS

A novel by

ANNA J.

Q-Boro Books
WWW.QBOROBOOKS.COM

An Urban Entertainment Company

ISBN-13: 978-1-933967-17-2
ISBN-10: 1-933967-17-X
LCCN: 2006936961

First Printing September 2007
Printed in the United States of America

10 9 8 7 6 5 4 3 2

Cover Copyright © 2006 by Q-BORO BOOKS all rights reserved
Cover layout/design by Candace K. Cottrell
Cover photo by Jlove Images; Model: Jeniffer
Editors: Anita Diggs, Candace K. Cottrell

Q-BORO BOOKS
Jamaica, Queens NY 11434
WWW.QBOROBOOKS.COM

Acknowledgments

When I first decided that I wanted to be a published author, I was scared to death. I wasn't sure that I had a hot enough product to put out there, and here I am three novels and several short stories later. Only by the grace of God am I able to keep making this happen, and all praises are due to Him for giving me a vessel to express myself. Thanks for keeping me humble.

First, I'd like to thank my family for being so supportive. To my mom, my sister, and dad for being my biggest supporters. Paul, you have especially been riding out for me since day one, and I fools with you because you are not afraid to challenge me to do better. We see the same vision, and I'm glad I have you in my corner.

To the crew: Karen, Sandy, and Michelle. Thank you so much for everything. Karen, didn't I tell you it would get better? God already has a plan. We just have to slow down long enough let him do his thing. Sandy, seems like you back on top, huh? Girl, I'm so happy for you, and I'm glad that everything with you has gotten better. Michelle, I know it's been an uphill ride since Harry passed away, and believe me when I tell you that we miss him, too. You doing your thing, though. Stay strong, baby girl. Keep living. So, I'll guess we'll all be meeting up at Red Lobster soon, huh? Yes, Karen, you're back in the group. ☺ I gotta taste for some of that seafood gumbo and a Bahama Mama, so when we gonna make it happen?

To my cousins: Tisha, Shardae, Marquella, Shalysa, Donetta, Sorayah, Nyser, Tynajah, Daja, Delita, Kashief (man . . . did I spell that right?), Keisha, Malik, Gerald, and Rayshun. I know everyone keeps thinking y'all lying when you say we related, so hopefully this will give y'all some proof. Thanks, y'all, for the love and support, and I'll see y'all at the next cookout or issues party.

To my uncles: Herb and Bobby. Bobby, it was truly nice talking with you. It's been ages, I know, but you definitely have family over here in Philly that's thinking about you. Keep in touch. Herb, you know how it is between us . . . we'll just keep it at that. Oh, and Herb, this is just a word of advice. You don't have to wait for the call to come in to do the right thing. You know what I'm talking about.

A special shout out goes to my grandmother, Anna L. Forrest, whom I was named after. We bump heads a lot, but you always support me no matter what. Good looking out, and I promise I won't sell any more sex books in church . . . unless someone asks me for one. (smiling)

To my God Mom Dee, Thanksgiving dinner is at your house this year, right? Thanks for all of your love and support, and thanks for spreading the word about me around the way.

Along the way I've met a lot of authors that gave me some useful advice, and were just all around cool as hell. Dywane D. Birch, you know you're my future baby father. ☺ You already know that I think you're the hottest author walking the planet. Keep doing what you do, boo . . . our kids gotta eat. (Just jokes, folks!) Seriously, Dywane, I have been a fan of yours since *Shattered Souls*, and I'm glad that we became good friends along the way. Keep doing it to 'em. And to the readers, if this is your first time hearing about Dywane, you are truly missing out on a good thing. Go pick up all of his titles A.S.A.P. *Shattered Souls* will make you laugh, cry, and talk out loud. *From My Soul To Yours* will make you look at life at a different angle, and *If Loving You Is Wrong* will be just what you need to make you look at how your relationship is going. All of these are must-haves for your collection.

Brittani Williams, first let me welcome you to the QBB family. *Daddy's Little Girl* was a hit, and I'm looking forward to what's to come. Thanks for always being just a phone call away when I need to vent or bounce an idea around, and for just general conversation. Thanks for always coming out to my book signings and going on road trips with me also. You know how nervous I get.

King Jewel, glad that we met, and I wish you all the success in the world with *Thirteen and a Half*. We have definitely become good friends, and it's good to know that when I'm in Maryland I got someone to chill with. I can't wait for your next book to drop, and good luck with your publishing company.

Kenneth Whetstone, we came from *Stories to Excite You* together. Congrats on *Rise of the Phoenix*, and I wish you the best of luck on all of your future endeavors.

To the rest of my author friends: Brenda Thomas, Treasure E. Blue, Marlene Ricketts, Erick S. Gray (you know I'm your number one fan!), K'Wan (You killin' the game right now. Keep doing the damn thing), C.J. Dominoe, Nancy Flowers, Azarel and K.Elliott (thanks for letting me participate in the hottest collaborations on the scene), Noire (thanks for the interviews), Allison Hobbs (you are a force to be reckoned with), J. Tremble (enjoyed both of your books), Tu-Shonda Whitaker, La Jill Hunt, Dwayne Joseph, Kiniesha Gayle, Gayle Jackson Sloan, T.L. Gardner, Dejon, Dynah Zale, Vonnetta C. Pierce, Mo Shines, and Madame K.. Keep putting those hot books out there!

Mark . . . book number THREE! Who knew all those years ago (okay, it's only been two years, but it seems like forever) that we would be here? Thanks again for believing in my projects. You know I'm always nervous about a new book, and I truly appreciate you giving me the confidence I need to keep putting them out there.

Candace, how many late nights have we been up brainstorming? Thanks for the hot book covers and your input in the editing process. Thanks also for just being a cool ass person to talk to and for believing in my work. My website is hot thanks to you, also.

Anita Diggs, you did the damn thing with those edits! I'm glad you enjoyed the read, and I look forward to working with you again in the future.

Nakea, you know we go back like a braid set. Thanks for all of the advice and for being the bomb publicist. Now it's time to get into the agent scene, and when you're ready, I'll be one of your first clients. Congrats on your novel, *On Air*, and I know you are going to be tops on the charts.

Thanks go out to Karibu, Urban Knowledge, Horizon, Hakim's, and every bookstore out there for carrying my titles. I wouldn't be known without you.

Gee, thank you, sweetie, for bringing me books when I need them. I really appreciate that.

As the Page Turns book club: thanks for your constant support. Frenchie, thanks for pushing my books at the stores even though you don't work there! ☺

Coast2Coast and Blackthoughtz: thanks for the love and continued support. Keep spreading the word!

Thanks to my people at the job: Keisha, Diana, Rochelle, Alicia, Nilsa, Connie, Markees, and Zakeda for always picking up a book when I bring them through. The support is greatly appreciated. Connie and Zakeda, I'll see y'all at karaoke night!

Jada, thanks for keeping my hair fly! I know ten at night is late as hell to be trying to get a full weave, but you always hook me up. Thanks, luv. Angie, keep spreading the word!

To my girls at Captivating Styles, Dorthea and Kim, and my people at Primp and Pamper, Cat, Roz, Kia, Dawon, Stacy, Glenda, Rasheeda, Lisa, Tawanda, and all of y'all in there getting that paper. Keep tossin' those heads up in there. Milton, I was fresh out of hair school back on 1996 when I started working there. Thanks for giving me a chance to show my skills, and after working there for seven years, you showed me what the real world was about. I appreciate the life lesson.

To my girl Shirrelle: man, how long has it been? Thanks for the constant support and the laughs while I'm doing your hair in my kitchen on the weekends. We are way too much alike, and that's why you're cool with me!

I don't consider too many people my friend, but those that are definitely at the top of the list are: Katrina Jackson and Janice Bond. It seems like I've known y'all forever. Thanks for always coming through and showing love.

Last but not least, thank you so much to all of my readers. I write for y'all, and every time I put out a work of fiction whether it be a short story or a novel I try to give y'all what's real from a different perspective. Thanks for challenging me to do bigger and better things every time. Keep spreading the word.

Anna J.

A Hustle Gone Dead Wrong

"**B**itch, what is you whispering for? I can't hear a thang you sayin'," my girl Karen yelled into the phone over the loud music playing in the background.

My heart was beating in my throat, and even if I had tried, I couldn't speak no louder than I was at the moment. I collected my thoughts as best as I could, but all I could hear were sirens, the clink of handcuffs, and bars shutting behind me. Something told me to leave the club when I first started to, but I stuck around. Now my ass about to be put under the jail.

"Girl, you gotta go get Shanna and get over here quick. I think I killed him, girl." By now, tears were rolling from the corners of my eyes like a run in a pair of stockings. I couldn't breathe, and my vision was blurring as we spoke.

"Over where? Black Ron's house? I thought you were in there pulling a caper?"

"Karen, listen to me. You have to go get Shanna and come over here now! I need y'all. I don't know what to do." I was screaming into the phone and crying hysterically.

"No problem. I think I just saw her pull up to the building. We'll be there in like three minutes."

Instead of responding, I hung up. Snatching my clothes from behind the chair, I slid into my gear quickly and went downstairs to wait for my friends. In my heart I hoped this nigga was just playing a cruel joke and was just trying to scare me. I couldn't go to jail for murder. I didn't have time to be fighting no bitches off me because I'm fresh meat, and, as sexy as I am, there's no doubt they'd be trying to get at me. Just the thought of going to jail had me shaking in my stilettos, and if the tears that spilled down my face were any indication of how scared I was, I knew I wouldn't last a second in the clink.

I paced the floor back and forth, wondering what was taking my girls so long to get there. Seconds felt like hours at that point, and I was about to lose it. Not even four minutes passed, and my girls were pulling up to Black Ron's door. I breathed a temporary sigh of relief as I opened the door to let them in, but the moment the door was closed, I busted into tears and fell into Shanna's arms. If my morning didn't start out bad, my night was surely ending in the worst way. I still can't believe he died right next to me.

"Mina, pull yourself together and talk to me. Where is Ron, and what happened?" Shanna said, making me stand up on my own two feet and wipe my face.

I sniffled a few times in an attempt to catch my breath. We took seats around the living room, and I ran it down to my girls. As painful as it was, I relived my day up to this point.

"I met Ron at the club last night, and we came here to handle our business. He was already drunker then a mu'fucka, so I knew getting ends from him was going to be a piece of cake. He was popping pills and drinking like crazy at the spot, so I gave him one of the els we soaked up in the fluid to puff on afterward. He was outside wilding out, and I didn't want someone else to snatch his ass up." I wiped snot and tears from my face. Me and Ron had been kicking it on and off for years, so it didn't take much for me to get close to him. He already knew what it was hittin' for.

Me and my girls were always about getting that money first, and for a while now we had been setting up dudes to take them for their cash. For the past couple of summers a lot of the guys out there in the Vill that smoke weed had been lacing their els with embalming fluid, better known as wiggles.

They claimed it was a high that you will never be able to achieve with just weed alone, but I'd be damned if I'd be trying it myself. It was supposed to have you so high that you think you seeing shit, but I remember one dude getting high off the shit and he thought he could really fly. He went up to the roof, thinking his ass was really Clark fucking Kent and jumped. He landed on top of a car that was parked below and died on the spot. I didn't need to be puffin' on shit that was gonna have me wilding out like that. When I saw that shit on the 10 o'clock news, I still couldn't believe it.

One night while sitting around blowing a couple of els with my girls, this cat from around the way named Cameron stopped by to chill with us for a while. That was nothing out of the ordinary because we were cool with a lot of the guys out there. We bought weed from them, so it was nothing for one of them to stop by and smoke with us at any given time.

Now, I had never personally seen anyone high off wiggles because we didn't get down like that, but Cameron was known for lacing his shit. So when he pulled out his Dutch and asked if we wanted to puff, we all declined. Sitting back watching him was enough to boost our high anyway, so he smoked his shit and we smoked ours. He was high as a damn kite and barely standing when he got there so I was surprised that he still had enough energy to raise the Dutch to his lips.

We were all cool for a while, but halfway through his Dutch, Cameron starting talking out loud as if he was having a conversation with someone we couldn't see. Me, Karen, and Shanna sat back and watched his ass, cracking the fuck up at him. He was really out of it, and didn't even feel it when Shanna dug up in his pockets and took his cash. By the time he got done smoking the entire Dutch, his head was resting on his chin, and his eyes were so heavy he had to fight to keep them open. Finally, he gave in and passed the hell out.

Shanna didn't want him to wake up in her spot and notice that his cash was gone, because who else could he blame but us for his money being missing? So, we slid him down the steps and propped his body up against the wall on the first floor and left him there. That way when he did wake up, he would just think he was robbed by someone outside.

When we got back upstairs, we were busting it up about what happened, and was trying to figure out how to get dudes fucked up just like that. It would be so much easier to get the money and jet, because nine times out of ten, they wouldn't remember what happened the night before anyway. My uncle Thomas owned the funeral parlor next to the church over there on Woodland Ave., and I knew for sure I could get up in there to get at some embalming fluid in a jug, but we didn't know how to put the shit together.

Two days later, we saw Cameron again and he still looked like he was in a damn zone. I asked him what exactly he did with the embalming fluid, faking like we puffed his el with him the other day and wanted more. He gladly told me what to do. I mean, if all I had to do was roll and el and dip it in embalming fluid and let it dry before smoking it, then I didn't need to get a significant amount, just enough to get us by for a second.

The very next day after work, I went down to the parlor to holler at my uncle and see exactly where he kept shit. I had a juice container in my pocketbook that was almost done so that once I finished drinking it, I could fill it up with the embalming fluid. My uncle was of course happy to see me, and in the cold room where he kept the bodies, I could see huge canisters of fluid sitting up on a shelf.

Me and him were talking over a body when the bell on the front door chimed indicating that someone had come in. He

told me he would be back in a second so I took that op
nity to swallow what juice I had left in the container and replaced it with a full container of embalming fluid. I already
had the container tightly closed and back in my pocketbook by
the time he came back in with his customer. When he went to
pull out the customer's family member, I used that excuse to
leave.

Calling Karen from the corner, I told her to meet me on
63rd Street and I started walking down until I saw her car.
When we got back to the crib, we did what Cameron told us
to do and rolled up three els, each putting one in our purses.
As to not look suspicious we had another el in our pocket that
we kept separate. When it came down for the pass off, we
could be smoking too so whoever we were with wouldn't get
suspicious.

Ron was already fucked up, so when I passed him the
Dutch, he took that shit to the head without second guessing
it. I stood on the sidelines and watched him, but when I saw
that other chick trying to get close, I snatched his ass up and
took him home before she or anyone else had a chance to
scoop him up. She would not be fucking up my money that
night.

I went on to tell them how Black Ron, the largest coke
dealer in all of this side of Yeadon, was popping Xanax like
they were lifesavers. He had already been drinking way before
I saw him at Dixon's, a local night spot over there on Hook
Road in Sharon Hill where all the ballers hung out. He was up
in that piece flashing money like he had just won the damn
Power Ball, and I was on his ass before any of those other smut
bitches could take advantage of his weak state of mind.

Now keep in mind that Dixon's ain't all that big. It's a little
hole in the wall no bigger than the downstairs of someone's
house. It had booths and tables set up all around, and the
dance floor was as big as my kitchen. They tried to pack as

many people as they could legally pack in at twenty bucks a head, so most of the time it was standing room only.

What made it hot was the drinks were reasonable and they weren't watered down. The deejay was off the chain too, and the party popped until about three in the morning. Ballers from all over the tri-state area (New Jersey, Philly, and Delaware) came through, and it was fair game to any sister trying to get laid, paid, or both.

We left there around two in the morning and I ended up having to help him to his car and drive to his crib so he wouldn't kill me and any other unsuspecting motorists behind the wheel. By the time we got to the crib, he was able to walk a little straighter, and he made it upstairs just fine.

My plan was to fuck him to sleep and help myself to a little bit of that money when he was out like a light. I would then ask him for money in the morning because I knew he didn't know how much money he was throwing around last night. I mean, the late great Notorious B.I.G. said it best: *"Never get high on your own supply."* A chick like me will catch you slippin', and then the next thing you know, it's curtains.

By the time I got finished taking a shower and came back into the bedroom, that nigga was lying back in the bed with his dick in his hand watching *Bottom Heavy Hoes* on the television. Silly me thought he would be out for the night because I watched him take that entire Dutch to the head, and judging by the effects it had on Cameron, I was expecting the same reaction with Black Ron. But I guessed I would have to work for my money this evening.

"You feeling better?" I asked him, inching closer to the bed. He turned his attention my way for a split second before looking back at the television. The girl moaning was a distraction, and was already working my nerves. Dude didn't seem like he knew what he was doing, but when you on tape, you do whatever to make your money.

"Yeah, my head is pounding a little, but I'm cool. Thanks

for seeing that I got home. Out of all the tricks I fuck with, you're the only one I truly trust."

I didn't say anything in response; instead, I toweled my body dry and began to apply some of the lotion he had on his dresser. I was waiting for the el that he puffed to take full effect because I could see his head getting heavy. A part of me was hoping that he would pass out before I had to actually do something. I pretended not to pay him any mind, but I saw him go from watching me to watching the porn movie. I made a display of massaging my breasts, and spreading my legs acting the entire time like he wasn't in the room.

"Girl, get over here and ride this dick. What you puttin' all that damn lotion on for anyway? You just gonna be ashy in the morning all over again."

I continued to lotion my body like I didn't hear what he said. He was stroking his dick in a long, slow motion, and I'd be damned if I didn't want some of it. Black Ron was definitely working with some shit. I figured I might as well make it a two-for-one deal. Get the best nut of my life, and the cash to go with it. The fact that his dick curved upward and to the left wasn't lost on me either. It was heavy too, and I knew for sure he would be knocking against my g-spot. My pussy was looking forward to it.

Walking over to the bed, I waited until I got to the side to drop the towel. Through half closed eyelids, Ron watched me give him head while he finger-fucked my pussy and smacked me on my ass. I was wondering for a second if he would be out before I was done because his head dipped to the side at least three times during the professional I was giving him. I started to wonder if I had used enough embalming fluid on the el I passed him.

I knew I gave him the right one because the one I had stashed on the side for my own use was already smoked down halfway from me pulling this same shit on two other dudes. I positioned myself on the side of him on the bed, and bent over

Ron so that my breasts rested on his thigh and my legs were open for easy access. Deep throating Ron was a task in itself, and once I got into a comfortable rhythm, it was on.

Now, this nigga had been drinking Henney all night, so I thought this was gonna be forever. My head skills were impeccable, but put up against double shots of Hennessey, the tongue doesn't have the same effect. To my surprise, in no time flat, I was swallowing all of his babies, but his dick was still standing at attention.

"Damn, girl. If you used your head for anything else, you'd be a genius. Get up here, and ride daddy's dick," he said in a slurred voice with drool running from the corner of his mouth. I could see the effects of the "special" Dutch I gave him, all the pills he took, and the liquor starting to work. It was only a matter of time before I dipped up in his pockets.

Ignoring the comment he made, I did what I was told; riding him like I've been taking horse riding lessons my entire life. I guess my momma's dreams of me being a ballerina was crashed, because the woman I became was nothing like the little girl I was back in the day.

I was on his dick hard, knowing the payout at the end of the night would be marvelous. He flipped me on my back and stretched my long legs out in all kinds of directions, and I could have sworn I heard him saying something about loving me before he pulled his dick out and busted yet another nut in my face. I pretended like I enjoyed it while he panted all hard in an effort to catch his breath.

Reaching over to the side of the bed, I grabbed the towel to remove his children from my face. This dude was a beast, and although I could see him falling asleep, I knew it would be on again in the morning. I took that moment to take eight one hundred dollar bills from his pants pocket, and put it in my wallet before lying in the bed next to him. He snuggled up close to me, and before I knew it, I was asleep, too.

I woke up in the morning to him sliding his already hard

dick into me from the back, and I had to clear the cold out of my eyes so that I could focus. This nut was a little quicker than last night, and I was grateful. I laid back in the bed and watched him stumble around the room, almost falling into the hallway over one of his Timberland boots. I laughed, but not out loud, because Black Ron was crazy and had been known to knock a chick upside the head for less. When he came back into the room, his eyes looked bloodshot, and he damn near crawled to the bed to get in it.

"You gonna be okay, B.R.?" I asked, noticing his breathing was getting heavier and he was breaking out in a sweat. I didn't know what was wrong with him, but I couldn't just leave him like that. I still had to get paid for my services.

"Yeah, I'm cool. Those damn pills got me trippin'," he slurred as his eyes closed, and his head fell to the side.

"How many did you take?" I asked, scared as hell. I didn't know what was happening, but I couldn't call the cops because I knew that nigga had drugs or something up in his camp, and I'd be damned if I was going to jail for conspiracy.

"Like four of 'em this morning, but I'm cool. I just need to sleep it off."

I didn't answer. I just moved closer to him and let him put his head on my stomach. Not too long after that, he was snoring, and I was able to turn him on his back. I watched him for a little while, but before I knew it, I was asleep, too.

"And when I woke up, he wasn't breathing and was foaming at the mouth," I concluded my story in a loud wail. *Lord, please, if you get me out of this one, I promise I'll stop being a ho.*

"Girl, he prolly just thirsty. Let's go see what's crackin'," Karen said, and we all got up and followed her upstairs.

When we got into the bedroom, he was the same way I left him; sprawled out on the bed, ass naked with his dick pointing to the ceiling.

"Damn, that nigga working with that? I had no idea," Karen said as she got closer to the bed.

I stayed my ass by the door, because I didn't know if he was going to jump up or what.

"Damn, girl, I know you said you had a killer pussy, but I didn't know you was for real about that shit."

While Karen and Shanna stood there laughing and high-fiving each other, I was a nervous wreck standing in the doorway. I killed a man . . . I think, and I didn't know what to do. How was I going to get my hot ass out of this mess? I tried to console myself by blaming his death on the liquor and pills, but I knew there was a strong possibility that the Dutch I gave him could have easily knocked him off.

"Okay, I got a plan." Karen's loud-ass mouth brought me out of my trance.

At that point, I was open to anything, as long as no one pointed the finger at me. I should have just let him leave the club with some other broad. There I was thinking about my pockets, and now I had a dead man on my hands. On the same note, every chick in there had the same motive, and that was to get paid. In my eyes I ain't do nothing wrong. If anything, I helped him out.

"Okay, what is it?" Shanna scoped the room out. I was sure she was looking for something to take, and I could care less. I just wanted to leave.

"Mina, wash him and dry his body off. Fix the sheets around him when you're done. Shanna, go get a trash bag out of the kitchen. It's clean-up time."

"I ain't touchin' his dead ass. You do it!" I yelled at her from in the doorway. I wasn't about to go nowhere near Black Ron. The next time I would see his ass was at his funeral.

"Bitch, that's your pussy juice all over him. You want the jakes to come and get your ass?"

I stood there for a second more before I ran to the bathroom to throw up. I couldn't believe the turn my day took, and I knew if nothing else, I had to walk away clean. Taking the rag I used the night before from the sink, I soaped it up and went to the room to handle my business. It was hard for me to clean up Ron's dead body, but what could I do? If I wanted to walk away with a clean slate, I had no choice. I didn't want to get caught so I had to handle my business.

In the meantime, Karen had found his stash, along with his jewels and a couple of brand new button-down shirts with the tags still on them for her uncle. We cleaned as best we could and was out of there in no time.

Back at Karen's crib, she counted the money we took from Ron's while Shanna rolled one of five Dutches. I stared out of the window, watching the world pass me by. I couldn't believe the life I was living. I knew after today, things had to change.

I got up and changed into a pair of Karen's sweats, taking the club outfit I wore the night before and throwing it in the garbage. I didn't want anything to remind me of that horrible day. I came back in the living room just in time to get the blunt passed to me. Inhaling deeply, I hoped the effects of the illegal drug clouded my mind long enough for me to make some sense of what happened. I was scared to death, and even though my girls told me I would be cool, I knew I was waiting for what happened to come around to me.

"So, what do we do now?" I asked Karen and Shanna. The weed started to take effect, and I wanted to enjoy my high as long as possible.

I didn't want to necessarily deal with any of this today or ever for that matter. *I was just trying to get paid. I didn't know his ass was going to die.* That was the thought I replayed in my head to try to remove the day from my memory.

"We wait. I'm sure someone will find his body soon. We just act like we don't know anything and keep it moving. We got a couple of thousand to spend. Focus on that," Karen said.

I knew Karen was right, but I couldn't help but think about it. I wasn't sure if it was the pills or the embalming fluid that killed Black Ron, but I was the last one seen with him, and that was my biggest fear.

My girl Cindy worked in the pathology department at the University of Pennsylvania hospital where they would most likely be taking his body, so I would definitely be hitting her up for the report when the time came. For right now, I would do my best not to worry, but like they always say: "What you do in the dark always comes out in the light."

The Crew

Shanna and I met Karen back in high school when me and Shanna tailgated a game that Bartram was playing against Lower Merion High School. Me and Shanna were already friends from our days spent in Morton Elementary and Tilden Junior High School. Karen went to Lower Merion high school while we were in Bartram.

Shanna had a crush on this guy named Desmond, the power forward for LMH, and when she saw Karen hugged up on him before the game, it caused a problem in Shanna's head even though Desmond and Shanna weren't together. Shanna was the type of chick that just knew that every guy out there was riding her hard. She had a body that was a curvy size fourteen frame, Mary J. Blige's complexion, and Sanaa Lathan's facial features. Shanna was a definite cutie and made sure everyone recognized it. I wasn't a mud duck myself, and people often told me I looked like Nia Long in the movie, *Love Jones*.

In our neighborhood school, the guys fell all over her like her shit ain't stank, but when we got out there to those suburban schools, they preferred white chocolate. When we blew through, we didn't get any play.

Normally, the white kids out there dressed like dorks and weren't into the latest fashions, but Karen dressed like she had some money and looked like she stepped off the pages of *Teen* magazine. She looked like a thick Paris Hilton, and she had the bling to match.

She was in the yard after the game talking to Desmond. Now, at the age of seventeen when you decide that someone should be with you, the first thing you do is make it known. At the time, we were thinking that Karen was just some lily white chick who went to school out there and would back off easily. We soon found out that it wasn't going down like that.

We cheered and partied with the crowd from our school during the game, but when the game was over, we made it our business to be one of the first out so that when Desmond showed his face we could approach him. Shanna checked her lip gloss for the hundredth time by the time he came out, and when he did show his face, Karen was right next to him.

We walked over to him and stood around waiting for everyone to finish. That was when Shanna made her move. He adjusted his book bag on his other shoulder so that he could hold Karen's hand, but Shanna stepped in between them to introduce herself.

"Hey, wassup Des? I know you don't know me, but I've been checking you out. I'm Shanna; I came here for the Bartram team."

"And I'm Karen, Desmond's girlfriend. Nice to meet you."

Me and Shanna had to take a look at Karen because we didn't expect her to come at us like that. We thought for sure she was just going to fall back, but this chick had definitely been raised around black folk. I knew Shanna had to have been salty, but we both knew we couldn't let her get away with that.

"Oh, you're his girlfriend? Wow, they really look over us when we get to this side of town," Shanna came back.

Karen's face turned beet red, but she still held her ground, letting us know she wasn't scared.

By then a crowd started to form around us, both a mixture of Bartram and Lower Merion students. I took my earrings off because I knew we would have to get it poppin' if we planned to have any respect when we returned to school on Monday morning.

"Here we go with the '*oh she's white*' shit," Karen said, taking off her earrings also and handing her book bag to Desmond.

He just stood there with a smirk on his face not saying a word. I'm thinking to myself that he probably didn't even like her ass, but that wouldn't save her from this ass-whipping we was about to put on her.

"Well, you know what they say," Shanna came back and popped her earrings off as well. I knew what she was about to do, so I braced myself to throw the next punch after she swung. Even though it wasn't my fight, she was my friend so when she had beef, so did I.

"No, bitch, I don't know. What do they . . ."

Before she could finish her sentence, Shanna threw a right hook, connecting with Karen's jaw. I followed up with the left, causing her to hit the ground. We both ran up on her and prepared to stomp the life out of her when the school security ran up on us and broke it up.

They took all of us to the office and tried calling our parents, but both me and Shanna's parents were at work. Hell, we lived in the ghetto in Philly. Our parents ain't have the luxury of just sitting the hell home. The principal asked us what happened, but none of us would talk, not even white-ass Karen. A part of me felt bad because Shanna did start with her, and I'd be digging in her ass about that when we got home.

After a half hour of trying to contact me and Shanna's parents, they finally let us leave. When we got outside, we were just in time to see Karen get into a shiny new Benz. She stared at us while we walked toward the bus stop, and a smirk was on her face.

Lower Merion High was a long way from the projects, and

it was a little chilly outside so I was pissed. The buses out there didn't run the same as they did in the city, so the wait was longer. I was pissed because everyone else had left so it was just our two dumb asses standing out there. After about ten minutes I began cursing Shanna's ass out, and when I looked back up, Karen was rolling up to the bus stop in front of us.

"What this bitch want?" Shanna said to me while looking the other way. I just knew this chick wasn't rolling up on us to finish shit. The way I was feeling, she would definitely get fucked up.

"Which way are you guys headed?" Karen asked from the inside, leaning toward the window that she rolled down.

Shanna acted like she ain't hear her but I spoke the hell up.

"Southwest Philly." I bent down in the window.

"Hop in, I'm going that way."

I didn't think twice about that shit and hopped in the car. Shanna was acting like she wanted to stand on that dark-ass bus stop, and at this point I was ready to leave her.

"Shanna, get in the car," I said to her from the back seat.

I sat back there on purpose so that she would have to say something to Karen. How you want to fight somebody over a man that ain't yours? She stood there like she wanted to be outside, so Karen started to pull off. We didn't even get a chance to move three feet before Shanna hopped her ass in the car, and we were off.

That night we sat around and talked at Shanna's house since her mom was still at work doing a double. We had copped some weed from Andrew and 'em up the top and sat back and got blazed. Karen told us that her and Desmond wasn't really an item. She was just using him for sex. She admitted that her parents had cash, but she didn't act all stuck up like them.

We ended up squashing the beef the two of them had, and Karen would come out to the Vill every weekend to hang with us. We would go shopping and all that, and come to find out, she was cool as shit. Even after we graduated from high school and she went to Drexel for a while, we stayed the best of friends.

The bond just got tighter over the years. That's why when all of this Black Ron shit went down, I knew who I had to call. Karen was the rational thinker, Shanna just didn't care, and we were all about that paper. At the end of the day, that was all that mattered.

Front Page News: The Present

We smoked all five of those Dutches to the head before heading out to the mall. Karen and Shanna were having a ball, picking out the latest in spring fashions and trying on sandals. I, on the other hand, was trying to find a black dress for Ron's funeral.

Yeah, I was over there on some get money shit, but me and Ron went back like four flats on a Cadillac. We'd known each other since grade school, and it would be weird not seeing him around.

Word around my way spreads fast, and I hadn't heard anything yet, so I know his body was still waiting to be discovered. I just felt bad for his mom. Who wants to bury their child when it's supposed to be the other way around?

Meeting Shanna and Karen in the dressing room, I sat there and stared at myself in the full-length mirror while they tried on outfit after outfit. Any other time, I'd be getting mine along with them, but today I was truly feeling blue. I couldn't shop knowing I just left a dead man only a few hours ago.

The five thousand dollars I had in my pocket eased my stress a little, but it was Ron's money that I was spending so I did still feel a little guilt. After Karen counted the cash she stole from Ron's house, five thousand apiece was the breakdown, but it was blood money, and I felt funny about the entire situation. Karen and Shanna ain't give a fuck, and spent that shit happily. I still had the eight hundred I took from Ron's wallet before all this shit went down, and that's what I was using to buy my outfit.

I knew I would have to get out of there and get my head together, so I was trying to plot a way to get a family leave or something like that from my job so that I could have a couple of days off. I thought maybe I'd go to Atlanta or something and get up on one of those football players. I knew the Eagles were supposed to be playing the Falcons in like a week or so in a preseason exhibition game, so maybe I'd just head on down and get some NFL paper in my pockets. I also knew that the mall closed early on Sundays, so whatever I was going to get I had better get it, or I would have to come back later in the week.

"Do I look fat in this?" Shanna asked, modeling a tangerine and cream sundress by Big Sexy.

Now, Shanna wore every bit of a size fourteen, but this bitch was convinced that she could still squeeze her ass into a ten. Sometimes I just had to look at her to see if she was serious about what she was asking. There's no way you struggle to get into an outfit that you know is too damn small and have to ask if it looks right on you. Ain't that much denial in the world.

"Do you feel fat in it?" I frowned in disapproval. I'm all for squeezing into an outfit, but some shit you just gotta let go. Ain't shit worth cutting off my damn circulation.

"Fuck you, Mina. What do you know about fashion when you buy everything too big?" She twirled around in the mirror trying to hold in her gut under the too small dress.

"I'm just tryna let you know you look like a stuffed sausage squeezed into that tight-ass dress. You got more rolls than

Pillsbury, but if you insist on not breathing for a whole twenty four hours, be my guest. And for the record, I don't buy my clothes big, bitch. I get shit that fits properly. That's why your stomach got that black line around it now," I replied dismissively. I wasn't the one who had to wear the shit, so I could care less.

"Y'all two fight like a married couple," Karen laughed as she came out in another Big Sexy original.

Now, Karen had a lot of class, and even though she was a gold digging ho like the rest of us, she liked to look professional at all times. She was sporting a cute cream two-piece skirt set that accentuated her size twelve curves perfectly. Her shoulder length wrap laid lovely and completed the outfit nicely. My mind was elsewhere, and I couldn't even begin to look at any more clothes right then. I was just focused on getting through the day.

I did pick up a pair of Jimmy Choo pumps to finish off my outfit. Even though I was going to a funeral, I still had to have my shit straight. Everybody and they momma would be out there, and I'd be damned if they caught me slippin'.

Word gets around faster than a New York minute in Southwest Philly. By the time we left the mall and got around the way, the cops were everywhere. Shanna and I don't live but a few blocks down from Black Ron's house with him living right there on 54th and Grays Avenue, and we had to go past his house to get to the mall. I just leaned my head on the window and closed my eyes after seeing the EMT's bring his body out covered in a sheet on the stretcher. I found it amazing that his dick was still standing straight up, causing the sheet to tent in that area.

I stayed in the car while Karen and Shanna went to investigate. From my viewpoint, I could see his brother, Young Rodney, holding his mom and sister up as Black Ron's covered body was put into the back of the ambulance. There were more chicks crying outside than I could count, and I shed a few tears in his memory as well. True, Black Ron was crazy, but he always looked out.

I mustered up the strength to get out of the car and make my way over to my friends. A few chicks gave me looks of death, and I could see a few whispering and pointing at me as I walked over to where my friends stood. The police gave Black Ron's mom a piece of paper and instructed her to come by the hospital in two days for the autopsy report. I couldn't take all of the crying and tears. We offered our condolences so that I could go lay down.

Karen and Shanna walked ahead of me toward the car. I turned back to take one last look at the house. It was a good thing I did, because out of nowhere I saw a chick coming toward me with her fists balled up, ready to jump on my neck. Before she could connect, I sidestepped and hit her with quick jabs to the nose and throat, causing her to lose her balance and fall on the ground. When I looked down, I saw that she was the girl I saw all up in Black Ron's face the night before at the club. I got one last look at her before the crowd and police swarmed around us.

Karen and Shanna pulled me up the street and into the car, pulling off before the door could shut all the way. I looked back at the crowd and I could see people trying to hold her back. We were up the street by now, but I could hear her screaming that it wasn't over. I knew what that was about, but then again, I didn't. Black Ron never claimed just one chick, and just about everyone from here to West Philly done had that dick, so I don't know what she was all emotional about. All I knew is I had to get right. Right now.

By Monday morning, Black Ron's face was all over the news and on the front page of the newspaper like he was a ghetto celebrity or something. They showed a few pictures of him from when he was young and some of his family in tears. He left behind one unborn child, and it couldn't have been anyone else but the chick who tried to sneak me. The newscaster said that it wasn't confirmed, but he apparently died from an over-dose of Xanax and that he may have had traces of embalming fluid in his system.

His mom, Ms. Rita, was on the news saying how good a man Ron was and how he took care of the community. She had the tears and all while she told the reporter that her son never touched drugs and something had to have gone wrong with the report. I was thinking to myself the entire time that she must have had her head in the clouds because Ron stayed high, and apparently everyone knew it but Ms. Rita.

My mouth fell dead open after seeing the girl who tried to fight me crying on television and holding her stomach. She looked a good ghetto mess, and I could see her eyes starting to get black from the punch I threw at her face. Damn, I done hit a pregnant bitch. I just hope she don't press charges.

I knew two things for certain: the funeral was going to be wild, and I hoped to get in and get out as quickly as possible. I called my job and told them a family member had passed. It wasn't a total lie because Black Ron was like family, and I would truly miss seeing him around. Instead of getting up from the bed, I rolled back over and went to sleep. I hoped when I woke up, all of this had just been a dream.

Rainy Days and Mondays

Young Rodney came by Shanna's crib a couple of days later with the postcards for the funeral, and confirmed my suspicion of Black Ron's death. Of course we all offered our condolences again, and he was cool with it, even thanking me for driving his brother home that night. That just made me feel like shit because his brother was fucked up like that because of me, but I'd be damned if I'd be the one to tell him.

We chatted a while about some of the good times we had with Ron while smoking a Dutch, then Young Rodney excused himself, saying he had more funeral cards to drop off.

I made sure to schedule my time off for the funeral with my supervisor when I got back to work. We had a good working relationship, and I barely asked for time off, so she didn't even bother to ask for the funeral card. I told her that the funeral was being held in North Carolina on Monday and that me and my family would be going down there for a few days to be with our family. She didn't need to know that the funeral was actually on Friday and that Ron wasn't related to me at all. That's why I love white people. They pretty much believe anything you say. She okayed the time gone since I had vacation time to use. They allowed two days for bereavement that I could also use.

Once that was cleared up, Karen got cracking with making reservations for us to go to Atlants because she was trying to get up on some of that NFL money also. Once we confirmed that the Eagles would be down there for the exhibition game, she made sure to book our rooms at the same hotel they would be checking into. Her cousin worked for the travel agency that the Eagles use to make reservations, so it was easy to get the information we needed. All I had to do was get through the week.

I had trouble sleeping all week. Every time I closed my eyes and got into a good sleep, Black Ron's ass kept showing up asking about his money. I was so upset that Karen and Shanna took turns staying the night with me, but by the fifth night, they were both like, "get over it!" Black Ron wasn't coming back, and there was no need for me to be stressing. I didn't shove the drugs down his throat, so I didn't understand why I felt so guilty. All I did was pass him the Dutch; I ain't light the shit for him and make him puff it. Besides, we didn't know of anyone who had died from it without actually jumping off a building or some shit, so what could we do about it?

Okay, so Black Ron didn't completely belong to me, but we shared a bond that didn't need explaining and I didn't expect anyone else to understand. We went back to like the fourth grade when he used to pull my hair and make me cry. As we got older, that hair pulling made me cum and it was welcomed.

I stayed in the house buried under the covers and only getting out of the bed to pee and get something to drink. My mom had called me a couple of times, but I just let the phone ring, listening to the messages that were left on my answering machine and commenting to myself on what was said.

My girls were at my house by nine-thirty on Friday morning dressed more like they were going to the club than a funeral. Karen had on a bright orange halter-top and white capri pants with matching stiletto heels. Her hair was pulled up into a tousled ponytail and her make-up was neatly done. She was working my nerves spraying all that damn White Rain holding spray, but she swore by the shit saying that it gave her hair the bounce it needed since she had to wash it every day.

Shanna was dressed just as loudly in an electric yellow slip dress that hugged all of her unwanted curves and some Jimmy Choo mules that strapped up to her knee that she stole from DSW. She must have been up all night putting that weave in, because Lord knew she was as bald as a cat, and surprisingly, I didn't see one track showing. These bitches were out to get a man at a damn funeral, but why was I not surprised? I was the only one dressed in black, but then again, I was the only one really mourning Black Ron's passing.

"Tell me that's not what you're wearing," Shanna said with a disgusted look on her face like I was mixing polka dots with stripes.

"Ummm, just in case you two heffas didn't get the memo, we are on our way to a funeral," I said with a lot more attitude than they were expecting. Ron and I were more than just fuck buddies, but I didn't expect them to understand that. When all you know is paper-chasing, your humility vanishes along the way.

"Exactly my point. That's why I'm wondering why you're dressed the way you are. Do you know how many ballers are gonna be there?" Shanna replied as if I were the clueless one.

I swear her tasteless ass never failed to amaze me.

"Girl, you better get with the program and quick. You're gonna need someone to replace Ron's ass, bless his heart. If you haven't noticed, we got rent and bills to pay in these projects, ya heard?" Karen chimed in. Her and Shanna slapped five and cackled like true hens.

Karen had some nerve because her ass didn't even live in the projects. Unless her staying in a twelve hundred dollar a month condo in the heart of Center City is considered the hood to her rich-ass parents, then she's rolling right now. Karen tried to be down, but on some real shit, she didn't have a damn clue. I just shook my head and continued to put items in the Fendi bag I was carrying.

"Well, at this point I'm not looking for a replacement. I'm going to see a friend of mine get put in the ground, and this is what I'm wearing."

"Well, do you, boo. But you catch more flies with honey," Shanna replied nonchalantly while adjusting her bra in the hall mirror.

"Hell, or a thong with honey on it!" Karen laughed out loud, the two of them amused by the entire situation.

I just grabbed my keys and headed toward the door. I had my own shit to deal with, and didn't have time for their nonsense.

We all hopped in Karen's car and drove the seven blocks down to The Church of Jesus and His Disciples on the corner of 65th and Woodland Avenue in Southwest Philly. When we pulled up, there were people lined up like they were giving out free food or something. Cars were everywhere, and we ended up having to park three blocks down from the spot because they had Woodland Avenue on lock. By the time we walked up there, Shanna was complaining about her feet hurting and Karen was scoping the crowd looking for men.

"Damn, this line is moving slow as hell," Shanna complained as she hopped from one foot to the other, trying to relieve the pressure from the corns on her baby toes.

"Bitch, if you stop tryna squeeze your size eleven and a half's into them eights, you'd be alright. Hell, half ya heel is hanging off the back of them joints. Blame ya momma for those big ass feet." Karen laughed out loud while flirting with a bunch of guys standing on the opposite side of the street in front of the Rite Aid. She got a few laughs from some of the people within earshot who were standing outside with us.

"All right now, y'all. At least be respectful of his family."

Both of them looked at me and rolled their eyes and I returned the favor. There would be plenty of time for flirting and all that later on.

This could have easily been mistaken for the set of a G-Unit video with all the ass-shakin' and bling-blingin' going on. On the drive by it would have never been obvious that there was a dead man on the other side of the church's doors. As I stood in line I said a quick prayer for Ron's salvation. Ron did some crazy stuff, but he had a good heart.

After about twenty more minutes, the line finally started moving. I looked around at the people that were outside with us and tried to read the expressions on their faces. One thing was for sure; I was about the only one dressed appropriately for the event. Everyone out there was dressed like we were gathered at the Plateau for a Greek show. Ass and titties were everywhere, and there where more bald horses in the United States than ever before because just about every chick out there had a weave.

My uncle had the church set up very nicely for Black Ron's family. By the time we got inside, we had to take a seat in the back because there was no room. So many people showed up they had to start seating folks in the balcony and pretty soon it was standing room only. Young Rodney did his best to hold up his mom and sisters as the preacher spoke about the life and times of Ronald Barkley.

I found it amazing that no matter what funeral you went to, it didn't matter whether the person was good or bad. They could have murdered eighty children on a school playground and got shot down by the police There were always nothing but good things said about the dead. There was definitely sadness in the air when they showed a slideshow of photos from Black Ron's childhood up until now. I almost lost it, especially when they showed a picture of me and him on the dance floor at the Club Lethal last summer. Ron was always the life of the party.

I sat back and watched through my tears as woman after woman went up to view Black Ron for the last time. Some kept their composure, and some acted like damn fools, falling all over the place and screaming at the top of their lungs. One girl almost knocked the body out of the casket as she attempted to try and give Black Ron one last blowjob before he was put into the ground. I just shook my head and cried silently to myself. Karen and Shanna were too busy checking out the selection of men in the house and getting numbers to be caught up in the scenery.

Young Rodney gave his brother a wonderful going home service with doves on both sides of the casket that were scheduled to be let go at the burial site. A funeral paid for by drug money. My uncle called for the family to go up for their last viewing, and despite the nasty looks she got, the chick who was supposed to be carrying Black Ron's baby went up their with the family to say her goodbyes. After another theatrical performance, the casket was finally closed and everyone was seated.

Just as the pallbearers turned the casket around to wheel it out of the church, the doors busted open out of nowhere. A woman walked in toting three kids that looked just like Black Ron behind her. You could see she was a classy woman. She was dressed in all black with her face partially covered behind a sheer black veil. She looked like new money, and her kids did too. I could see from my seat that she had her make-up applied perfectly, and looked to be a very pretty woman.

Naturally, everyone was wondering who she was, and murmurs could be heard throughout the crowd as we all waited to find out how this mystery woman was connected to Black Ron. She didn't acknowledge anyone; she just walked to the front of the church, pausing for dramatic effect at the casket before she walked up to the podium.

Taking her place behind the microphone, she instructed the three Ron clones to stand straight as they looked out into the crowd. She stood there looking at everyone before she began to speak. I wished at that moment I could see everyone's face from her viewpoint because I knew there were at least ten broads in the audience ready to bum rush her ass in front of everyone.

"First, I would like to thank all of you for showing up for my husband's funeral today. I just wish someone had told me about it," she replied, pausing for effect as the crowd started up again.

I had no idea Black Ron was married, and apparently no one else did either. From the ice this chick was wearing, I could see that she was well taken care of. Black Ron kept this one on lock. She let the crowd comment and take in what she just said, causing all kinds of havoc in the audience. She didn't seem fazed at all by the controversy she'd just caused. She merely cleared her throat to get everyone's attention and continued with her speech.

"I heard about the funeral from Ron's cousin Anthony. I thought it was only fair that his kids get to see their father before he is put into the ground. I didn't come here to stir up any trouble. I just want what's rightfully mine."

She went on to explain how she and Black Ron had been married for the last eight years, and even though his mom knew, she kept the secret tight from everyone as long as Ron continued to keep her pockets fat. Their oldest child was seven and the youngest three with a five-year-old boy in the middle. She also informed us that she was four months pregnant with his last child.

I, for one, was shocked. Who would have thought that their mom was sheisty like that? Ms. Rita was a really nice woman, but damn. She kept that one under wraps, which was surprising as much as she was in other people's business. You could hear a mouse piss on cotton in there as Ron's wife finished up her speech and came down from the podium. My uncle opened the casket back up so that they could view Ron's body. I was wondering if something was gonna break out. Sure enough, it was on and popping.

When Ron's wife bent over to kiss Ron on the cheek, the girl who sneaked me jumped up and snuck her from behind, landing a hard blow to the right side of her face. I couldn't believe she did that shit. Next thing you knew, the two women were fighting and the men were tying to break it up. In the midst of the tussle, everyone kept bumping into the casket. Suddenly, the casket tumbled over and Ron's body was laying facedown on the floor.

All hell broke loose up in there, and we broke for the back after we heard the first gunshot go off. Lord, they were shooting in the church, and all I remembered seeing before we disappeared through the doors was Ron's mom trying to protect his dead body from being trampled on by the crowd that was trying to get out. The doves got loose from the cages and were flying around and crapping on the people in the sanctuary. It was a sight.

I couldn't believe the events that took place, and once we all got to the car, we decided we had enough excitement for one day, opting to skip the repast that was to be held at Ms. Rita's house. Shanna walked the three blocks back barefoot, and was sitting in the back picking pieces of rock and glass out of her feet. Her and Karen recapped the events while Karen drove toward the McDonald's down there on 62nd Street, looking in the mirror at every red light, and counting the numbers she got from the guys at the funeral.

I, on the other hand was just glad it was over, and I couldn't wait to get home. I wondered briefly if Ron could see what was going on. I knew for sure that if my funeral would be like that, they could save themselves the time and money and cremate me. I'd rather do without the aggravation.

NFL Weekend

Karen dropped me and Shanna off so that we could go pack for our weekend in the ATL. I was excited because I needed to clear my damn head. This Black Ron shit was getting to be too damn much, and all I wanted to do was lay up somewhere and relax my mind. Karen had to go check on her father and get her luggage so that gave us a little time to get it together.

I ran home and pulled out my Louis Vuitton luggage and prepared to make it happen. Opening my closet door, I carefully browsed through my clothes and only selected the cream of the crop because I had to be on point if I planned to land me an NFL star. They always went for white girls on some Kobe Bryant shit, so I had to make sure I stood out. I didn't plan to wear any panties the entire weekend, but I packed some just in case. We would definitely have to go shopping when we got there, because I knew there would be parties popping all over the place, and I needed some fresh shit to floss in.

Our flight was scheduled to leave at nine that night, and Karen wanted to get to the airport at least by 7:30 so we could check our luggage in and have time to fall back. I changed from my black ensemble to a sexy little pair of cut-off jean shorts that barely covered my ass and a halter-top that dipped low in the front.

I finished it off with a sexy pair of Baby Phat wedge sandals and my jewelry matched perfectly. Before I left, I pulled my hair up into a ponytail and threw on my Donna Karen shades. I wasn't about to be dragging no luggage around the corner, so Karen would have to bring me back to get it. After locking my door, I went around Shanna's to see what she had on and what she had packed.

When I walked into her apartment the music was blasting and I could smell the remnants of previously smoked weed. She had all the lights on, but I guess you can afford that luxury when you ain't got no electric bill. When I walked in the room, she was sorting clothes on her bed, and was only dressed in a thong.

It was a good thing we were cool and I was used to seeing her ass-naked. I sat in the chaise lounge chair and watched her pack and unpack at least five times before I got up to help her decide what to take. She had enough shit packed for a month and we were only going to be gone for four days, but a woman needs options, so I understood.

I helped her put her room back in order, then we sat in the living room watching TV and waiting for Karen to come back. Both of us dozed off for a while, and were awakened by Karen coming in the door.

"I know y'all bitches ain't sleep and we about to get our party on," she said all loud. She flopped down in the chair across from me and pulled a Dutch out of her pocketbook.

"Girl, I had to close my eyes for second, but I am so ready to go," Shanna said, all of us getting hype about our weekend vacation.

"Well, I contacted a good friend of mine that lives down there now. Y'all are going to absolutely love Monica and Yolanda. Monica is dating one of the Eagles players, so we'll be able to get in any party that's popping down there," Karen informed us as she continued to smoke on her Dutch.

We already decided that we would only dip a few Dutches in the embalming fluid to take with us because none of us wanted to have a murder on our hands or any incidents while we were in Atlanta. Shanna spoke with Cameron and he told her that you only needed a few pulls off the el once it was dry to have you beyond faded and that smoking the entire el would put you in the ground. That made me feel worse because Ron did bang the whole thing, but it was time to move past that. We were about to go chill in Atlanta and I had money to get.

"So who is this Monica chick anyway?" I asked Karen, curious to see what kind of person I would be dealing with. I ain't got the energy to be around some stuck-up ass chicks, so I needed to know what I was getting into.

"Monica is the bomb, y'all. She used to live here in Philly, but she got into some shit with this married couple. Let's just say it was better for her to relocate. I met her at an art exhibit that my dad had donated money to a couple of years ago, and we just clicked. I didn't know that me and her sister Yolanda knew each other from Tasker projects until after the fact, but they both cool as shit."

"Oh, that's what's up," Shanna replied while preparing the three Dutches we rolled to take down there with us.

"You remember the boy Rico that used to run shit before he got knocked in prison?" Karen asked between puffs.

"Yeah, I remember him. Word on the street was that some chick he was fucking with got him locked up and that his own boy got him knocked in the clink," Shanna responded.

I had heard about the situation but I wasn't really sure how it all went down.

"I don't know that much of the story, but I do know that was one of the reasons Monica relocated," Karen said while flipping through channels on the television.

This Monica chick sounded like trouble, but hell if I cared. I just needed to get away.

"Whatever, I just want to get the hell out of here. What time are we leaving again?" I asked.

"We're leaving at seven, and instead of staying in the hotel, Monica said we could stay at her house. She had a beautiful house when she was here, so I know her crib down there has to be off the chain," Karen came back.

I was so ready to leave, and after a while we decided to call and see if we could get an earlier flight. Karen's dad has connections everywhere, so after making two phone calls our flight was moved up to 6:30, and by this time, it was already five on the nose.

We moved as fast as we could, each of us grabbing one of Shanna's bags and heading downstairs while she checked to make sure we had everything we needed and locked up the place. It only took us a few minutes for us to grab my stuff, and within a half hour, we were at the Philadelphia International Airport, checking in our bags and eating pretzels from Auntie Anne's while we waited to board the plane.

I was nervous as shit because I'd never flown before, and my ass couldn't swim if the plane fell in the water. By the time we boarded, I felt myself hyperventilating and I had to lean my head on the window and count down from a hundred to get my breathing together. I made sure my seatbelt was buckled tightly, and before the pilot made any announcements, I was fast asleep. When I woke up, we were in Atlanta.

The exit off the plane was quick, and as we were getting our luggage, Karen's friend Monica and her sister Yolanda were walking toward us. Karen dropped her bags and ran over to Monica, making it obvious that they hadn't seen each other in a while. Me and Shanna checked them out from a distance and tried to keep straight faces. Monica seemed like she was cool, and her sister was just a tad ghetto, but I liked it. You could definitely tell they were related because they had the same facial features, but Monica was dressed a little classier as opposed to Yolanda coming out barely clothed.

After a few more minutes of hugs and kisses, Karen finally introduced us to her ATL friends. They were both so down to earth and cool that I relaxed instantly. They were even nice enough to have the escort service in the airport come and get our stuff and take us to the car. I swear if we would have had to walk it, we would've never made it.

We pulled up to Monica's home a half hour after leaving the airport. Her crib was laid. I could have done without all the pink, but the way she had the different shades blended, it all came together nicely. She had black art hanging around her home and I noticed that she always made herself a part of the picture. I was even more shocked to see some of Philly's more prominent people in the pictures, including Judge Stenton and a couple of police officers I saw in passing around town. I wanted to ask her what her story was with these people, but I decided to let it be what it was.

Monica gave us a formal tour after we were unpacked, and I knew I had to have a crib like that one day. I mean, this chick had a portrait of herself painted at the bottom of her pool and shit. Who does that? But from what I understood, she was really rolling in the damn dough, so I wasn't mad at her for flossing.

Since it was Friday night, Shanna and I were definitely ready to party. Monica decided that we would visit this club called Masquerade that was located on North Avenue, not too far from where she lived. Her Philly Eagles friend informed her that they would definitely be partying there after the game they were playing now. We originally were going to watch the watch the rest of the game from the skybox, but we all wanted to chill before we got dressed.

We took turns using the two bathrooms that were located in the hall, and we all got dressed in Monica's room. I was having a ball because that was exactly how we did it at home, but for some odd reason I felt like Monica was watching me. I was sitting on the extended ledge she had under her window putting on lotion. I had my thong on, but my breasts were still out. I didn't see a problem with it because all of the girls were either topless or naked, but it felt like she was just watching me.

I pretended I didn't notice and kept on doing what I had to do, but I would definitely be asking Karen what was up with her girl later on. After spraying on a little Light Blue by Dolce and Gabbana, I slipped into a hip-hugging, sparkly peach mini dress that fell right below my round ass and accentuated my hips just right. The weather outside was warm but not too hot, a nice eighty two degrees. Warm enough to let my hair down out of my wrap and I just pinned the top back.

Karen had on a Big Sexy original, of course; a cute halter dress in cream with a high split. She had body to be white, and I swear her breasts sat up perfectly. Shanna chose a black mini and halter to match, and Yolanda had on these tiny shorts with half her ass hanging out. Monica, of course, was in a pink halter dress. We all wore sandals to match.

After getting our hair right and make-up set, we were out the door. To our surprise, Monica had a limo waiting for us. She had Moet waiting for us inside and of course we had some weed. Monica didn't smoke, but Yolanda was like a vacuum, and she was sniffing some powder on the side as well. That was way over the top for me.

Thoughts of Black Ron entered my head briefly, but I pushed those thoughts to the side. I was there to get him and that crazy episode out of my mind, and that's what I would be doing. Taking a sip from my cup, I leaned back into the seat and chilled. Karen asked was I okay, and I assured her that I was. We talked amongst ourselves, and I was listening as Monica was telling us the problem she was having with her son.

When we pulled up to the building, the music pulsed in our

veins. I hadn't been back to the club since that night I was there with Ron, so I would definitely be making the most of it. I was there to get money, and from all the well dressed men I saw lingering around outside, I knew it would be an easy catch tonight.

Club Masquerade

When we got to the door, the bouncer hugged Monica and Yolanda like they were regulars at the club. Monica introduced the rest of us, and shortly after we were all ushered to the VIP section. There were mad Eagles and Falcons players up in there, as well as guys that I assumed were ballers in the area.

We shared a table with a famous Eagles quarterback, who Monica was dating, and one of his friends. Karen was all over dude like they knew each other for a while, and it shocked me because I'd never seen her act that way. Shanna was star struck for a while too, but our mission was to get this paper so, just as I was doing, she was looking for a victim.

The pickings were on point, so naturally I searched the room for a guy that was already on his dip. Initially I planned to scoop up one of those Eagles players, but I didn't want to get caught up on the news with the shit I was about to pull. I had my eye on this one dude who was sitting in the corner by himself, looking out on the dance floor.

I caught his eye a couple of times, but he would only look my way then turn his head back around. I decided to send him a drink, but when the waitress approached my table, she sat a drink down in front of me.

"I didn't order this," I said to said to her over the loud music. I thought maybe Monica or one of the other girls ordered it for me, but when I looked around, they were all engaged in their own thing.

"That guy over there sent it to you," she said in my ear.

When I looked over to where she was pointing it was the same dude that I had been eyeballing. When he looked my way I held my glass up in salute, and he returned the gesture. Before the waitress walked away, I put the drink back on her tray. She had a puzzled look on her face, so I motioned her closer to me so that she could hear what I was saying.

"Tell him I will only accept this drink if he lets me come over and talk with him."

She looked a little confused at first, but when I slid that twenty on her tray she did as she was told. Moments later he was motioning me over to join him. The closer I got to him, the sexier he looked, but it was obvious that he was high off something by the look in his eyes. His head bopped to the music, but his eyes looked glazed over, and that's when I knew I had this one in the bank.

"What's your name, sweetheart," he slurred. I wondered if he was going to drool, but he seemed like he was trying to get himself together.

"I'm Mina, and you are?"

"Lucky that I saw your pretty ass," he responded.

I swear, men are the same all over the globe, they just have different accents. He was nice and fucked up, so I decided to test him and see if he got down like I did. I pretended that I was amused by what he said, and leaned into my laugh so he could get a good look at my breasts.

"Lucky, huh? Okay I hear that. Well I just wanted to thank you for the drink. Have a nice night."

I moved to get up from the table and he grabbed my arm. I

looked at him like he was crazy, and he loosened his grip. Things were going exactly the way I had planned.

"Ma, don't leave. Dance with me at least. Let's get to know each other."

I let him think I fell for the okey-doke and we got up on the dance floor. He was actually a good dancer, and we ended up dancing through five straight songs. He was feeling all over my body while we were grinding to the music. It was almost hard for me to stay focused on the money I had to get.

"You smoke weed?" I asked him over the loud music as I led him to the front door of the club. A light breeze blew by every so often when we got outside, but the air was a welcome change to the heat inside the club.

"Yeah, I do. Why, you got some?"

"I sure do," I said reaching into my pocketbook for the two Dutches I rolled. I gave him the one I had dipped in the embalming fluid.

"Listen, let's get in my car and drive over to a hotel or something so that we can get comfortable. No sex or nothing; I just want to smoke this in peace and chill," Lucky said to me like I didn't know shit about niggas.

I sent Karen and Shanna a text message to let them know I had left, and to not leave me. There was a Motel 6 a block down, so we chose that one to pull up in.

He took he Dutch I gave him and ran into the building to get the room, practically skipping like he was really about to get some ass. I was cracking up because I knew these ATL dudes weren't ready for no Philly bitch. After a couple of pulls of that Dutch I gave him, he would be out like a light.

He returned with the key and then drove down to the room and parked the car. Within seconds, we were inside. I immediately lit the Dutch I held in my hand so that he wouldn't try to pass me the laced one I gave him. He sat down on the edge of the bed and took of his shoes, immediately lighting his Dutch and taking a big pull off it.

"Damn, this some good shit here," he said between coughs and trying to catch his breath.

"That's that Philly weed right there. Ain't nothing like it."

His chest looked like it was going to cave in from the cough, and I thought I was going to have another Black Ron episode. He got it together after a while and took another hit. Scooting back on the bed, he moved up until he was able to rest his head on the pillow and his eyes were closed. I began to massage his body to further relax him, starting at his feet. By the time I got up to his pockets, he was already out and I took the liberty of removing the money I found. He would be out at least until the morning. I wasn't concerned because I'd be long gone by then.

I searched his wallet and to my surprise this fool had four numbers written next to his signature on two of his debit cards. I took both and left everything else. Creeping out of the hotel room I grabbed his keys off the end table and drove his car back to the club, parking it out in the back with everyone else's and leaving the keys in the inside panel of the door. I was sure he'd figure it out.

When I got back inside the club, I stopped at the ATM to see how much money I would be adding to the three hundred I took out of his pocket. I punched in the numbers in when prompted for the code, and they were exactly the ones to give me access to his bank account. The machine allowed me to take out a thousand dollars on each card, and afterward I stuck the cards in my pocket for later use.

When I got back up to VIP, I was just in time to get in on some pictures with some of the Eagles players. Some of the guys from the Falcons let us take pictures also. They were passing around bottles of bubbly and we were having a grand time. We didn't get back to the house until about four in the morning, and I was tore the hell up. All I remember was giving Karen condoms before I fell in the bed, and when I woke up it was morning.

By the time I got downstairs the football players were gone, but Shanna, Karen, and Monica had smiles on their faces. Yolanda wasn't anywhere to be found, and I remember her telling us she didn't live that far away so I assumed she went home. Monica had made us a huge breakfast, and we got our eat on before we all got dressed to go to the mall.

The limo was outside once again, and we headed over to the Mall of Georgia, located in Buford. We ain't have no shit like that in Philly, and you could easily spend hours up in there. I first tested "Lucky's" card in Nordstrom. They didn't even ask for identification, so I knew it would be smooth sailing from there. I guess because his first name was actually Lauren, they automatically assumed he was a she.

After that it was on, and I tore the mall up using his card in Nordstrom, Macy's, Dillard's, Fredericks of Hollywood and about ten other stores until both cards were maxed out. We sat down to eat lunch, and Monica was gracious enough to pay. We shopped a little more after we ate, and afterward we had to stop at the post office so that Monica could send off her child support check.

I was curious as to why she was paying child support, and why didn't she have her child. She didn't look like she ever carried a baby in her stomach; her body was gorgeous. She just said that her son was staying with some relatives back in Philly while she got herself together down there. I left it at that because it was none of my business.

We hit the club scene again on Saturday night, and on Sunday we just sat around the house and had a slumber party. Monica was cool as shit, and didn't seem half as crazy as Karen said she could be. She could make the shit out of a mixed drink also. On Sunday night, her sister came through and we did our 'waiting to exhale' thing and had a really good time.

On Monday afternoon after we sat around and talked about our weekend, we finally prepared to go, and I surely wasn't ready. Those Atlanta dudes were too easy, and I could be balling in no time out there. Monica rode with us to the airport in her limo, and it was a bittersweet goodbye.

Once we checked in, we were waiting in the boarding area watching television when a special news bulletin popped up. Apparently, Lauren, a.k.a. Lucky was found dead in the Motel 6. The owner of the hotel said that it looked like a robbery. Someone had broken into his room and beaten him to death, but the victim was intoxicated so there was no sign of struggle from him. They found his car parked a block down at a local night club, and he didn't have a wallet or ID in his pockets.

When they showed that guy's face, I almost lost it. I was so glad I didn't go into the motel when he checked us in, but I did briefly wonder if they would be able to trace the charges I made on his cards back to me. Karen and Shanna looked at me, but none of us said anything. When our seating zone was announced, we got on the plane and took our seats, hoping to get to Philly as soon as we possibly could. All I could think was that we had one more secret we would be taking to our graves.

Mina

A Year and a Half Later

"I thought you said you had connections, and you knew someone at the door because right now I can't tell," I said to Shanna in an agitated tone while literally shaking in my stilettos. The hawk was not only out, but it was mockingly pacing back and forth in front of us, occasionally blowing a bone chilling wind our way. To say I was pissed would be putting it mildly.

It had been a year and a half since that fiasco with Ron, and I didn't think I would ever get over the hump. I swear on everything I love that my plan was to give up the ho stroll and walk a straight line. I was doing good, too. Then, all of my prayers and promises to act right went right out the window once my funds started running low. But when it got to the point where I thought I was going to have to sell one of my Fendi bags I knew it was time for me to stop kidding myself and get that money. Hell, closed legs don't get fed, so I went back to what I knew best. Paper chasing.

That brings us to the situation at hand. Fooling around

with Shanna's crazy ass, I was out there in the dead of winter in summer clothes waiting in line to get into a damn club. If it wasn't for the fact that it was the *Don Diva* party, I would have been broke out on their asses. This chick said she knew the owner and we wouldn't have to stand in line, but we'd been doing just that for the past damn hour.

I was heated because instead of standing out there looking crazy with the rest of these hoes I could have been across town working this nigga out of his money like I had planned. Now look at me, a sexy popsicle with frostbite on my damn toes. It took us damn near an hour and a half to get in, and by then I had to pee and was thirsty as hell. Of course, the line to the ladies room was ridiculous, but once I got in there and did my thing, I was ready to make it happen.

I spotted Karen and Shanna at the bar entertaining some fools, and neither of them looked appealing. I started to go shake my ass on the dance floor but my toes were still a little numb from the cold, and I did want to get a drink or two before I started to sweat. On the way over to them, I made eye contact with a nice caramel dream. I knew he was from somewhere else because of the gear he had on, but he was fresh to death to say the least, and I was fittin' to be pushing up on that before the night was out.

We stared each other down, and I was the first to break eye contact as I got closer to my friends. I showed that dude what I was working with, being sure to show my entire ass while bending over the bar to get the bartender's attention. Before I could order, he sat an amaretto sour down in front of me.

"Ummm, I don't remember placing an order," I said a little flirtatiously because the bartender was hitting for something too.

"That guy over there sent it."

Following his finger across the room, my eyes landed on the caramel thug I was eyeballing on the way over. I lifted the glass in his direction, mouthing the words "thank you." He raised his glass in salute, and I smiled before turning my back to him. This was perfect because I had my eye on him anyway. He looked like he had money, and he was already tipsy so he'd be an easy target. This one would be a piece of cake.

"Let me find out you have an admirer already," Shanna yelled in my ear over the loud music.

I chose not to respond because I was still a little salty with her over the long wait to get in the club. And, to top it off, we still had to pay. As if waiting for Karen to wash her hair wasn't enough time wasted and shit. Instead, I downed the rest of my drink and made my way to the dance floor, allowing the alcohol to take effect and my body to move to the beat of the music.

The deejay was playing reggae music, and I was swaying my hips back and forth to "Kill the Bitch" by Sasha and watching my new friend through half closed eyes. I winded my hips and bounced my ass to the beat of the drums, giving him a show like me and him were the only two in the room. The smile on his lips told me that I had his full attention, and by the climax of the song he was out of his seat and on my ass, me riding him like the song lyrics spoke about.

We danced to three songs straight, and by the time Shabba Ranks started in with his *trailer load of girls*, the crowd was going wild. He was moving with me with ease, and I was throwing my ass back and grinding my pussy on his knee, letting him know how things could be if we were naked and alone. They say if you can dance you can fuck, and I would be seeing if what "they" said was true before the sun came up.

The deejay broke the trance when "Shoulder Lean" started playing, and instead of making small talk, I walked away from him, losing him in the crowd. I glanced back over my shoulder once to see if he was watching, and he was. That was how I knew I had him. Now all I had to see was how easy it would be to get his cash.

Grabbing a napkin off the bar, I made a show of wiping the

sweat from my brow and between my breasts, watching him out of the corner of my eye the entire time. He must have asked one of the guys who I was because they all turned to look at me at the same time. I continued to bounce to the music lightly on my heels, pretending like I didn't notice them looking my way. I only recognized one of the guys over there, and he looked like someone I had slayed in the past. No parent wants their child to be known as a freak, but that was what kept me flossy, so oh well.

"Damn, bitch. You were practically fucking dude on the dance floor. I swear you were like five seconds from sucking his dick," Karen laughed with her drunken ass, and Shanna joined in.

"Fuck both y'all bitches because I ain't seen neither of you lonely hookers out there yet, or are the cronies not biting tonight?"

"Damn, Mina, we're just joking with you. Must you be so sensitive?" Karen looked as if she was hurt, but I'm sure it was just the alcohol talking.

I chose to ignore their asses instead, and concentrated on getting with my dance partner on a more personal note. I knew this dude had gravy because they were popping bottles of Cristal like that shit was spring water, and neither of them niggas bothered to use a cup, opting to take the thousand dollar bottles of bubbly to the head.

"Yeah drink up, nigga," I thought to myself. I knew for sure I'd be on that ass and in those pockets by morning. Not that he had to be fucked up for me to get up on him, but I didn't feel like working hard tonight, and him being drunk as hell would make it so much easier for me to swoop down on his ass.

Me and him danced a couple of more times, and I found out along the way that his name was Omar and he was from Baltimore, Maryland. He got a little more free with his exploration of my body, and I allowed him to sample what he had to look forward to. At 3 AM on the dot, the lights came up letting us know that we didn't have to go home, but we had to get the hell up out of there. Before he could blink and get his eyes adjusted to the light, I put my plan into motion. There's something to be said about opportunists, and now was the perfect opportunity.

"Listen, shorty. Me and my homeboy got a room over at the airport Hilton. Why don't you get one of your homegirls and we can go and make this shit right?" he slurred. He dipped back and I thought he was either going to catch the floor with his face or slobber on his damn shirt. I had to laugh on the inside at this one. I felt like I just hit the damn lottery.

"Is that so?" I asked him, setting his ass up for the kill.

"Yeah, that's so."

It was obvious that he was nice and fucked up, and I knew once I put my ride game on him, his ass would be out for the night.

"Well, I can make that happen, but under one condition."

"What's that?"

"You give me everything in your pockets right now, and I give you the best night of your life. That goes for my girl too; just let me know which one your boy wants."

He looked as if he was contemplating what I said, then he called the guy that was interested over and ran the scenario down to him. I waited patiently for them to get it in their heads, and the next thing you knew, those cats were digging in their pockets.

"Listen, I ain't never had to pay for no pussy, but if your dancing was any indication of your fuck game, I'm almost certain it will be worthwhile."

I took the money from both men and discreetly counted out five hundred dollars from the stack of hundred dollar bills they gave me. I quickly summed it up to about three thousand between the two, but Shanna and Karen made me mad, so the cut would be eighty/twenty tonight.

"Okay, papi. I'll be right back. Which one did you like again?"

"Yo, that one right there. That one is right." Omar's friend pointed to Karen.

I instructed them to wait for us outside, and I went over to Karen to let her know what was really good. She was hugged up on the same loser that she met when we came in, but he had to be the thirstiest nigga in there, buying all that damn water. Maybe she thought he had potential, but tonight we had bigger fish to fry.

Omar's friend Cee-Lo made a good choice by picking Karen. White girls are into all that butt fucking and dick suck-ing, and with her ass being so damn tipsy I was sure that was how it would all go down. I ran the situation down to her, and after making sure Shanna was good, we met our rides outside and went to do the damn thing.

We pulled up to the Hilton, and once we were inside, I in-structed the woman at the desk to call my cell phone in an hour. That was more than enough time to do what we had to do and get ghost, and we would simply take a cab once we got down-stairs. Karen knew the routine because we had been doing that shit since we were teenagers. She was more sober now than when we were at the club, so I knew she was in the zone and ready to do the damn thing.

When we got up to their suite, it was laid out nicely. As much as I wanted to, we didn't waste any time looking around and admiring shit. I made sure the bolt lock was on the door so that none of their people could pop in on us. I'm all for a train, but only when done voluntarily. And besides all that, the three gees they paid us wasn't nearly enough.

Within a matter of minutes, we had both of the men un-dressed and laying next to each other on the bed. I was on my knees on one side of the bed and Karen was in the same position on the opposite side, both of us in a dick sucking contest. Omar definitely had the bigger dick, but Cee-Lo wasn't lacking either. Sometimes we did a little girl-on-girl action when we pulled a double party like this, but tonight would not be one of those nights. It was hit it and quit it time, and we had to stick and move.

Moving like synchronized swimmers, we made sure the Magnum condoms were secured on both men before taking position on their dicks. I was riding Omar with my back facing him, and Karen was riding Cee-Lo the traditional way, both men looking like they couldn't believe their luck. All you heard were moans and palms connecting with ass flesh while we rode those dudes like pros.

Halfway through, we maneuvered our bodies so that we were still riding their dicks, but we both turned to the side facing each other. Karen put her legs over Omar's sides, and I put my legs on top of hers because I'm the lighter of the two. We then leaned back on our hands and positioned our bodies into a crab position, bouncing hard on their dicks simultaneously until they were both begging us to let them cum.

Within seconds, we untangled our legs and wrapped ourselves around them, grinding hard until it felt like their dicks would come through our navels. I've never seen a grown man cry, but these two looked like they were close to tears. Arching my back, I bounced one last time and it was over. Omar was clutching the nightstand and pushing me back off him like he was about to have a heart attack.

It took us all a few minutes to get it together, and as soon as my foot hit the floor, my cell phone began to ring. I answered the phone pretending like I was upset that we were interrupted. My fake-ass conversation led to Shanna having trouble with her non-existent baby father and that, in turn, made us have to leave.

Me and Karen got dressed quickly after I came out of the bathroom, and after offering our apologies, we hauled ass up out of there and got home in record time. I made sure to give Omar my cell phone number before we left, and that was how it all went down. I must say, it felt good to be back in the swing of things.

Karen

"I can't believe you are hanging around with those types of women, and I use the term 'women' very loosely. It's bad enough they're black, Karen. I know I raised you better than to be keeping company with a bunch of paper chasers who don't have enough sense to get a job. What ever happened to that wonderful young lady Margo that you were friends with? She was so nice."

I had been listening to my mother drone on and on for the past hour about Shanna and Mina. I say "mother" because a "mom" is someone who gives you hugs as a child and surprises you by adding an extra snack in your lunchbox. My "mother" did none of those things; she just shipped me off to private school with the rest of the rich kids. I had a closer relationship with our housekeeper Inga than I did with her, and I liked it that way. There wasn't any type of love lost between us, and I swear she just had me to trap my father. That's why I'm an only child. I was an investment.

I didn't understand why she couldn't just let it be what it is. My dad didn't seem to have a problem with it, but then again, he had no backbone. He just did what my mom said and let her make all the decisions. I mean, the poor man was sitting there eating a plain egg white omelet because my mother wanted to be a vegetarian. Why couldn't the man have a piece of steak on the side? Damn!

Every Sunday we got together for brunch at one posh restaurant or another, and every damn Sunday I had to go through the same shit over and over again. I was so tired of hearing it, and I swear I bit my tongue so much that I was surprised I hadn't chewed it up and swallowed it by then. My mom lived in the days where white people didn't befriend blacks, but I'm not sure how she still had that mindset in this day and age. The one thing I did know was that it was getting old, and I was tired of it.

"Mom, nothing has changed since last week. Margo is in a drug rehab trying to get custody of her kids. Why do we have to go through this every time we meet up, and why does it matter that I have black friends?"

I looked at my dad for some support, but as usual, he was face down in his omelet, not wanting to be a part of this conversation. It wasn't like they didn't have black friends; it's just that I didn't want to hang with their stuck up ass kids. Just because I came from money didn't mean I had to walk around with my nose up at those less fortunate. And little did my parents know, Shanna and Mina definitely had money. They may not have gotten it through a hardworking job, but they did work hard at what they did. We all did, and if they knew their little girl was just like them, they would have probably had a damn heart attack.

"I don't have a problem with black people, honey. You know that," my mom said in a monotone voice that grated at my nerves.

I wasn't convinced that she believed what she just said and my face mirrored that exact thought. I'm sure she didn't have a problem as long as they were rich like my dad because Lord knows she never worked a day in her life.

"Then what's the problem exactly? We go through this every week, and for what? You and Dad aren't all that on point either."

"Yeah, but we have class, and that, my dear, is all that matters."

"How you figure that when I watched you paint one toenail because that was the only one showing through your shoe? My girls may not be rich, but all of their toenails are the same color."

As our conversation started to escalate, the restaurant got quiet and all eyes were on us. At that point I just didn't give a damn because I was tired of having to defend my friends. I felt out of place with my family anyway, and the hood was where I should have been brought up instead of being bused out to some damn private school. It's too bad we don't get to pick our family because if so, Shanna and Mina would have been my sisters for real. Being well off was nice, but I didn't feel like the aggravation.

"Karen, apologize to your mother," my father stated weakly, still not looking up from his plate. I took a long look at the both of them and decided enough was enough.

I threw my napkin on the table and grabbed my Dooney & Bourke bag from the empty seat next to me. I scraped the chair back loudly on the floor and separated myself from the madness that was going on at this table. They made me sick on my stomach, and the only reason I even showed up to these wack-ass brunch dates was to keep money in my account, and if I had it my way, that would be the last one. I had some shit set up that was flowing along nicely, and soon I'd be sitting on top of the game for real.

"Karen, wait. We haven't discussed what we will be wearing to the captain's ball," my mother called out dramatically like we were performing a stage play.

"I'm not going," I hollered back, not bothering to turn around. I could still hear her hollering out orders from the table, and that only made my feet move faster toward my ride.

Once I got comfortable in my seat, I screeched out of the parking lot and raced down to I-95 on my way to the Bartram Village housing projects to be with my girls. A few stray tears escaped my eyes, and I wiped them away, frustrated that I let my mom get under my skin again. I never thought in this day in age that racism would still be prominent, but my parents are living proof that it is alive and well.

"Fuck them. They don't know what the real world is about," I said to my hazel-eyed reflection in the mirror. I knew where I needed to be, and it wouldn't take me long to get there. I was just trying to get away from that tragedy as quickly as possible. In due time, everything would fall right into place.

Zigzagging through traffic, I pulled up to Gibson Drive with a screeching halt, damn near busting one of my twenty twos on a broken forty bottle. Throwing my pearl Murano in park and grabbing my bag at the same time, I made sure the door was locked before I took the stairs two at a time to apartment 3B, where Shanna lived.

The door was unlocked as usual, and when I came in I found Shanna in her usual spot cursing the television out. Shanna wasn't the least bit concerned about locking the door during the day because either me or Mina were always in and out, but at night all five locks that she had installed did their job at keeping unwanted people out.

Mina was nowhere to be found, and I briefly wondered if she was still asleep after that escapade we handled last night. On the low, I briefly chatted with Cee-Lo and Omar while Mina was in the bathroom to make sure things were going as planned. Mina didn't know that I knew exactly who Cee and Omar were, and that's how I had to ride it out for my plan to work. I knew she didn't let that honey she was on escape without sliding the digits. I took my seat by the window, and just as I was going to ask Shanna of Mina's whereabouts, she exited the bathroom.

"White bread, when did you get here?" Mina asked, walking over to give me a hug after drying her hands on the end of her shirt. White bread was the nickname they gave me when we first met back in high school. I had money, and was definitely white, so the nick name fit nicely. Only they were allowed to call me that, though. Anyone else would get cursed out.

"After yet another wasted moment of my life spent with my parents, I'm glad to be here." I kicked off my Nine West pumps and tossed them in the basket by the door.

Shanna's crib was laid for her to be living in the projects, but after all the fucking and dick sucking she did, it wasn't hard to see why. From the plush carpeting to the expensive black art on the walls to the butter Italian leather furniture and big screen television, Shanna was living like she should be on MTV *Cribs*, and she kept it real all the time. That's why I had to make sure she would be spared when it all went down.

"Y'all hoes rolled out on me last night, but it was all good. I met up with that nigga Chilae, and it was on. I walked away with about two thousand and the Rolex off that nigga's wrist. I'm a bad bitch, if I must say so myself," Shanna said, getting up to turn the radio on.

"It's Going Down" by Young Joc blared through the speakers, and all of us got up to do the motorcycle dance from the video. Soon after, it turned into a booty shaking contest, and we were all in there laughing at each other and trying to see who could get the lowest. I had a lot of ass for a white girl, and I could dance better than most black girls out there, even Mina and Shanna. But since we were girls, I didn't get too much into that. We danced through about two more songs then fell out exhausted on the couch. I was starting to feel a lot better. My girls always made that possible.

"Roll up a Dutch, Karen. It's time to get fucked up," Shanna said after turning the radio down.

I was already two steps ahead of her and had the Dutch cracked, emptied and filled with weed.

"So, where were those guys from?" Shanna asked me while searching through her Gucci bag for a lighter. That bag must have been new, because I'd never seen it before, and we shared almost everything.

"Maryland, I think. It didn't matter because they were paying and I was receiving," I said through a quick chuckle. I had a little salt on me because she walked away from dude with two grand, and all I got was a measly five hundred. Those Marc Jacob boots I saw at the mall were an easy seven-fifty, and that job was easily worth an entire grand. I started to question Mina on the money tip, but I didn't want her to think I didn't trust her.

"Girl, I'm sure that fifteen in your pocket was well worth dealing with their country asses. They looked like they were from the backwoods somewhere." She laughed and moved to give me a high five.

I leaned in to it, but had to pause to make sure I heard her correctly.

"What fifteen are you talking about? Mina only made a grand off that, and she gave me five. Right Mina?" I tossed a curious glance Mina's way.

I swear we hadn't gotten into a fight over money in years, but she would get her boots knocked if it came out that she was playing me. Not that I was strapped for cash, but I didn't play those games with my money being ran to me properly. That's a good way to end it all. Fuck with my cash, and that silly white girl shit goes out the window.

"Uh, yeah. I gave you your cut before we left the club," Mina said, avoiding eye contact with me and tossing Shanna a dirty look.

That didn't sit well with me because from experience, I knew that meant she was lying.

"Oh, if that's how it went down, then okay." Shanna shrugged her shoulders and went back to searching her bag.

"Mina, how much did dude give you for the night?" I asked

again, this time with mad bass in my voice. It wasn't about the money because I had plenty. It was the principle. In my book, half of fifteen hundred still wasn't five, so either my math was fucked up or a new way of doing division was suddenly created.

"He gave me a grand just like I told you, but afterward he slid me two more while you were on the bathroom rinsing your mouth out. I was going to break you off later on tonight as a surprise when we got to the club. You were going out with us for a little while later on, right?" she asked, trying to shift the blame.

"Yeah, I am. It was just that I didn't know about the extra money that's all," I said looking at her sideways. Mina and Shanna were like my sisters, but ever since Ron died, Mina been doing some dumb shit, and this was one of those moments. Her loyalty to the crew was wearing thin, and I wasn't sure if I could still trust her ass.

"Cool, as a matter of fact as soon as I'm done rolling this last el, I'll break you off. I couldn't have made it happen without you, and you know this," Mina came back, still not making eye contact.

Shanna must have peeped the scene, and instead of allowing the tension to build, she started laughing.

"Y'all some alley cat bitches, I swear. Bitch, spark this el and let's get this mutha fuckin' party started."

I let the incident go for that moment, and acted like everything was all good, but I would be watching Mina's ass. She had been talking about getting out of the game for a while, and she wanted to stack her cash. That's cool and all, but I'd be damned if it would be at my expense. Every ho in the game knows that either you marry a baller or become one. I was cool with that, but don't take it upon yourself to tap my damn pockets.

I took several puffs off the Dutch and leaned my head back on the lounge chair. I wouldn't think about it at this moment, but this conversation was not over. I swear, when it rains it pours and sometimes it storms, but I would come out on top. I had to. Between my mom's bullshit and the shit in these streets, I didn't know which was worse, but I knew people in high places, and it was time to make some calls.

Shanna

I was not getting into that shit with Karen and Mina. Ever since Ron died, Mina had been on some other shit that I was not even trying to understand. I knew she didn't run Karen's money to her correctly; that's why I asked Karen about the night before in front of her. Mina told me she walked away with over three thousand dollars, and when she wouldn't tell me how much Karen got, I knew she was up to some funny business. I hate a thirsty bitch, and Mina was acting like she was dehydrated.

A while back she expressed her concerns to me on her financial situation, but I just told her she wasn't grinding hard enough. I ain't worked a day in my life, and didn't plan to. All the fucking I did was going to pay for something, and that was why my place looked the way it did. I was trying to school her to the game, but she acted like she didn't get it.

On some real rap, we'd been hoes since like the seventh grade. How many days did my mother dropped me off to school only for me to walk into the building, wait for five minutes, then walk back out and hop into my old head's car and get fucked all day? To me, walking away with at least three hundred dollars and a new Gucci pocketbook was worth more than my education and that's how it always was.

Now don't get me wrong. My mom's tried, but the money she was pulling wasn't enough to pay for what I needed. You got to use what you got to get what you want. I learned that shit at the early age of twelve, and had been using it ever since. If those dudes wanted to treat me like my pussy was lined in platinum and diamonds than who was I to disappoint them? They knew that a bitch didn't move without karats and that's the way it was. I was the '06 Jessica Rabbit, you dig?

I could see the anger in Karen's eyes, but I knew she would probably just drop the situation. If I could help it, they'd definitely be discussing it again because Karen had to learn to speak up for herself. Either way, friends don't do that kind of shit to each other, and if we couldn't trust each other, then who was left to trust?

On the flip side of shit, I had been kicking it with this dude Chilae from G-Town, and his paper was so long it was ridiculous. He was the only nigga riding around Philly in a Bentley, so I'll just leave the hint at that. If you from this end, you know exactly who I'm talking about.

Of course he had all kinds of bitches on him, but when I came through, those chickens didn't exist. I had gotten into so many confrontations about him it was sad, and what was even more sad was he always left with me. That's why I didn't see why they even bothered. No, I wasn't his girl, but Chilae knew what time it was when I blew through, and it was hitting for just that the night before.

I got the call while I was in the club, and I knew I was going to be out. The guy that I met on the way in was a real loser, with his thirsty ass, and I was using him for laughs while I ordered drink after drink and all this nigga had was the same bottle of Voss water he had when we walked in the damn door.

I already knew he couldn't even afford to have the conversation we were having, but I entertained him anyway. He gonna tell me he don't drink alcohol that's why he got water, and me and Karen almost fell out in amusement. That was the best line I ever heard. I wouldn't have been surprised if that bottle was from the week before and he kept filling it with tap water.

I saw Mina freaking some dude on the dance floor and me and Karen was watching our girl work from the sidelines. I knew what Mina was setting up because I peeped dude when we came in, too. Hell, if she didn't get every dime he had, I would have. He had a different look about him, like he knew he was in a strange place but was trying to floss out of control. He was also tipsy as hell, and all that did was make him an easy target.

I was watching Mina the entire night, and I saw the exchange when the lights came up. It definitely looked like he gave her a knot of cash, and when I saw her count out five bills I knew she was up to some shady shit. I found out soon after that she made over three thousand from that, but the look on Karen's face said she didn't get broken off properly.

Yep, I was starting shit because I would want the same treatment. If the deal has always been fifty/fifty then keep it that way and don't be changing shit up halfway through. All that'll get you is an ass whipping you probably don't want. Hell, if she didn't want to share, she should have just rolled out on a threesome and kept Karen out of it. It ain't like she ain't never had a train ran on her ass before. A part of me thought she welcomed it.

Back to the situation at hand. When Chilae came and got me from the club, all eyes were on him and me as I got in and gave him a tongue-down that promised a wonderful time later on. I also wanted all those jealous hoes to see that shit so that they knew what the fuck was poppin' off. During the night I bumped into Chilae's baby mom once or twice, and the look on her face when she stepped up to get in his car and I got in was priceless. She knew not to make no moves, though. She and Chilae had been over for months.

A few minutes later, we pulled up to his spot over on Stenton Avenue and I walked up in there like it was my shit. He wanted to move me out the projects and up in there with him, but Bartram Village was my home. Besides all that, I wasn't giving up my shit to be put out by some nigga and be living on the street. I was cool on that, even though he always tried to convince me that it was a cool situation and he would never do that to me.

You know how that goes. As soon as a nigga thinks he got you hooked, he starts acting like a fool. Next thing you know you go from seeing him everyday to not seeing him at all, and the most interesting conversation you'll have is why some girl called his house phone asking for him by name and him denying it. That kind of drama I could do without.

I walked straight back to his bedroom and stripped naked, which wasn't much considering all I had on was a halter dress and sandals. Stretching my body out on his plush ass mink comforter, I waited for him to join me in the room. When he walked in, his eyes lit up, showing me he was pleased with what he saw. I spread my legs and pulled my knees up to my chest, letting him know it was time to eat.

Chilae wasted no time placing his face between my legs, and after that it was on and poppin'. Chilae was so damn sexy, and his head game was murder, but he was an average ass dude when it came to the size of his dick. It was about six inches or so, but it was thicker than a mug, and I was in there acting my ass off like he was knocking my damn kidneys loose.

See, I knew how to make my money, and all a nigga wanted was to feel good, whether you were faking it or not. It was all about busting a nut at the end of the day, and that's a small sacrifice to get paid major dollars. I gave Chilae a star studded performance acting like his stroke was the best thing since sliced bread, and by the morning I had two grand in my pocket, a promise to take me on a shopping spree, and his new Rolex in my pocketbook. Like I said, the power of the pussy works every time. You can believe that and take that to the bank.

If you think I'm bullshittin', I'll clue you in on what's real. If you wake up in the morning and that nigga is still sleep, that means either one of two things: you wore his ass out or he's just tired from being up late. Now, if you wake up in the morning to him trying to slide back in, he can't get enough of you. If he takes you to breakfast, that's just a courtesy, but if he cooks breakfast, you got his ass hooked. Needless to say, as I acted through another dick down this morning and smiled through the breakfast he made me, I knew for sure that I was the shit.

On the ride home in his other car, a BMW X5, he was chattin' his ass off. I just smiled and kept my eyes on the road as I thought about how I was going to spend the money he just gave me. I did see these sharp-ass Fendi boots that I wanted the other day, and thanks to Chilae, I'd be scooping those things up.

When we pulled up to the front of my building those same bum-ass dudes who were out there on a daily basis was grittin' hard on the X5 when we pulled up. Tonguing Chilae down once more so that these niggas could see what caliber of man I was dealing with, I made a show of slipping his Rolex off his wrist and sticking it inside of my pocketbook. Hell, he had about three of them so he wouldn't miss it.

"We need matching his and hers Rolexes," I said to him as I unclasped the catch on his wrist. "When you get mine, you can have yours back."

I didn't even wait for an answer. I just took my panties out of my bag and stuffed them in his top pocket. Then I got out of his truck and bounced up the steps to my crib. I'd be getting with him by the end of the week, so I wasn't worried about that. I saw Mina coming out of Cookie's apartment on the way up, and she said that she was going to run to the store and she'd be back at my place. That was cool. It gave me time to freshen up and roll me an el.

Chilae

It had been about a week since I saw Shanna, and I was ready for some more of her ass. She was a damn freak, but her girl Mina looked like she would knock some shit loose if you'd let her. On my way from dropping Shanna off, I ran into Mina coming off of Elmwood Avenue. Mina was a bad bitch; a lot sexier than both Shanna and Karen put together, but I didn't really know where her loyalty to her girls stood. I approached her a few times, and she always acted like she was interested, but she never took the bait. I ain't one to be sweatin' no chicks, so I always just let it ride, but she knew I was digging her, I'm sure.

Instead of the normal approach, I pulled up beside her while she was walking and rolled my passenger side window down. I watched her ass jump around for a while in those tight-ass sweat pants she had on before I said anything to her. I could see her nipples poking out through her wife beater from the side, and the sight made my dick hard instantly, which was amazing considering the work out I just got from Shanna. She didn't even have a thong on because her jacket rose up in the back, and her sweats rode low on her thick frame, almost showing her ass crack. I loved it. I briefly wondered why she didn't have her jacket buttoned up considering it was a little chilly outside at the moment, but who was I to be concerned?

"Hey girl, what you doin' out here this early?" I flashed a smile her way.

She turned to look at me, her face mirroring mine. It really wasn't all that early, maybe about 11AM or so, but that's early if you were out shaking your ass all night.

"I'm on my way home. I had to run to the store to get a few things."

"Let me give you a ride. Your bags look heavy," I said in an attempt to get closer to her. I could smell her perfume from where she stood on the curb. Light Blue by Dolce & Gabanna. It smelled good enough to lick off her skin.

"A loaf of bread and a gallon of milk looks heavy?" she said, her sexy smile brightening her face and her laugh music to my ears.

Every time I saw her I wished I had met her before I met Shanna, but what could I do about it? Something was telling me that I could still get it even under the circumstances.

"Not really, but it was worth a try," I laughed back, easing into the conversation. "You sure you don't want that ride?"

She lived around the corner from Shanna on Harley Terrace, so I didn't have to worry about running into her on the way back.

"No, I'm good. I can see my apartment from here."

"Well at least take my number, shorty. Hit me up sometimes, maybe we can politic over some coffee or something."

I thought she was going to wild out, but instead she reached into the car and took the card I extended her way, letting me know that her friendship with Shanna wasn't as tight as I thought it was. I smiled at her again and pulled off.

On the real, Mina would just be another jump off I added to my list. After what my boys from B-More told me about her and Karen, I knew I had to smash that. They said she did some shit to them that should be illegal. I was just waiting to slide up in there and see what it was hittin' for. I kind of figured she was better than the rest, though. Her ass was definitely fatter, and I knew I would have her ass stretched out in my bed sooner than later.

Hopping on I-476 south, I made my way up to the hotel where my mans O and C were staying at in King of Prussia. These were some get money niggas for real. They were a little bit country being from the south, but they were getting paper like you wouldn't believe. They were actually down here doing a drop off for me, but decided to stay overnight and hit up the club scene. They had the best dope next to the connection I had out of LA, and they were reasonable. They also didn't bullshit me on the price, so I always kept them in the loop.

Karen was into some deep shit, and I often wondered why she rolled with Shanna and Mina. They weren't on her level at all. I mean, she was the one who introduced me to Cee-Lo and Omar right after her dude got knocked last summer. She had been running coke up and down I-95 for them for the longest, and she got paid lovely. She kept that little bit of information from Mina and Shanna because she knew they couldn't handle no shit like that. In this business it's always about being discreet, and that was something Shanna and Mina were not. Karen came from money though, so this had to have been just something to do. I never got into how she met them, but when she turned me on to them, I let it be what it was.

I done already hit Karen a couple of times, too. It didn't seem to faze her that Shanna and I were kicking it, and those too were definitely tighter than her and Mina. Karen told me one night that she only tolerated Mina because she was Shanna's friend, but she really didn't care for her too much. That's all I needed to know to get shit moving. If shit went the way I wanted it to, I'd be tapping all three of them broads by summer's end.

I pulled up to the hotel before noon, just in time to grab something to eat and talk business. When I go to Cee's floor I could smell the weed in the hallway as soon as I exited the elevator. When he opened the door, a cloud of chief rushed out, damn near knocking me down. Those dudes got it in something serious, but they were so on point on the business aspect it wasn't even funny. Him and Omar was a couple of killers for real, so I just wanted to keep them as friends. I'd hate for some dumb shit to go down.

"My nigga," Cee-Lo said before giving me some dap after I came in.

The door connecting his room to Omar's was open, and I could see O finishing up an el while he counted coke out on the table. There were bricks piled up so high it looked like it was snowing in that bitch.

"What it do, baby? Tell me something good." I took a seat at the table next to Omar. He never even looked up as he continued to weigh and bag up the pounds of coke that I paid for. They would be heading back out today, so this would be the last of the business until it was time to re-up.

"Everything is everything. How are things looking on your end?" Cee-Lo asked as he sat down on the couch and scooped up the PlayStation 2 controller from the floor. The sounds of *Madden '06* filled the otherwise quiet hotel room. Omar didn't even flinch; he just kept a steady pace at what he was doing.

"I should have this moved out in no time. It's straight to the top from here," I replied in a confident tone. I only moved weight, and this was some supreme shit I was about to bring to the streets. The price they gave it to me for was ridiculously low, so I pretty much was about to quadruple what I put out in sales. I had a team so tight it was foolproof, and we had been working this shit for years.

"That's good to hear. We love happy customers," Omar chimed in, joining the conversation. He was done measuring my product and had it all packed up and ready to go. All I had to do was bounce; they got paid for it two days earlier.

"What's good with you and Karen? Is she still on the team?" I asked just to see what they would tell me. They were tight lipped about a lot of shit, so I wouldn't be surprised if they just shut me up.

"Karen is good; she's been bringing us a lot of money. That's why I can't understand why she flicked up with those hood ass chicks. She has so much potential," Cee-Lo said while never taking his attention off the game.

"I hear that. Well, fellas, until next time, be easy. I'll definitely be keeping in touch," I responded while grabbing the two duffle bags Omar packed for me. I headed toward the door. I didn't respond to their comments, because that would have shown a sign of weakness. Shanna was actually cool. Mina was the dick hound, but how important was that information going to be to them? My business there was done, so it was time to get it moving.

"Okay, Chilae. Happy hunting."

I didn't know what he meant by that. After a week, that coke they gave me had been moving like crazy, which gave me a free day to sneak up on Mina's ass. She'd been riding ya boy for the past half hour, and it was taking everything in me not to bust a nut.

Mina

"You gonna pay for this pussy, nigga. Lay ya ass still and take it."

Okay, so I knew I was dead wrong for laying up there with Chilae, being as though Shanna had dibs on him. I felt like this: every nigga is fair game, and since she ain't wifey and he wanted me anyway, why not? He gave me his number a week earlier, and I was surprised when I called him and he invited me over.

I did have a heart, and I was a little hesitant at first about actually going to see him, but I knew if nothing else Chilae had gravy and he was willing to break bread generously. Shanna said she only got two thousand and the Rolex off his wrist. I planned to walk out of there with at least five gees and the keys to his whip. The power of the pussy works, ladies. That is, if you know how to work it.

I had this dude stretched out and handcuffed to the bed with a blindfold over his eyes. Chilae wasn't big on size. I guess it was just an average dick. Enough to ride on, but not quite enough to go buck, or the shit would fall out. Let him tell it, he had a dick down to the damn floor. He was thick though, so it was workable.

When I first got there we just chilled and blew a few els while we bugged off of Martin Lawrence's best movie ever, *You So Crazy*. I would laugh and touch his thigh on some real girlie type shit. I had on my tightest pair of jeans and a cute little sweater that stopped just below my breasts. I left the bra and panties at home on purpose, you feel me? Wasn't no need in restricting a brother.

It wasn't long before we moved our little touching game to the bedroom and soon after, I found his head between my legs. His head game was on point, but it *had* to be with a dick that size. By the time it came for me to ride him, we ended up going at it raw because the damn condom kept coming off. Why this delusional nigga thought he could fit in a Magnum was lost on me. Maybe he thought his dick was as big as his bankroll. I was just going to leave, but I had money to make. Besides, Shanna never complained about any pussy problems, so I was sure it was cool. Shanna was my girl, and she was one of the cleanest people I knew, so I just handled my business like I came there to do.

Now, the downside to all that was I wasn't on any birth control, but I just figured I'd pull it out before he came. Even if I did get pregnant, an abortion only cost like three hundred, and that was a drop in the bucket for a nigga like Chilae to shell out. Like I said, I had no worries.

So we gettin' that shit in something serious and I'm caught off guard by this nigga cummin' early. I wasn't even mad because it's always about him getting off when you are bound to get paid. Only thing was, I didn't have time to get off the dick, so I'd just have to wait and see. As quick as that shit was, it was probably a damn blank.

We fucked a few more times throughout the night and by the morning I was dropped off at my crib with thirty five hundred dollars in my pocket and a woman's Rolex. Something was telling me that he purchased it for someone else because it was in a gift bag, but oh well. He'd just have to buy another one.

I didn't even let him come to a complete stop in front of my building. I jumped out on the slow roll and sprinted up the steps to my apartment. I didn't want to risk running into Shanna or Karen. Once inside, I stopped to piss and then crashed in the bed with my clothes still on. For him to have a short dick, my pussy was a little sore, but that wasn't nothing a hot bath couldn't fix later on.

Around three that afternoon my peaceful sleep was disturbed by the phone ringing. I stumbled out of the bed and crawled across the room to answer the phone with my eyes still closed. I was sleepy ass hell, but knew it couldn't have been anyone but my girls on the phone.

"Yizzo," I spoke into the phone in a groggy voice, hoping whoever was on the other line would get the picture. I really didn't feel like talking and just wanted to sleep a little while longer.

"Bitch, I know you ain't still sleep. It's three in the afternoon, and you know we about to hit the mall up," Karen said in an annoying fake ghetto voice that grated on my nerves. Sometimes she overdid it. Damn, bitch. Be original.

"The mall? I forgot all about that. I'm tired as hell, though, so I'm gonna have to take a raincheck," I said while getting up off the floor and walking back to lay on my bed and get comfortable. I really was tired, but truth be told, I didn't want to confront Shanna just yet. A little bit of guilt done set in about what happened with Chilae, and I couldn't look her in the eye right then.

"Girl, since when did you being tired stop you from spending some dough? Your ass was out all night so I know you got some ends in your pocket. Besides, it's our annual shopping trip, you have to go."

"I know, but Chi . . . I mean Charles had me up all night last night and my coochie is still hurting. I didn't get any sleep at all until I came home this morning. Can we do it tomorrow?"

Damn, my ass almost slipped up. I was just hoping Karen didn't catch on to that. She didn't sound suspicious though, so I just assumed I didn't have anything to worry about. Something was telling me they weren't taking no for an answer, so I had better get ready.

"Tomorrow? What are you wearing to Get Ruff's party tonight if you ain't shopping today? Did that nigga Charles sneak in a shopping spree that we didn't hear about?"

"No, but I'm . . ."

"Be ready in an hour. I'm just waiting for Shanna to get out of the shower, and then I'm hopping in. If it's a cash thing don't worry about it. I got my dad's Black Card."

"But, Karen, I . . ."

"No buts, be ready in an hour."

She didn't even wait for me to respond; she just hung up the phone. It seemed as though I didn't really have a choice in the matter, so I got my tired ass up and prepared for the day. *Fuck it, I might as well go and spend some of this money Chilae gave me last night.*

An hour later I emerged in a sexy little Donna Karen jean cat suit and stiletto knee boots that scrunched on the side. I threw on my leather jacket that stopped just below my breasts and popped my collar. I was in diva mode for real, and I knew once we got to the mall all eyes would be on me. By the time I got done putting on a little make-up, Karen and Shanna were calling me from downstairs.

Both of them did a double take when I came out of the building. There were a few guys up top too, and all eyes were on me. I was so loving the attention. All conversation stopped and I saw a few mouths drop open. I threw my shades on and walked to Karen's whip like I didn't notice what was going on.

"Bitch, the party is tonight," Shanna said while looking me

up and down with a frown on her face. I knew she'd be the first to hate. That was why I'd enjoy spending her man's money even more.

"I know when the party is, damn. A sistah can't get dressed to go to the mall?" I was acting like I was pissed and I didn't know what they were talking about, but I definitely got the picture. They were dressed in sweats and Timbs ,and there I was looking like I was about to rip the runway. What can I say? Bitch rule number one: always be prepared.

"Oh, a bitch most certainly can't. . . in mall gear. We laugh at chicks just like this every time we go shopping. Slipping and sliding around the damn mall in stilettos," Karen said while high fiving Shanna who co-signed.

I kept a straight face because I wasn't in the mood.

"Well this is what I'm wearing, so let's get moving. If I go upstairs, I stay upstairs, so I'm not changing."

I didn't even wait for an answer. I just opened up the back door and got in. Karen and Shanna exchanged one last glance before hopping in also and we were off to the mall. On the ride up I was in my own little world, holding back a sigh as we passed Black Ron's house. I really wasn't paying much attention to the conversation, but I did hear Shanna say Chilae dropped her off some money this morning. He must have stopped there after he dropped me off. Sorry-ass nigga. I tell you, guilt will eat cha ass up if you let it.

Once we got to the mall we did our thing, going from one store to the next dropping cheddar all over the place. Partly because of Karen's dad and his Black Card and partly because of the money both me and Shanna got from Chilae. It wasn't until about three hours went by that we stopped and got something to eat. I had to trade my boots in for a pair of slides from the Chinese hair store in the mall because my feet were killing me. I didn't know how those young girls did it, but it would be my last time.

Halfway through lunch Shanna, jumped up from the table

in the middle of our conversation and sprinted across the food court. Both me and Karen followed her eyes, and once they landed, I was staring at Chilae. He and Shanna exchanged a passionate kiss, and I couldn't help but think about how those same lips were just kissing my pussy a few hours ago. That's exactly why I don't kiss niggas. You just never know.

I was a bit disgusted to see them all hugged up, and from our view it looked as if he gave her a gift. I tried not to show any emotion but I was getting a little salty. No, he wasn't my man . . . yet, but we were just together not even twenty four hours ago. How could he act like I didn't turn his ass out?

When Shanna returned to the table with a Rolex watch just like the one he gave me last night and a fist full of money, I acted like I was happy for her ass, but inside I was screaming. I knew I would really have to work Chilae over to get him to treat me like he did Shanna, and that would be happening soon. I haven't met a man yet who could resist good pussy.

"Girl, I'm going to have to get me one of those," Karen said while admiring Shanna's new watch. I just shook my head and looked from the sideline, knowing I had one exactly like that in the crib. Groupie bitches, I swear. It was hard being on top.

We finished up our lunch quickly and made our way back to the hood, promising to be ready to go by ten tonight. That gave me plenty of time to get some beauty sleep in and to get fresh to death. If they thought what I had on earlier was over the top, wait until they saw what I was dipping up into to out. Now that I had Chilae lining my pockets, it was on. *Look out, bitches. The game has just begun!*

Karen

The very next day I was over Chilae's house getting my back twisted and wearing a Rolex better than the cheap shit he gave to Shanna and Mina. The one they got was a basic gold Rolex that cost Chilae about ten grand. The one I picked out—the Rolex Oyster Perpetual Lady in platinum with the diamond bezel—ran him about the price of a new ca . . . about fifty grand.

See, Mina and Shanna were my girls, but they were hood. All they knew was they had a Rolex. They didn't know the value of it, and Chilae knew they didn't know too. You would think they would have learned something from being around me, but who knows what goes on in the minds of fools? Knowing Mina, she'd be pawning hers soon. She'd rather have the cash in her pocket and a Timex on her wrist. That's why when it came time to get mine, he came correct and let me pick out the one I wanted. Oh, I paid for it later that night, but my frozen wrist was well worth it.

I actually came over to handle business, but we got into a little something, you know how it is. At any rate, we would need a new mule to transport from here to Maryland, and Chilae was considering bringing in Mina for the job. We both knew that she couldn't know I was involved in the entire operation, but my skepticism went beyond that. Mina got dick dumb when it came to men, and we couldn't let that be something to fuck the game up. I tried to talk him out of it, but he insisted that we move forward with the plan. He said he would talk to Omar and Cee-Lo about what they thought and then we would see what's up.

"I don't think it's a good idea, Chilae," I said between puffs of the Dutch I was smoking on.

Chilae didn't get down, but he allowed me to do my thing. We were laying here still naked from our earlier session, and he was sipping on a glass of Hypnotiq while we talked.

"How you figured it wouldn't work? Mina is about money first, and we all know that playing with someone's money could get you killed in this business. She doesn't want to die, so why would she fuck up? Besides all that, she would do anything I tell her to do."

"Yeah, but we both pulled some shit on Omar, and I think she really liked him. Wouldn't that pose a problem later on?"

"First of all, Karen, she didn't pull shit on Omar. You set shit up, remember? Secondly, Omar ain't letting no broad get in the way of his funds. So they might fuck while she down there? So what? You getting dick, so why can't she?"

"Yeah, but can she be trusted?"

"Hell, can you? Both of y'all are fuckin' me, and you know me and Shanna is kicking it. So I can pose the same question to you. Tell me what the difference is?"

Something told me Mina was seeing Chilae. When she made that little slip up on the phone, I acted like I didn't notice it, but he just confirmed what I knew to be true. I didn't even bother to respond. I just puffed on my Dutch instead.

Chilae did have a point, though. Mina was about her

money, and I honestly thought once he explained the importance of her job, she'd do right. My thing was she might have to layover one night before coming back to Philly, and she couldn't be getting dicked down and end up sleeping late. That would be a problem on both ends.

We also needed her to get back and forth without getting caught because the one thing they wouldn't tell her is that if she got knocked, they wouldn't be bailing her ass out. That's what happened to the last one, and it ain't shit you can do. Mina didn't even know that Chilae really wasn't his name. The same as Omar and Cee-Lo. Those were just the names we used to communicate with each other, so even if she snitched who would they be looking for?

I was deep in thought contemplating the situation when Chilae smacked me on my ass. I knew what that meant, but I didn't rush. He had me feeling some type of way about the entire Shanna comment. Truth be told, I'd been fucking Chilae way before he even met Shanna, so fuck what he just said.

We never hooked up because we knew it would be bad for business, but if he couldn't trust anyone else in the world, he knew I had his back. It stung a little that he thought so little of me, but it was cool. This wasn't a business where you could get your heart mixed with your feelings, so I didn't say anything about it. He'd pay, though. Like he had been doing. I'd definitely be hitting up those pockets before I rolled out.

Tapping my el out in the aluminum foil ashtray I hadmade next to his bed, I set the remainder of it on the nightstand and climbed on top of him. This nigga swore he needed a damn Magnum, but I chose to just leave the condom out of the equation. I could make him nut faster without it, and the sooner it was over, the better.

I had to go to my parents' house when I left there, and I wanted to get that done and over with while I still felt like it. My father hadn't been feeling well lately, and I wanted to check on him before I went home. My mother wasn't shit, and I knew she wouldn't make sure he was cool. What his insurance didn't cover, I paid extra for in home care for him so that he got his meds on time and all that. I knew my mom couldn't wait for him to die, and if it were left up to her, he'd be in a damn nursing home.

I hated my mother to the fullest extent of hating someone. How could a person be so selfish? I understand a person wanting to be secure in their future by keeping that money right, but at other people's expense? I was just wondering when my father was going to realize she married him for money and nothing else.

Squeezing my walls tighter, I had Chilae's dick on lock inside of my pussy. I milked his dick until he couldn't hold it anymore, and he finally exploded inside of me. I wasn't concerned about getting pregnant because I took my birth control religiously and it hadn't failed me yet. I never had an infection or disease from Chilae either, so that was the furthest thing from my mind.

After making sure I drained every ounce of cum from his dick, I jumped up and took a quick shower. He tried to join me, but I had to go. While I was getting dressed he went to the safe behind the picture of his mother on the wall and pulled up a stack of one hundred dollar bills totaling about five thousand dollars. I hated that picture. It felt like his mom was watching us fuck every time I came here.

"Give me by the end of the week to get shit straight with Mina and I'll tell you what's crackin' from there. I already know she's going to confide in you and Shanna even though I'll tell her not to say nothing, so just act surprised. We'll talk more later."

I didn't even bother to respond. I just took the money out of his hand and stuck it inside my Gucci bag. Grabbing my car keys from the table, I took the steps down two at a time and jumped in my jeep, making a mad dash across town to check on my daddy. I didn't feel like the shit with my mom tonight, so my visit would be brief. I just wanted him to know he still had me in his corner if no one else was there. My business class also started at eight-thirty and I didn't want to be late.

My dad's money was old money, passed down for nine generations. Back in the day the men in his family invested in the oil trade and came up big time. Over the years they took that money and invested in different stocks and companies and by the time me and my cousins came along we were extremely well off. My father owned several restaurants, car dealerships, and spas in Philly and the surrounding cities. He also had a ton of money invested in several companies that kept his shit growing.

We talked a while ago and he told me that if he passed I would be in charge of everything. He didn't even include my mother in his will, so I couldn't wait to see her face when that all went down. As a part of his will, I had to have my degree in business in order to take control of everything, hence the reason why I was in school. My dad wanted to keep it all in the family, and I didn't mind that at all. So when I tell you it's never a money thing with me, my word is bond. Believe that shit and take it to the bank.

Pulling up about twenty minutes later, I let myself into the house and walked straight to the back where I knew my dad would be. Considering it was a Sunday night, I knew he would be watching football in the den. My mother was out at one of her many "married wives" club meetings, so that was a relief.

I stood in the door and watched my dad for a while before going in. He looked a little on the pale side, but he did look a lot better than he did the last time I saw him. I noticed that when my mother wasn't around he seemed so happy. I often wondered if he ever considered divorcing my mother, but you know what they say. It's cheaper to keep her, so why bother? I watched him for a second more before walking over to him and placing my hand on his shoulder.

"Hey Daddy, how's it going?" I said, moving around to his side and taking a seat on the chaise across from him.

His face brightened up instantly.

"Hey pumpkin, I didn't hear you come in. How is everything?"

"Everything is good. How is everything for you?"

"I couldn't be better. The doctor told me the chemo treatments are working and I should be able to slow down pretty soon. The nurse you sent me is wonderful also."

"That's good to hear. Did you eat today?"

"Yes. Inga made me some . . ." before he could finish his sentence, he went into a coughing fit that looked painful.

The cough shook his body from the feet up, and I jumped up to pat his back and offer him some water. He took the glass out of my hand and, when he pulled his handkerchief back, I noticed a few droplets of blood on the white material. I didn't say anything about my observation, but I would be mentioning it to his doctor the next time we went.

He took a few more minutes to get his head together and finished his glass of water. I poured him another cup so that he wouldn't have to get up. Just as I was going to ask him what time his next doctor's visit was, my mother made a loud entrance into the house. I already knew it was going to be some shit, so it was time to pull up. My dad understood. I could tell because he had the same look I had on my face.

"Well, Daddy, I have to get going, okay? I'll be here to go with you to the doctors on Thursday, and I'll call you for the time later. I love you." I kissed him on his forehead and blinked back tears just as my mother walked in.

"Okay, pumpkin. You be safe."

I was trying to leave the house without any confrontation with my mother, and it almost worked. I was hoping that she had walked upstairs or into the kitchen, but just my luck she was sitting in the foyer flipping through mail. I was just going to walk by without saying a word to her, but of course she had to take me there.

"Karen, what a pleasant surprise. I didn't know you were coming," my mother said sounding like a fake ass Vanna White.

I just smiled and kept it moving. "I was just leaving."

"Leaving so soon? Let me guess, you're rushing to go hang with your little ghetto friends."

"Mom, whatever. I'm not in the mood today."

"I just want the best for you, dear. And if you haven't noticed, a dark tan and a black name doesn't make you black. You are a white woman, and you're just bringing yourself down by hanging with such filth."

"Don't you have black friends? And why every time I come here, we have to get into this race shit?"

"First of all, watch your damn mouth in my house. Secondly, my black friends all have money and manners. Something your friends lack. Hopefully you'll see soon how damaging this all will be to your career and social status later on."

"Well, you're damaging to my social status now. This conversation is done," I said while opening the door.

I could still hear her saying smart shit while I was getting into my truck, and just as I sped off, she ran to the door and yelled out to me some shit about getting a gown for the same ball I told her I wasn't attending.

I swear if life wasn't so hectic for me right now I would take my dad out of there and let him live with me. I just didn't want him caught up in no dumb shit, but soon I'd be on point and he would be with me. I got to class ten minutes late, but it was cool. All of this would be behind me soon.

Mina

To my surprise, I received a call from Chilae about two weeks after I saw him and Shanna acting a fool at the mall. I mean, who kisses in public anymore? Anywho, he told me he had to talk to me about something and that he wanted me to come over as soon as possible. I was nervous as hell because from what I heard, the last time Chilae told someone he wanted to talk they ended up at the bottom of the Schuylkill River.

I tried to jog my memory to see if I possibly burned his ass, but I hadn't been with anyone unprotected besides him, so if some shit popped off it was on him. I was told to be at his house by eight, and I waited until 7:59 to knock on his damn door. I was literally sweating bullets and it was cold as shit outside. My wait was brief, and just when I decided that I would skip out and just call, he opened the door wearing nothing but a damn towel.

I slid past him like I didn't notice the water that was beaded up on his smooth chest and running down his stomach, and went and took a seat in his living room. I didn't know if that shit was a set up or not, and I didn't want his naked ass clouding my judgment. A few minutes later he came into the living room with a pair of boxers on his ass and a Corona bottle in his hand.

"Wassup, Mina? Glad you could make it over," Chilae said with a serious look on his face.

I was scared to death because I didn't know what was about to go down. All I knew is I didn't do shit. That's my word and I'm sticking to it.

"Nothing really. Just chillin' I guess," I came back followed by a nervous laugh. I was trying to appear cool and collected, but it came off all wrong.

He sat and flipped through the channels and sipped on his beer, not even bothering to offer me anything to drink. We sat in silence for a good twenty minutes, and I was wondering when in hell he was going to say something. Looking at my watch as a gesture of impatience, I waited ten more minutes before I decided to say something. I was stuttering like a scared bitch until I realized that I had nothing to be afraid of . . . yet.

"Yo, Chilae. I know you didn't call me over here to watch television. You said you had to ask me something. Shoot straight. I got places I need to be."

I came at him with serious attitude, and it got his attention. He stopped mid-sip and looked over at me like he was seeing me for the first time. I gave him the screw face right back, and dared him to pop fly. He continued to sip his beer before he spoke to me.

"Where you need to be that you can't be here with me?" he asked, and waited for me to answer.

"I got money to make."

"Good thing you came by then, huh?"

"What?"

He threw me off with that one, and I'm sure my facial expression showed it.

"Since you in a rush, I'll just put it out there. I got an opportunity for you to make some money that you can't refuse."

"Is that so? And the opportunity would be?" I automatically thought he was going to be on some getting ass type shit and that was cool as long as he paid like he weighed.

"I need you to transport for me," he said with a straight face.

"Transport what? Where?"

"Weight from here to Maryland and back. An overnight trip that can put at least five gees in your pocket."

I thought before I responded, making sure to mask what I was thinking so it didn't show up on my face. *I could use some extra money, and I get a trip out of town, so why not?* I acted like I was really weighing my options, but in reality, I had already come to a decision.

"So if I do this, when do I get paid and how long will I have to do it for?"

"You'll get your money as soon as you get back, and you'll do it for as long as I need you to. What else you got to do with your time? They can't be paying you but so much at that little billing job you're working at or you wouldn't be doing the things you do, right?"

"What is that supposed to mean?" I asked with an attitude. Okay, I wasn't making bank at my job, but I didn't have a little minimum wage gig either. It paid the bills. What I did on the side supported my lifestyle.

"I ain't tryna ruffle ya feathers, ma. Chill out for a second. All I'm saying is can you make fifteen thousand a week at your job?"

"So are you saying is that I'll only have to make three trips a week?"

"So you can count, huh? For now it'll just be a trip a week, then we'll up it as needed. Is that cool?"

"Yeah, that's cool, but you need to keep in mind that I have to work. I may not be making millions, but I need my benefits. A bitch needs to be able to get her pussy checked every so often, and the last I checked the drug business didn't offer health care services."

Chilae looked at me to see if I was serious, and my face showed that I was. That was just one of my concerns. Since I was stepping into the drug game, I needed to have something legitimate on the side just in case I got caught out there. I needed to have a source of income that supported my spending habits.

"Okay, ma. I feel you. So this is what you have to do . . ."

Chilae broke it all down on how I would be transporting money and coke from here to Maryland without getting caught. He would drop a backpack off to me in the morning with money in it for the trade before I went to work. He said for me to keep it with me at all times until I got to where I had to be after work. The money was placed in the lining of the bag, and the bag was stuffed with school books just in case they had to check it before I got on the bus.

The ride from Philly to Maryland was only two hours, so on some days I would be able to come straight home. Chilae said for now I would be taking the bus back and forth until they got me a car. Nine times out of ten, a female driver wouldn't be stopped, so I would be cool. I would go straight to Omar's stash spot where the drop would be made. I would have to chill for a while until the Greyhound employees changed shifts. He said he didn't want me looking suspicious getting right back on the bus. Then I'd be heading back to Philly, where he would meet me at the bus station.

We talked for a while, and it was a lot to take in. We sat at the kitchen table and he told me how much money I would be taking down there, and what I should be bringing back up. I made sure to pay careful attention to what he was saying to me because I needed this shit to go smooth. At the amount of money they would be paying me a week, I'd be living it the fuck up.

"So, do you have any questions?" Chilae asked after he was done.

I was a little hesitant to ask, but I figured I might as well get it out now.

"Actually I do."

"What is it, ma? Shoot straight."

"Umm, if I get caught, what do I do?"

"Don't get caught," he said with a straight face.

That shit didn't sound right to me, and if I knew then what I know now, I would have taken heed to that shit.

"But if I do?"

"Then we'll cross that bridge when we get there, okay?"

"Okay."

Chilae got up from the table and went back into the living room. I followed suit and took my seat back on the couch. My mind was running a mile a minute, and I was just trying to make sense of everything. This shit seemed like it was going to be easy. The hardest part would be making that first run, but I was sure once I knew where I was going and what to do, I'd be good.

"So, Chilae, when do I start?"

"I'll call you this week to let you know what's what. Just remember that we don't talk drug business over the phone, no matter what. That is very important for you to understand."

"I got it."

"Oh, and keep this between me and you. I don't need Shanna and Karen in my business. I know y'all are girls and all that, but this is on another level and I don't need too many people knowing what moves I'm making, understand?"

"I understand."

"Good."

Chilae went back to watching television, and I got up to leave. I had butterflies in my stomach like I was about to lose my dinner, and I just wanted to go and lie down. I'd be better able to think at home.

"So you just gonna leave like that?" Chilae asked just as I was putting my hand on the door knob. I turned back to look at him with a puzzled look on my face. He already told me what he wanted me to know so what more did he want?

"Umm, yeah. I got to get ready for work tomorrow."

"Oh yeah? Well let me give you something that will put ya ass right to sleep."

When he got up, his erection, as small as it was, was poking through the slit in his boxers. I really didn't feel like being an actress, but what choice did I have? I had yet to tell him no, so why start?

Removing my coat as I walked, I went straight back to Chilae's bedroom and began to undress. I noticed a pair of women's panties on the floor by his dresser that looked like a pair that Shanna just got from Victoria's Secret, but I didn't mention it. I wanted to get this done and over with as soon as possible.

I laid down in the bed, and Chilae put his face in my pussy. Normally I came from his tongue working me out, but I had too much on my mind and was faking the shit out of an orgasm within minutes. Chilae moved to slide in me, and I flipped that shit on his ass and flipped him over so that I could ride him. We weren't even five minutes into it before he was talking that "oh I'm cumming" shit.

"Mina, girl, you gonna make me cum," he said through clinched teeth as his body tensed up and he grabbed for the sheets. I was thinking in my head that he always came quick, but I let him have his moment.

"Oh, yeah? Cum for mami. Cum in this pussy."

"Girl, talk that shit. Talk to daddy."

Bored with him and this lame-ass conversation, a twist of my hips ended it all, and Chilae came all up in me. I grinded down on his dick until his shaking subsided before I got up to put my clothes back on. He was still stretched out in the bed panting like a damn dog. By the time I went to put my shoes back on, he was in his safe pulling out money for me.

"This is just to hold you over until we get started. Don't be nervous; you'll do fine."

"I'm good."

"Cool, and remember to keep this between me and you."

"Don't worry, daddy. Your secret is safe with me. Now get dressed so you can take me home."

He didn't object at all, and a few minutes later we were in front of my building. I saw Shanna's light on in her apartment as we drove past, so I knew I would have to make a dash for my building. He leaned in to give me a kiss, and I gave him my cheek. If he did half the shit to Shanna that he did to me, I wanted no parts of it. Chilae had no problem licking my pussy, ass, titties and toes. I knew Shanna wasn't letting his ass slide without all that going down, so his lips would never ever touch mine.

"Mina, keep this shit tight, you hear me?"

"Don't worry about me. Telling your business would be putting my own shit out there, you dig? Don't sweat it, my mouth is closed. Just have my money right when I get back here."

"Girl, have I ever shortchanged you?"

"Never," I said with a smile although I wanted to say that I got shortchanged every time he gave me the dick.

"We gonna be rich together, just watch. I'll talk to you in a couple of days, okay?"

"Okay, baby. Talk to you later."

He moved in to try and kiss me again, and I used that opportunity to jump out of the car and sprint upstairs. He was catching the raps, and I didn't want Shanna to see me getting out of his jeep. Plus, I still had some thinking to do. He told me not to say anything, but I had to talk to someone.

Shanna

Mina came calling me at six in the damn morning like my ass wasn't just out all night. I ain't heard from the bitch in like a week, so I was surprised she called. For some reason she got an attitude when Chilae rolled around, but I just brushed that shit off. Her and Karen hadn't really been clicking either, and I was starting to wonder what was up with my girls. We'd been rolling tight for years, so I didn't really know what it was.

She was acting real shady with Karen too. Not running her money right, and just straight giving her ass to be kissed. Karen was underestimated because she was white, but if push came to shove, I would straight stand back and let Karen wear Mina's ass out. She might have to do that to get her respect.

I don't like late night phone calls, or early morning calls for that matter. It normally ain't shit but bad news at that time of day, and I don't need to hear nothing negative at six in the morning. The phone rang about eight times, so I figured whoever was on the other end really wanted to talk.

"Hello," I spoke into the phone around the thickness of my tongue. My damn mouth tasted like I was eating zoo dirt, and

I had to get up and at least gargle. Good thing she couldn't smell that shit through the phone.

"Girl, we need to talk."

"About what? Do you know what time it is, bitch?"

"Yeah, and I'm on my way to work. What you doing later? I need to stop by there."

"Why can't you tell me now?"

"Because I can't talk over the phone."

"So let me get this straight," I said into the phone, now fully awake and getting a major attitude. "Your simple ass called to tell me that you wanted to talk but you can't right now? So what the fuck did you call for? Why didn't you just stop by later instead of waking me the fuck up out my sleep? You know Chilae be keeping a bitch up all night."

I threw that shit out there because Chilae already told me that he asked Mina to transport for him. I was pissed because he didn't ask me after I heard how much he would be paying her, but then he came back on some ol' why would he put his girl in harm's way and all that. I let that shit slide, but I would be tapping his pockets double time now. He also told me that he told her not to say shit, but I'm almost certain that's what she wanted to talk about.

"Shanna, please just hear me out, okay? I have a decision I need to make, and you are the only one I can trust to talk to about it. Just be home when I get there."

"Whatever, bitch. Just be here before my man come get me. We goin' shopping today."

"I'll be there by five."

I didn't even bother to respond. I just hung up the phone. I knew Chilae wouldn't be trying to hit up no mall at that time of day, so I would be calling his ass around ten. Plus I wanted Karen to be there to hear this shit so I wouldn't have to repeat the shit later. After taking a piss and gargling with some Listerine I laid back in the bed until ten, making Chilae my first call of the day.

His phone only rang three times before he answered and it sounded like he was at a damn party. I was thinking to myself that he better not had left town and he knew we had money to spend.

"Hey, baby girl, what you doing up this early? You miss big daddy already?"

"You know I do, boo. What time you taking me shopping?"

"Is that today? I thought I told you some time this week?"

"You said tomorrow. And that was yesterday, so that would be today, or was this pussy making you talk all reckless?"

I was starting to get an attitude, because I already called my girl Charmaine and told her I would be by to get those Gucci rain boots they had in the window of her store. She worked at Macy's part time and got a discount on everything. Those boots were two hundred dollars, and I wanted to get an outfit too. Chilae was starting that amnesia bullshit, and I swear on everything I love that I would take out all the windows in his jeep if he starts acting dumb.

"Okay look, be ready by two and I'll take you out to King of Prussia."

"Chilae, we need to go before two. Mina called saying she wanted to talk and I want an outfit too. Can we go at twelve so we can be back at two? Please?"

"Baby, hold on," Chilae said into the phone before talking some real grimy shit to whoever was standing there. It sounded like some commotion was about to pop off, and I didn't want to bear witness to none of that shit.

"Okay baby, be ready by twelve and be on the stoop. When I roll around and you not there I'm keeping it movin'. I got a lot of shit to do today and I really don't have time to be in no damn mall."

"I know, baby, and I really appreciate it, but can we go out to the Springfield mall? It's closer with less traffic and I can be in and out. Charmaine works at the Macy's right there."

"Cool, be out there or I'm gone."

I hung up the phone and hopped my ass out the bed. I needed to be dressed and outside at least five minutes before he pulled up. I took my time and washed every inch of my body, making sure to smell delicious for my baby. Deciding on a pair of True Religion jeans that fit my ass perfectly and a cute little boat neck sweater that showed my shoulders to match, I was looking fresh to death.

I retouched my curls and chose a cute pair of Nine West stiletto knee boots to complete my outfit. I don't usually wear stilettos to the mall, but, since I was going with Chilae, I had to show those mall rats who was the boss bitch up in there.

At five of twelve I was on the stoop and at twelve on the dot, Chilae was pulling around the corner. I sauntered off the stoop like I was walking the runway, giving him a good look at my outfit. His eyes showed he was pleased, and once I got into his jeep I leaned over and gave him a kiss on his lips that promised a great time later tonight.

He looked me over once with lust in his eyes and then we were off, hauling ass down Lindbergh Blvd toward I-95. While he was driving I flipped through his CD's and the radio channels, something he hated. Ask if I cared? Within a half hour we were pulling up outside of the Macy's department store in the mall, and Chilae was walking around to let me out.

When I jumped down, he pinned me to the car and gave me a kiss. I was stunned because I wasn't expecting it, but something told me I had missed something just that fast. I gave into the kiss, but I kept my eyes on everything as we made our way into the store.

When we walked in, Charmaine was right up front setting up a new Coach display by the entrance. We spoke briefly, and just as our conversation started getting good, Chilae reminded me that he had somewhere to be. I apologized to Charmaine then began to look around for an outfit. DJ Smooth Beats was having a listening party for this new rapper, Big Thug, on Friday night, and I made plans to be at the after party. There were going to be all kinds of ballers there, and even though Chilae was my boo, there was money to be made.

I moved around the store quickly, trying to find an outfit that would pop, and halfway through, Chilae told me that he would be walking down to the food court to get something to drink. I was cool with it because that would give me time to at least try on some stuff before I decided.

I must have been in the dressing room for at least twenty minutes and Chilae hadn't made it back yet. I took the liberty of looking around for another pair of shoes even though in the back of my mind something had my gut twisted. It don't take that damn long to get something to drink, and when forty-five minutes had passed by and that nigga wasn't back yet, I knew some shit had popped off.

"Charmaine, let me go get Chilae from the food court. I'll just sit my stuff right here."

"Okay, girl. I'll just move it to the side when I'm done with this. You picked out some cute stuff."

I didn't even bother to respond because my mind was already out the store and down the hallway wondering what the hell Chilae done got into. My walk was brief because I was only halfway to the food court when I saw Chilae hugged up on the wall with some low budget bitch, tonguing her down like they weren't the fuck in public.

I ran up on they ass like a bat out of hell and just started swinging. That bitch or Chilae ain't know what hit them, and I had all intentions of tearing the food court up. I snatched the bitch by her hair and was trying to put her face through the damn wall. It took Chilae and two flashlight cops to pull me off of her. I was going the fuck off, and had mentally checked out for all of four seconds.

I was cursing and threatening to kill everybody up in that bitch while Chilae literally had to drag me down the hall. The chick he was kissing on was holding a towel under her broke ass nose with blood all over her winter white coat looking confused as ever. It was obvious she didn't know about me, but that ass-whipping would be a constant reminder. *Chilae is off limits, bitch!*

By the time we got back to the store, I had struggled out of his grip and walked straight to the counter with my hair all over my head and a ripped coat like ain't shit just happened. We came there to go shopping, and I wanted my shit.

Chilae tried to act cool and paid for my items in a hurry so as to not draw any more attention than we already had. I ain't say shit else. I just snatched my bags and his car keys off the counter and walked the hell out of the store with him not far behind me. Using the keyless entry I opened the door on the passenger side and hopped in, dropping his keys on the ground outside the door before I got in. Chilae didn't say a word; he just picked up his keys and walked around the other side to get in.

I was tempted to open up the door and bust his damn head open when he bent down, but I kept my composure. I had better ways to get him back without physically harming him.

He got in and started the car without a word, and I just stayed looking straight. I didn't even want to look at his ass at that moment. Mind you, I wasn't pissed because there was another bitch because Lord knows Chilae had hoes everywhere, but the blatant disrespect was just too much. Do whatever when I'm not around, but he came to the mall with me, so he should have known. Now I knew the reason for that kiss when we first arrived.

We got stuck in a little traffic on the way back, and it was so quiet you could hear a mouse piss on cotton. He tried to explain his self, but once he figured out that I wasn't saying shit back, he just let it go. Halfway home, he took off his jacket and laid it on my lap like it was cool. In fact it was because I took the liberty of searching his pockets and wallet and removing all the cash he had in there. I was so petty I even took the change he had in his ashtray.

When we pulled up to my building I grabbed my shit and got out, slamming the door with half of his Rock-A-Wear jacket hanging out of the door. He was still trying to talk. I just kept it moving, going on inside my building like he was invisible. If Chilae wanted to play that game, that's how we would do it. I had my eye on this honey they called Jarrell who lived over in the Divine Land projects in Trenton, New Jersey. That nigga was balling out of control, and him and Chilae were known enemies. What better way to get back at his ass then to start fucking the competition?

Karen

Shanna called me all hype when she got home from the mall, telling me I had to get over there A.S.A.P. I came through with my Timbs and sweats and my hair pulled back ready to make shit pop. Here I am thinking we about to thump and all this bitch had was hurt-ass feelings from fucking with Chilae. I sat my bag down and got her some tissue and a glass of water, and then I made myself comfortable so that I could listen to my girl vent.

The one thing I noticed about women, especially women like me and Shanna was that as tough as we were sometimes we let our heart slip up in there, and that almost always fucked the game up. The sad thing was, we were sitting there in love with the same damn dude and neither one of us wanted to admit it. Furthermore, I definitely couldn't say shit because it was her man I was digging on.

I half listened and commented as she ranted and raved about how Chilae did her at the mall. I wasn't surprised. There was a time or two when I was over there kicking it and Chilae had an unexpected visitor. I didn't hate. I just told the nigga to invite the bitch in. Fuck it, let's make it a threesome. She acted like she didn't want to leave, and I damn sure wasn't, so what was it gonna be?

When I tuned back into the conversation, she was telling me about Chilae wanting Mina to transport for him and how she was so upset that he never considered asking her. I was thinking to myself that she has got to be a damn fool if she's pissed about that minute shit. Why put yourself out there to get fucked when you already getting what you need from a nigga? That's hustlin' backwards if I've ever seen it. I just kept my thoughts to myself and heard her out.

"You going to K Breezy's party on Friday?" she asked as she finally stopped crying and got her shit together.

"Yeah, I'm just showing my face for a minute, though. I gotta take my dad to his therapy appointment on Saturday morning."

"Cool. I hope to run into that nigga Jarrell there. I need to see what it's hitting for with him. I'mma have to show Chilae that his ass can be replaced."

"And you plan on doing that by hooking up with Jarrell? That dude's number one fucking enemy. I give you too much credit because you got to be as dumb as they come. You must want to end it all at the young tender age of twenty six, bitch."

She looked at me like I was speaking Portuguese or something. Shanna knew she was playing with fire, and this fire would be an inferno if shit got out of hand.

Jarrell, also known as Killa 1, was from the Donnelly Page Homes, better known as the Divine Land Projects. Those Trenton mutha fuckas were real life fuckin' killers. I spent a little time over there in them projects when I used to fuck with Jarrell's homeboy, Benny Bronco. He was a sexy Puerto Rican that could rip your fuckin' heart out your chest with his bare damn hands. Flexx and Big Keith were some murdering mutha fuckas too, and it all happened down in the gut.

Every project has a good part and a bad part, and the gut was like South Central, only it was in Jersey. Martin Luther

King Boulevard. was the most dangerous strip, even in the daytime. The cops they had walking that beat turned a blind eye to it all because they were either on the payroll or they were scared to damn death. It was serious business, and the dudes that rolled in that crew were in it for life. *Jersey born, Jersey bred . . . and when I die I'll be Jersey dead. North Trenton mutha fuckas!*

I loved it over there, and after I had to knock a few bitches back, it was all good. We were living it up over there until the heat got too damn hot and my baby got sent up. This young chick they called Reminisce was moving shit for them back and forth, and just like Mina she was cool at first. She was fucking with Omar and Cee's boy Beanz, and let the dick cloud her judgment. She was supposed to go down there and make a drop and head right back to Philly, but good dick made her stay and she didn't realize that the law had been tailing her ass and watching her every move for a couple of weeks.

On the way back down, she was speeding her ass off because she slept late and she knew if she ain't have the drop off Jarrell and 'em was going to be pissed. Just before she crossed the Maryland/Delaware line, the cops pulled her over and searched the car. She had a good ten keys in the trunk, and after thoroughly searching the vehicle, they found half a million dollars in the spare tire in the back and guns with the serial numbers scratched off under the floorboards. When she called Jarrell to let him know what all went down, he had already got the drop from one of the detectives he paid in the bureau and by the time she got her one free call, all the cell numbers were changed and she was forgotten.

Three weeks after that, she took a plea bargain and dimmed them all out, opting to go into the witness protection program. On that night I was having dinner with my parents when the spot got raided. They had clear 8x10 photos of all of us, but my dad had pull in high places and I was spared. I stayed away from Jersey for a while and started running the strip myself, but that got to be too much after a while. Shortly after that I met Chilae. We did have a few chicks run for us, but either they got scared and got ghost or locked down, so we had to fall back for a while.

We were just kicking it at first, but Cee-Lo and Omar was missing that Philly money and wanted me to put them down with someone. It took me a while to see what Chilae was really about before I put him on, but after about a year of seeing this dude make crazy amounts of money, I wanted in. What I liked about Omar and Cee was they stayed loyal and worked with me until I figured out my next move. That's why I had mad love and trust for them.

That's the kind of shit that I kept tight from Mina and Shanna. They were my girls and all and we had come a long way, but haters jump out the woodwork if they think they can't shine like you. So I just let them think I was a clueless white girl who was living off of her father's gravy, and that kept the peace.

Two years later, Jarrell was somehow able to manipulate the system. He was let out on parole because his lawyer found a loophole on his case. Big Keith and Flexx soon followed and I was doing good until I found out that my baby Benny got murked in the pen. I'm still not over that shit.

When Jarrell got back in town, he picked up right were he left off and then some, moving his shit down to West Philly, and keeping rank up in Jersey. Chilae felt the pinch when word got out that Jarrell had a better product and he was selling it for less. The war began when Chilae sent stick-up kids to raid Jarrell's spots down west, and the nation soon found out why he was donned the nick name Killa 1.

They have been at war ever since, and although it had died down some, there was definitely known beef there. Shanna was just trying to get Chilae's attention, and she would, but not the kind her ass could handle. Never cross enemy lines unless you plan to stay there. The rules of the street are deep, but I guess some people have to learn the hard way.

When Chilae asked me to get Omar, Cee-Lo, and Mina connected, I knew the best way to do it was to put her in the position were she felt like she was in control. I knew O would be paying her for sex that night, but after the shady shit she pulled, I knew for sure that I would be watching her ass like a hawk from now on. Chilae never told me how they would be connecting until I was at his house that night, and at that point I was done trying to save desperate bitches.

Mina could actually come out on top if she played her cards right, but Shanna was just begging for a funeral of her own. The thing about Shanna was once she'd made up her mind, there was no talking her out of it. I'd be talking to Jarrell before the party though, because I knew them niggas was gonna be there. Any party thrown by K Breezy is bound to bring out Trenton niggas, so it was on. I just wanted to give him a heads up so if it ever came down to it, he might just spare her life in a desperate situation.

We talked a little bit more about Chilae and Mina, and before we knew it, five o'clock had rolled around. Shanna said Mina would be there by then, but we were supposed to act like we didn't know what was up with her and Chilae. It's crazy that Shanna didn't think they were fuckin', but I'd be damned if I'd mention that shit.

I knew I was hungry as shit. I guessed we could wait for Mina to get there. I felt like hittin' up Ms. Tootsies for some smothered turkey chops. That was just a quick trip down South Street, so we would be there in no time. I mentioned this to Shanna, and she agreed, so I ran down to the car to grab my duffle bag so that I could put on something more presentable. I went down there in fighting clothes, and since wasn't shit poppin', I figured I might as well play my part.

Just as I was closing my trunk, Mina was coming around the

corner. I acted like I just pulled up, and hopefully Shanna would follow suit. She walked toward me briskly, and for the first time, I noticed that Mina was kind of cute. She had her shit together, and I could see why men sweated her. If she could just get that desperate-ass look off her face, she'd be cool.

"Hey, girl, how was work?" I asked, making small talk as we climbed the stairs to Shanna's third floor apartment.

"It was as cool as work can be. I can't complain."

I couldn't really judge what was going on because she answered real nonchalantly, and I was trying to pick up on her mood.

When we walked in, Shanna was ruffling through her pocketbook and looked surprised to see both of us standing there. I was hoping she rolled with what I started outside, and she did.

"Hey, ladies, what it do?"

"Ain't nothing. How you?"

"I'm good and fucking hungry. Karen, when did you pull up? Let's go get something to eat."

"That sounds good, let me change my clothes."

I could hear Mina and Shanna conversing in the living room while I changed in the bedroom, but I couldn't understand what they were saying. I took my time getting dressed because those hoes had that shit on and I was not to be overlooked. I borrowed some of Shanna's smell-goods from the dresser, and as I was putting it back, I noticed a little white packet of powder resting between her jewelry box and baby powder.

I refused to believe that my girl is dippin'. Maybe she had some scab-ass nigga over or something. Sticking it into my bag, I would be asking Chilae what it was about later. When I walked into the living room, Mina stopped talking abruptly. I already knew what it was about, and she'd be telling me before the night was over.

"Let's go, hoes," I said and walked toward the door.

Mina frowned her face and Shanna just laughed. I think that bitch is smoking wiggles, and I'd be finding out.

We held small talk on the way to the restaurant, and I had plans to get Mina fucked up so I could see where her mind state was. I was also hoping that Shanna would have a change of heart also. They made me sick sometimes, but they were my girls so I guess I'd just have to hope for the best.

Mina

I couldn't even concentrate at work today. I was beginning to wonder when life for me got to be so damn complicated. I was cool with just getting money from niggas and getting the dick in the process, but I done moved on to some shit that I wasn't sure I could handle. At the same time, the money was too enticing to walk away from.

Halfway through the day, I started to fake sick just so I could leave and go talk to Shanna, but I needed all my ducks to be lined up in a row just in case the law came at me sideways. I did ask my supervisor if I could work through my lunch break so that I could leave an hour early, though. At 4:15 my ass was packed and out the door, and I was on my way home. I didn't even stop at my apartment to piss like I usually do. I ran straight to Shanna's block, and to my dismay, Karen's jeep was parked out front. *Damn, does this bitch ever go home?*

I really didn't want to get into details in front of Karen, especially since shit between us hads been kinda shaky lately. But I knew if I didn't tell her with my own mouth, Shanna would give her rendition of the situation and have it all ass backwards.

Running up the steps as fast as I could, I turned the handle on Shanna's never locked door and ran straight to the bathroom. After getting some relief, I addressed my girls with a serious ass look on my face. Chilae told me to keep shit tight, but if something went down that was out of the ordinary, someone had to know what to tell my momma.

"Wassup, y'all? What did y'all day look like?" I said while getting comfortable in the corner and taking off my boots.

When I finally looked up at Shanna, she looked like she had been through the fire. Her hair was all over her head, and she had a small red line under her eye like someone had scratched her face. On the flip side, I saw a few Macy's bags sitting by the couch. Whatever went down, I was certain she came out on top.

"Girl, fucking around with Chilae at the mall done gave me a damn headache. I don't know why I fuck with that nigga, but he gonna see what the real deal is real damn soon."

I looked at Karen for some kind of clue, but she just looked clueless like she didn't know what Shanna was talking about. I was almost certain they had already discussed the shit before I got there, but I played along. Fuck it, I ain't gonna beat it out of her. I decided to let that simmer for a second while I got some juice and rolled a Dutch. I was ready to burst from the anticipation, but I didn't want to seem inconsiderate of Shanna's situation.

"So, what got you all in a huff, Miss Thang?" Karen asked. Although I didn't really want to say, I was happy that she initiated the conversation so that it wouldn't seem like I was brushing them off.

"Well, I got some shit I need to run past y'all, but you have to swear that it stays in the circle. It's a matter of life or death."

"Done. Now spill it," Shanna jumped in, not taking her eyes off the T.V. screen. The sound was muted, but I bet she could read the hell out of some lips.

"Okay," I began nervously, not knowing how she was going to take what I was about to tell her. Shanna could be a bitch about a man, and I didn't feel like the nonsense. "Chilae asked me if I would transport for him for a while . . ."

I went on to explain to them exactly what he wanted me to do, and how I would benefit from the services I'd be performing. I stressed the point that it could not get out that I was making moves with Chilae because first off, I wasn't supposed to have said anything, and secondly I had to keep that aspect of my life separate. My biggest goal was just staying the hell out of the clink. I barely escaped it with that Black Ron shit, and there my ass go right back into the hot-ass frying pan.

"So, Shanna, I need to know what your thoughts are. If it's a problem, I'll call it all off."

"Girl, make ya money. I'm not worried about Chilae's ass right now. I got my eye on a bigger fish," she responded with a nonchalant attitude.

I looked at Karen for some kind of clue or conformation, but she had the same look on her face as I did.

"Since when are you not worried about Chilae? You act like that nigga is your source of oxygen or something."

"Since that nigga decided it was cool to be hugged up on some gutted bitch while we were out shopping together."

Both me and Karen's face registered shock. Now, I knew Chilae was a damn dog. Hell, me and him done got it in on a several occasions, and I wouldn't be surprised if he done tapped every chick in Bartram Village, but that's how it is when you fucking with a drug dealer. Bitches stay floating around like flies on shit. It comes with the territory.

"So, what are you planning to do to get him back?" I asked.

I mean, bitches were expendable to dudes like Chilae, so I needed to know why her ass was so special.

"I heard that Jarrell is back on the scene, and I plan on pushing up on his ass at the party on Friday night."

For like the hundredth time that night, my eyes bulged out of my face. If you didn't know who Jarrell was, that was a great thing. Ignorance is sometimes bliss, and this was definitely one of those cases. He was bad news all the way around, and his street name, Killa 1, was just as bad as it sounded.

"Bitch, you can't be serious. Do you have a damn death wish?" I asked more out of fear than anything. Either way Shanna went, be it with Chilae or Jarrell, when either found out what was what, it would be an all-out war.

That would be a straight dummy move on Shanna's part, and I hoped that my girl thought that situation through thoroughly. It was no secret that Chilae and Jarrell had a personal problem with each other, and even though Shanna "technically" wasn't Chilae's girl, he done dropped some major paper on her and he would definitely be taking that shit personal. That's just like having a shirt you really don't wear, but as soon as you see your sister in it all of a sudden you want to wear it. In this case, it wouldn't necessarily be the pussy they would be feuding over. It would be the principal, and Shanna would be dead wrong in this case.

"Are you sure you want to do that, Shanna? Do you know who you getting in with? This shit could end in murder," I asked again just to drive my point home. Why die over some simple-minded bullshit?

"I won't let it go that far. I won't be actually doing shit with Jarrell but spending his paper. I just want Chilae to see what he's missing."

Karen and I must have been thinking the same thing, because once again we shared the same facial expression. If he didn't give a damn about his baby's momma, and she gave that nigga three boys, then why would he give a damn about Shanna's ass? Shanna was borderline retarded sometimes, but hey, that was her shit. I had other things to think about. Excusing myself, I went home to give Chilae a buzz and to let him know it was on.

Chilae

Mina did just what the hell I thought she was going to do, although it took her longer than I thought it would. Karen came to my house two days after Mina called to let me know she had spilled the beans. That was cool with me because at least if some shit popped off, they'd know she had run her mouth.

Shanna was still mad, and frankly I didn't give a damn. Okay, so that was a tad rude of me to be hugged up on the bitch in the mall when I knew Shanna would wild out if I was caught, but I thought she would be shopping a little longer than she did. Shanna be trying to buy the whole mall, so I thought I had time. Plus the chick I was on could deep throat a damn two liter coke bottle, so I knew I had to keep that shit close. I was almost caught when I saw her walking toward me in the parking lot, so I had to wave her off and distract Shanna. Otherwise, we wouldn't have even made it in the damn building. All hell broke loose anyway, but I wasn't sweating it. That ain't nothing a little shopping spree can't fix.

So, I set everything up with Cee and Omar. Mina would be making her first trip out on Monday morning. As a thank you,

I took her to the mall so that she could get an outfit for the party tomorrow night, and twisted her back all crazy afterward. This was the party of the damn century, and I was hoping that I wouldn't have to murder anyone. I didn't really fuck around in Jersey, but my boys wanted to make it happen, so it was on. I always came in peace until I had to act otherwise, so that's how it would be. If me and Shanna weren't made up by then, it wouldn't matter. I'd just get a bitch at the party and work the hell out of it.

What I needed to do was get my ass up off the couch and go handle business. I had to get some shit lined up before Mina did her thing, and I needed everything to be right by the weekend. There was no room for mistakes, you dig?

On my way to West Philly I couldn't help but think about the pinch that Jarrell was putting on business. He'd only been out for a couple of months now, but that dude was moving quick and covering a lot of territory. I knew if I was going to come at him I would have to have an army like no other. Now, don't get me wrong. My soldiers were serious business, but I needed more niggas like them. For some reason I'd been running across some mush-ass dudes faking as men and come to find out they had bitch all up in 'em. I needed niggas that were gonna bust guns without a second thought because with niggas like Jarrell and his crew in the way, we had to hit hard, and we only had one chance to get it right. When them niggas said they were guilty as charged, that meant in all aspects and they were dead serious.

When I pulled up on 52nd and Pine to one of my many safe houses I had around Philly ,I could see my mans and 'em going into the house. You could hear the music from Choppa's Yukon at the end of the block. I done told that nigga about making himself obvious, but you can't tell dudes nothing. By the time I got to the end of the block, he was going in, and I took advantage of the free space behind his whip.

Following suit, I went up into the crib and was greeted by

Brenda, whose house we were using to store shit. Brenda had to have had the biggest ass on the planet. I mean, you could sit a meal tray on that thing and it wouldn't even tilt. Everyone in the crew had hit that, and she didn't seem to mind us rotating on that ass either. As long as we kept her rent paid as agreed and broke her off some cash, she was willing to cooperate.

My boys Sonny and Dave were already there bagging the rest of the shit up that we got from Cee and O on the last trip. That was the purpose of Mina making this move because we had no choice but to re-up in spite of the situation. I slapped Brenda on the ass on the walk by, which she made easy because all she had on was a t-shirt and thong. I walked into the kitchen to see what she had cooking.

"My nigga," I said to Dave while giving him a pound. He was the one who cooked the coke and measured shit out. It was comical because Dave was a chemistry major going to school full time at Temple University. Hard times make the street look good, and when he came looking for work, I didn't turn him away. He proved he was down for me early, and that was why he held rank in the crew.

"What it do, baby?" Dave replied. This nigga swore he was from down south, and as far south he went was South Philly. He was man, though, so it was cool.

"You know, just tryna make this money. What it looking like?"

Me and Dave went over some figures, and he broke down how much money we had in each safe house. When we hit Jarrell up we came up on some nice money, but his product wasn't shit. Word on the street was that he was doing it, but I had to practically give his shit away to make a profit. We were looking up on a couple of million though, and if Mina played her part right, we'd be good for real this time. I always heard niggas talking about getting out of the game, but with the kinda cash we was pulling in, there was no way of going back to a 9 to 5.

Brenda fed us, and we sat around and talked business for a good while afterward. I was about to have Philly on lock for sure, and the shit felt good. It's hard being the man, but who better to be the man than me? I also knew shit was going to get real sticky, and I was looking into some property over in Delaware; somewhere I could hide out and no one would know where to find me. I was being clocked 24/7 as it was, so I needed somewhere I could get some true sleep in, and not have to worry about the law or some knucklehead banging my door in. That was where Karen would come in.

Pulling up from there after midnight, I did my patrol to make sure everyone was where they were supposed to be, then I called it a night. Tomorrow was Friday, and I couldn't wait to get my swerve on.

Shanna

I spent the better part of my day pampering myself. This would be the last party we would have worth going to before the spring rolled through, and it was time to step the game way up. At Captivating Styles you heard all the scoop on what was going on in the hood. The trip I took to South Philly once a month to get my weave done could be a little tedious, but it was well worth it.

Dorthea, the owner of the shop, was the truth when it came to straightening out some nappy roots. You'd walk in there looking like Kunta Kinte's little sister and would come out with more bounce in your wrap than a big girl's ass. Jaydah and Kim were beast too, and they always knew all the damn scoop. Dom, the shampoo girl, always kept me informed on what was what while she washed my hair, and although a weave could get a little pricey, it was well worth it.

Everyone was hyped about the party tonight, and I used that opportunity to see how available Jarrell's ass really was and what the word was on the street about Chilae. I hadn't spoken to him since that mall incident that happened two weeks earlier. He called me nonstop the first couple days, but his calls eventually dwindled down to nothing. I assumed that he was seeing some other unsuspecting victim.

"What you wearing to the party tonight, Jaydah?"

"Girl, I got this sexy little jean cat suit that's about to hug all up on all this," she replied while running her hands up and down her plus-sized frame in a sensual manner. Jaydah was only about 5'4", and she had a little thickness on her, but not too much. She had her shit together, and that's all that mattered.

"I hear that girl, do the damn thing. I heard Jarrell went all out for this party."

I threw that shit right out there to see who was going to take the bait. Chilae's baby mom's sister, Aja, was in Dorthea's chair getting her hair pressed, and I know she was dying to call and let her know I was in the shop. Dorthea was my girl and all, but I hoped for the sake of everyone in there that I wouldn't have to tear the shop up this morning.

"Yeah, I hear that too. They said they were giving out a bottle of Cristal to the first hundred ladies that came through, and my ass plans to be the first in line. Somebody getting this pussy tonight, so I might as well get to' up in the process," Kim said, bringing forth all kinds of laughter.

"I wonder if Chilae gonna show his face. I ain't seen him in a while."

I looked to gauge Aja's reaction, and to my surprise, she kept a straight face. Everyone acted like I didn't say nothing wrong, and the conversation went on. I wanted the bitch to say something so that I'd have a reason to fuck something up. She ain't never did shit, but her sister did, so she was guilty by association.

To my disappointment, she didn't take the bait so we talked about a bunch of other shit until I rolled out. Once I got my feet and nails done, I didn't get home until around four in the afternoon, so that gave me time to chill for a second before I had to get ready. Karen and Mina were supposed to getting dressed at my place so we could all ride together.

After stripping naked, I stretched out across the bed, careful not to mess up my hair, and closed my eyes for a quick second. I had just gotten comfortable when the phone started ringing. My first thought was to ignore it but it might have been Karen or Shanna and I didn't want to miss their call. I rolled over and jumped out of the bed so that I could get the phone before the fifth ring. I barely made it after I fell into the table, stubbing my toe on the side.

"Hey ma, you been avoiding me?" Chilae asked.

My heart began to beat a little faster, but then I remembered how he did me at the mall, and getting back wouldn't be easy.

"What do you want?"

"Damn, baby. You can't hate me that much."

"Of course I can, now state ya purpose before I hang up."

"Shanna, come on now. After all we been through, this is how you treat me? We done been through the fire together."

"Fuck you and the fire, Chilae. I got shit to do. Now what do you want?"

"I was calling to see if you wanted to roll with me to the party."

"Fuck you, nigga. I'm good. Get that bitch from the mall to be your arm bitch tonight. I got my eye on bigger niggas."

"Bigger than me? You have got to be kidding me," Chilae laughed into the phone. I wanted so bad to tell him he was no bigger than my damn pinky finger, but why bother? Besides, I might have to hit his ass up at a later date, and it wasn't no point in stopping a possible cash flow.

"Look, Chilae, I'm about to get in the shower. I'll see you at the party."

"You sure will, but don't be mad at me, okay? I gave you a chance."

I just hung up on his ass. Damn, I swear he made me sick. Flipping on the television, I watched the soaps, knowing full well that real life was just like that shit. I was laying there thinking about how I would get next to Jarrell's ass, and I must have fallen asleep because before I knew it Karen and Mina was knocking at the door at around nine o'clock.

"Its party time, bitches!" Karen came in hollering with a bag from Doll House clutched in her hands.

Mina was right behind her with a garment bag and backpack ready to get her party on too. We took turns in the shower and we all got dressed in the room. I ended up having to bump my hair out again, but soon after I was fresh to death and ready to party. We piled up in Karen's jeep at quarter to ten, and an hour later we were paying valet to park her car.

Tonight would be interesting. I walked up in there like I owned the bitch and spotted my target as soon as I walked in. Of course he had a bunch of bitches around him, but that was a minor inconvenience. He'd be mine and I'd be riding that dick by the end of the night. Guaranteed.

Karen

Jarrell was the first person I noticed when we walked into the dimly lit club. I looked at Shanna to see if she saw him too, and from the look on her face I could tell she had. She was getting into some unnecessary bullshit by trying to play Jarrell and Chilae against each other, but you couldn't tell her shit. These niggas were drug dealers. They could care less about a money hungry bitch on a paper chase, and I tried to tell her that, but it was like talking to a damn wall. Fuck it, she'd have to find out the hard way.

I took post by the bar so that I could get a good view of the room. Shanna and Mina were there, and I'm almost certain that between the three of us, we done hit at least half those dudes in there at one time or another. You know how bitches can be. In short, I needed to know my element just in case I had to hurt something.

Jarrell was looking better than the last time I remembered. Dressed in a Sean John sweat suit from his exclusive line and some mesh Timbs to match, my man was doing it real big. His ear, pinky, and wrist were blinging like crazy, and the simple medallion chain that rested on his chest spoke volumes. He was definitely eating. And I wasn't mad at him.

I spotted a few enemies in the room and some regular bitches that didn't mean too much to me. I sent him over a bottle of Cristal, and it wasn't until he looked up and acknowledged me from across the room that I made my way over to him. I could smell his Unforgivable by Sean John way before I reached him. I was a little bit nervous at first because I hadn't seen him since he came home. Although it wasn't right out there for everyone, I was working with the enemy now, and I wasn't sure if he knew. An easy smile spread across his face the closer I got to him, and I knew for sure we were still family.

I walked right into his embrace and accepted the warm hug he offered. Jarrell and I were close at one point, but under the circumstances, I was sure things had changed. How much was beyond me. He brushed off all the chicks around him, and we took a seat at a table by the bar and caught up.

"Jarrell, you looking good, pa. Life treating you well I see." I lightly fingered the medallion on his chain before laying it back on his chest. Talking to him brought back memories of how me and Benny used to kick it, and I got a little misty-eyed. Just when I thought I was over him, all those feelings came rushing back.

"You doing it real big too, ma. I see you still got that figure, and you wearing the hell out of those jeans."

I blushed a little at his comment. Although I didn't get all decked out, I was killing them in my formfitting Doll House jeans that I had carefully tucked into my calf–high, dark chocolate Manolo Blahnik Bobfeti boots. I had on a sheer blouse that was cut open from my neck to just under my breasts, where it fit tight at the bottom. Only a small portion of my stomach was out, and I had my naturally curly hair pulled up off my neck with my curls framing my face. Being one of few white women in the club, I had to make sure I was on point.

"You know how I do. So how's everything going? Business is obviously going well for you," I responded, watching Shanna out of the corner of my eye. I could see her circling around us like a damn hawk, just waiting to dive down in on her target.

We made eye contact once more before she was at our table pushing up on him. I got to admit that Shanna was smooth with her shit. I'm certain that Jarrell had all kinds of pussy being thrown his way since he been home, but Shanna had a way of making a dude think that her pussy was the best thing since M&M's.

My biggest concern was how Chilae was going to act when he showed up. You know how territorial guys could be, so this right here would be interesting to watch. Shanna already had Jarrell under her spell, so I discreetly excused myself from the table, and went to go find Mina.

After circling the club twice, I finally found her in VIP with Scoop and 'em from back street. Over in South West Philly there was a strip of houses on one side and empty lots on the other that began on 52nd street and Greenway and stretched to 54th on the same strip. All you saw was the backs of folks houses so it was lovingly called "back street" by everyone that hung out that way.

Taking a seat at the table, I avoided eye contact with the other guy that was sitting there and danced in my seat while I people-watched. Shanna was killing it over there with Jarrell on the dance floor. I knew at that point, she was in there. Jarrell wasn't no cheap nigga, so she'd be walking away from that with a nice knot in her purse.

We partied hard for a good while and just as suspected, five after midnight Chilae comes walking through the door with a bad ass chick on his arm. I ain't one to hate, so I'll be the first to say that this chick had her shit together. Shanna was my girl and all that, but this one was murdering folks with her body. Curves were all over the place, and she had a pretty butter pecan complexion that looked like she was lying up on the beach for the past couple of months. Her shoulder-length wrap flowed with her walk and it looked like it was all hers, too.

I looked Shanna's way to see if she peeped them coming in and she had. She looked a little uptight for a second, but then she started giving up the ass to Jarrell big time on the dance floor. Chilae didn't seem like he was fazed by it. He just made his rounds, showing love to those he knew. He stopped along the way to give hugs to a few of the chicks that were already there partying, and that had to be the biggest mistake he made all night. Shanna wouldn't have ever went for him hugging up on no other bitch. Being as though this one just stood to the side and didn't say a word made her an easy target. She'd be getting abused and bumped into for the rest of the party, and that was just the kind of shit that Shanna was into.

When Chilae crossed Jarrell's path, it got tense up in there right quick. Everyone stopped what they were doing, and some even ducked behind the tables, not knowing what to expect from the two trigger-happy men. Chilae acted like he didn't see Jarrell, but he did look Shanna right in the face before stepping around them on the dance floor. Everyone breathed a sigh of relief, but who knew how it would be when we got out of the club later on?

Shanna was a damn good actor, because on the outside it would appear that she wasn't bothered but I know she was fucked up on the inside. She just got straight dissed, but she put herself out there, so what could she do about it? I kept on getting my party on, but I did watch Shanna from a distance to make sure she didn't get too tipsy and do something stupid.

As the night went on, Shanna and Jarrell got a little closer, and I knew for sure she'd be leaving with him tonight. None of the women who were surrounding him earlier were anywhere in sight, but I saw a lot of those bitches hating from the sidelines. Mina had even managed to hook up on Scoop, so that left me to get home by myself. That was cool because my mind was really on this drop Mina had to make on Monday.

At three on the dot, the lights came up in the club, indicating it was time to roll up out of there. Since neither of us had coats on, we all waited outside for our respective rides. I was waiting to see if anything was going to pop off with Chilae and Jarrell. Rumor had it that Chilae's boys was sticking up Jarrell's safe houses last summer, and even though they had gone to war, I doubted that it was over.

To my surprise Jarrell came up from out the club and snatched Shanna up on the way to his whip the valet conveniently had ready for him. I saw Chilae's whip being pulled up three cars behind. We said our goodbyes, and they rolled out. To my surprise when Chilae came out, Mina followed him to his car. It had to have been the liquor for them to be so outright blatant. I was suddenly glad that Shanna had already left.

Just as I was getting into my car, I got a call from my parents' house. Something told me to ignore it, but I couldn't. My dad hadn't been doing well lately, and my gut tightened up at the thought of something happening to him. I was supposed to have gone and seen him three days earlier, but hadn't made it there yet. Damn, the guilt was setting in already.

Racing to my parents' house across town, I pulled up just in time to see the ambulance bringing my father out. His body wasn't covered, so I knew he wasn't dead, but all the oxygen and stuff hooked up to him made me crumble to the ground. I didn't even bother to park my car. I just pulled off behind the ambulance, leaving my mother standing outside with a look of shock on her face. I figured I'd deal with her later; right then I had to make sure my dad was cool.

Shanna

Jarrell's crib looked like a mini mansion. I was prepared to see guard dogs run to the gate when we pulled up and all that on some real Biggie Small's *Ready To Die* shit. When we walked in the door, I damn near hit the floor. He had a real baller's crib equipped with plush furnishings and a state of the art surround-sound studio system. He didn't give me a tour or anything; he walked me straight to the bedroom.

I knew what I was there for, so I didn't waste any time stripping his ass naked and working the shit out of him. He was definitely bigger than Chilae, and I found myself running from the dick several times during the act. I knew if I was gonna keep his ass around and keep a steady hand in his pockets, I had to take control of the situation, though.

Jarrell was hammering into me like he had some shit to prove, and maybe he did. He knew I was Chilae's "girl" kind of, and just to be able to brag about snatching up some shit Chilae previously had was all he really wanted. I wrapped my legs around him real tight and clamped my pussy muscles down on him, causing him to go into instant convulsions. He was shaking and flopping around like a fish out of water, and that's how I knew my job was done.

He laid on top of me with his head on my chest for a few minutes before he rolled off. I took that opportunity to wash my hands in the adjoining bathroom and slip into one of his bathrobes. He was lying on the bed looking at me like he was in love and shit. I was enjoying all the attention.

I left the room and went downstairs, walking around until I found the kitchen. That thing was decked out with modern appliances, and all of that shit looked like it had never been used. I was skeptical at first, but was glad to see the refrigerator fully stocked. I rifled through until I found some cold cuts and lettuce, and made him a sandwich that would definitely knock him out for the night.

"So, Shanna," Jarrell said sleepily while still watching T.V. "What you doing with a mark-ass nigga like Chilae?"

I had to take a good look at him to see if he was serious before I responded. I knew he would try to get me for some information, but I didn't think it would be this soon. *Let me find out he a nut.*

"That was just something I happened to get into," I said, choosing my words carefully. I was mad at Chilae, but I ain't no song bird. Whatever he needed to know, he damn sure wouldn't be finding out from me.

"Oh, you just happened to fall into it, huh? The same way you fell into me?" he said with a sly look on his face.

"Yep," I said, returning the expression. I already knew how shit was gonna be with Jarrell, and I was gonna make sure I got all I could from this nigga before he brushed me off. He would only keep me around long enough to piss off Chilae. As soon as he decided Chilae ain't thinking about me, my ass would be history.

"Okay, ma. You got jokes I see. So what I gotta do to make you happy? You gonna be my girl?"

"I'll let you know along the way," I responded before I

leaned over to suck his dick. He was really laying it on thick, but little did he know, I was hip to the game. The tables were already turned. He just didn't know it yet.

I was juggling his balls in my mouth and jerking his dick at the same time, causing him to screech and moan like a damn girl. Either I was really doing the damn thing or he was a hell of an actor. I would let him think that he was juicing me for info on my man, but he'd definitely be paying for it. Minutes later I was swallowing his kids and riding that nigga to sleep.

He was out like a light, so I used that opportunity to look around his crib to see what was cracking. He had three other bedrooms besides the one we were in, all immaculately decorated. He had a beautiful bathroom connected to his room, and the one in the hall was nothing to sneeze at. The black and white marble Jacuzzi and the double chrome sinks were to die for.

I crept down the stairs. His living room had to have been decorated by a female, because no man could have ever thought of that layout. A long hall next to the small restroom in the living room led to a studio booth and a sitting room with all of the equipment needed to produce records. *Let me find out Jarrell is a rapping drug dealer.*

I walked back past the kitchen to look out at the pool that was just beyond the wood patio, and that's when I felt like someone was watching me. I was almost certain that Jarrell and I were the only ones in the house, but I still felt like there was another presence in the room. Choosing not to take any chances, I walked around the island back through the kitchen, quickening my pace.

Just as I reached the steps, the hair stood up on the back of my neck. When I looked back, there were two snow white pit bulls growling at me and showing their teeth. We made eye contact, then I just broke up the steps. The dogs were right on my heels.

I took the steps two at a time all the way up and I barely

made it in the room, shutting the doors on the dogs and falling to the floor. My heart was beating a mile a minute, and all I could do was rest my head against the hard wood and try to catch my breath. When I looked up, Jarrell was staring at me with a smile on his face. I didn't know what to say. I just shook my head and got up off the floor. I was more embarrassed than anything, and it showed on my face as I walked toward the bed.

"I see you met my girls, huh?" Jarrell laughed like the shit was comical.

I was ready to fuck his ass up.

"Why didn't you tell me you had dogs in here?" I asked him angrily. Considering we had sex with the damn door open, he should have warned me of my damn surroundings. "What if those dogs would've smelled us having sex and started acting a damn fool? What would I have told Chilae if I was attacked?"

"That's what's happens to nosey bitches. Now get ya ass in the bed. If I wanted to give you a tour, I would have done that when we first walked in."

I did what I was told, turning my back to him and laying my head on the pillow. I was ready to jet, but with his those bitches out in the hallway I had no choice but to chill until the morning. He would definitely be paying for this one. I couldn't wait to tell my girls this crazy shit.

When we woke up, he was energized like he just slept for ten days straight. I, on the other hand, was still pissed about last night. I was up all night, scared to piss, just waiting for them damn dogs to bust up in the room and eat my ass alive. I finally dozed off to sleep around six in the morning, and there this nigga go jumping up at nine like a damn rooster. I knew I had bags under my eyes and everything, and I didn't give a fuck. I just went and washed my face, opting to wash my body when I got home. I ain't even want breakfast. I just wanted to get back to Philly.

He wasn't in the room when I came out of the bathroom,

and the bedroom door was open. My first instinct was to run back in the bathroom, but there was no way he'd just leave them damn dogs out there knowing I was scared to death. I quickly dressed and went downstairs to find him in the kitchen eating breakfast. My plate was already made and on the table, but I didn't make a move toward it. I had to go.

"Good morning, ma. How you sleep last night?" he asked between bites of eggs and sausage.

I've never felt more played in my life.

"Cool, what time are we leaving?"

"Sit down and eat your breakfast."

He totally ignored my question, and I obliged, not wanting to start shit with him. For the first time I felt like I made a mistake coming there. That shit with Chilae was minute, and I had to go and blow shit out of proportion. I took a couple of bites of food just to shut him up, and sat there fiddling with the rest of it until he was done.

When he was done, he took my plate without asking if it was cool and walked toward the door. I followed behind him, not knowing what to think. When we got outside, those damn dogs were out there, and they acted more like precious puppies around him as opposed to the vicious man-eaters they were the night before.

I didn't care either way. While he was being a loving dad, I made my way to his car, happy as hell that the door wasn't locked. I was cursing myself out the entire time, and after fifteen minutes he finally came to the car. I wanted to call Karen, but I didn't want this crazy nigga snapping the hell out.

When he got in the car he pulled off like he was in the Indy 500 or some shit. My heart was beating in my chest a mile a minute the entire ride. I didn't know where the hell we were headed to because last night it was dark and I was drunk so I didn't remember which way we had come to get to his house. All I knew was we were on I-295 headed toward Philly, and I couldn't wait.

A half hour later I could see the projects and I had never been happier to be home. When we pulled up, I saw Chilae out there talking to Bam and them on the corner and I just ignored his ass. Running up to my apartment, I locked the door like someone was chasing me and breathed a sigh of relief. I didn't get a chance to get any money from Jarrell, but I'd be more on point the next time. I'd be damned if he would play me twice.

Picking up the phone, I called Karen and her phone went straight to voice mail. I didn't bother to leave a message, deciding to just give her a call later. I called Mina next and she said she hadn't heard from Karen since the night before. Hell, it was Saturday, so I was sure she'd be coming around later. At that moment, I had to take a bath and get some sleep. I would be giving Chilae a call later too. I had to at least patch shit up with him so that when I was done with Jarrell's nut ass, I'd have him to go back to.

Karen

My daddy was dying. I felt so helpless watching him lay in that hospital bed hooked up to all those tubes. The reception on my cell phone wasn't working in the hospital, so I couldn't call anyone. I was calling from the room phone, but neither Mina or Shanna picked up, and since it was after hours, they wouldn't be able to call back to see who it was.

My mother didn't even bother to come. After the ambulance pulled off, she went back into the house like nothing ever happened. If I didn't have to go and be with my dad, I would have knocked her ass straight out. Her own husband, and she couldn't even see about him. I understand that she was in it for the money from the beginning, but have some compassion. You learn to love someone after a while, but with her, I guess it never happened that way.

I thought I had cried all the tears I could cry, but I just couldn't take it. Without him, I had no reason to even visit my parents' house. He just looked so at peace lying there, and that was a first. He was supposed to be finishing up on his chemotherapy that week, and now here we go with this. The doctor told us that there would be a possibility of a relapse, but he had been doing so well.

As the day went on, I just kinda chilled out and watched a couple of shows on television that I knew he liked, hoping that it would bring him out of it. I had been there since three that morning, and sleeping in that chair had my back cramped tight. Around mid-afternoon I ran down to get my books from out of the car so that I could get a little schoolwork done. I would be done with school in a couple of months. I knew he'd be happy about that. That's all he ever really wanted from me. I couldn't really concentrate, but I had to do something to keep my mind off of my father's condition.

At around eight the nurse that would be taking care of him overnight came to let me know visiting hours would be over soon. She offered to get me a comforter and a pillow if I wanted to stay, but I opted not to. He was in stable condition, so I was cool for now. I wanted to just go home and think. I hated hospitals, but this was the only exception.

I watched the nurse get my dad settled for the evening and, after she left the room, I approached the side of his bed. I felt like I couldn't live without my daddy, so if he died, I figured I might as well die too.

Pulling the blanket up to his chin, I gave him a kiss on the cheek and told him I loved him. The tears were starting again, so I gathered my bags as quickly as I could and left. It wasn't until I pushed the down button on the elevator that I allowed my tears to flow freely. My dad was a good man, and it seemed that bad shit always happened to good people. When the elevator opened, I was surprised to see my mother standing there. I didn't even acknowledge her. I just stepped into the elevator and let the doors close. She was probably just up there to see if he had died yet.

I was in a zone on my way to Shanna's house. I just needed to be around someone who understood my pain, and my girls always made me feel better. Damn the club tonight. I just needed to stay in the house and get faded.

When I pulled up, I saw Chilae's truck parked at the other end of the block. He must have hooked himself another hood rat out in there in the Vill. I just shook my head. I swear he acted like a girl sometimes, and nine out of ten he was out there to make Shanna mad. The two of them were a damn mess.

When I got upstairs, Mina was already there wearing the same exhausted look that I had on my face. Shanna looked a little vexed too, so I was sure that we were all in agreement that tonight was a good night to stay in.

"What's up, y'all? How is everything?" I asked, not wanted to be the first to put my burden on anyone. Aside from that, I knew I would cry, so I wanted to be the last to go.

"I'm nervous as hell about Monday. Chilae suggested that I still go to work, but I don't even think I'll make it through the day," Mina said, like she was second guessing the decision she made to help Chilae out. Little did she know, the agreement she made was set in stone. There wasn't no turning back now. Calls had already been made to set shit up.

"Girl, what you about to do is a cakewalk. All you got to do is get on the bus, make a drop, pick up some shit and come back. Just don't let the Maryland niggas sidetrack you. Keep business just that."

"Girl, I know, and Omar can definitely be a distraction. I'm just scared the law is gonna run up on me. I ain't made for jail."

"Girl, just relax and don't be looking all suspicious and shit. If you go down, Chilae stands to lose a lot of money, so I'm sure you'll be cool," Shanna butted in nonchalantly in a bad attempt to ease Mina's fears. Normally she was a little more understanding, so something had to be wrong. I knew she left the club with Jarrell, but it was apparent that shit didn't go well.

"Fuck what you just said, Shanna. You're not the one putting your life on the line."

"Bitch you getting paid for it, so relax."

"Bitch? Why I got to be all that? You just mad because your man chose me."

They were about to seriously get riled up in there, and a part of me started to let them. At the same time, we had been at each other's throats a lot lately, and I knew we were tighter than that. We needed each other more than ever, so it was time to stop all the madness.

"Y'all two need to get it together. We're sisters. If you need to vent, do that, but at the end of the day, we are all we got. Shanna, something is obviously bothering you, so say what it is, damn."

Shanna looked at me like she was ready to fuck both me and Mina up, and with the way that I was feeling, I wanted her to be froggy and leap. She would get the ass-whipping of her life today, that was a guarantee. I needed to talk to my friends, and after seeing my dad laid up in the hospital, it made me realize how short life really is. Now was the time for us to be with each other, not against each other.

"Well, as y'all know, I left the club with Jarrell last night," Shanna began, wisely taking heed to what I said.

Mina still looked like she had some attitude with her, and I paid her ass no mind. I saw her leave with Chilae, so let's keep shit in perspective.

"So what happened?" Mina asked as if she was really interested.

Anything would work to keep the spotlight off me for right now.

"Err thang was going good. I was giving it to that nigga, had him screaming my name and all that. I mean, I put his ass to sleep in no time."

"And I know that's right," I came back with all of us high fiving each other.

"So what happened next?"

"Girl, he had a beautiful-ass house. That shit looked like a mini mansion. He didn't bother to show me the place when we first got there, so after I put his ass to sleep, I took it upon myself to check everything out. Girl, I should have kept my ass in that damn bed with him because my ass was almost mangled."

Now by this point Mina and I were on the floor cracking up at Shanna's theatrical performance. When she told a story it was like she was onstage. I could imagine how it all went down, being as though we've all had sex in the same room at one time or another and we all knew exactly what we were capable of. She put her hands on her hips and continued with her story, me and Mina waiting eagerly for the outcome.

"Well, I'm looking around the downstairs and through his kitchen was a banging-ass pool. For some reason it felt like someone was watching me, and for a second, I thought maybe he had busted me walking around his crib. Girl, when I turned around there were these two giant-ass pit bulls looking at me like I was dinner or something."

At that point both our mouths were open, not believing the turn of events. That was some wild shit to be put up against, and pit bulls were the most vicious dogs out there. I would have hated for Shanna to have to walk around with a club foot.

"Chile, let me tell you how I turned into a crack addict and took flight. You know a crackhead moves fast. Well, my ass broke up out that kitchen like I was running from some nigga I done stole from. I barely made it up to the room and had the door closed just in time for those trifling-ass dogs to thump up against it. My damn heart liked to jump out my chest, and when I turned around, this nigga up in the bed laughing at me."

At that moment, I damn near pissed on myself from laughing so hard. Shanna looked genuinely pissed, but she had to admit that shit was funny after the fact. I'm sure she was scared shitless at the time, but when you look back on some shit, you see the humor in it.

"Girl, I know you were fit to be tied," Mina said while catching her breath.

Shanna and Mina had told of their concerns and how hectic shit had been, and now it was my turn. I didn't even want to bother them with my shit, but I knew they wouldn't let me slide out so easily.

"So, who you luck up on? I know one of us got some paper last night," Shanna asked while taking her seat. She tired herself out telling her own story, and immediately began rolling an el so that we could all fall back. I guess it was unanimous that we weren't hitting the party scene tonight.

"My dad is in the hospital. When I left the club, I got a call when I was on my way over to West Philly. By the time I got there, the ambulance was taking him away, and I followed behind them up to the hospital."

"You can't be serious. He was doing so well. How is your mom holding up?" Mina asked. She looked like she was going to cry, but tears were already rolling down my face.

"That bitch turned around and went in the house like he didn't even matter to her. I fucking hate her, I swear I do."

By then I was snotting and tearing all over the place and my girls gathered around to comfort me. My mother could be a bitch at the most inconvenient times. I never understood the relationship her and my father had, but one thing was as clear as the day is long. My mother was a get money chick, and the apple didn't fall that far from the damn tree.

"You have got to be kidding me. How could she be so

cold?" Mina tried to comfort me by rubbing my back, but all I could think about was life after my father was gone.

"Well, there is one thing you know for certain," Shanna said while puffing the el and passing it to me. I didn't hesitate to take it either. "He has to go to a better place from here. You just have to prepare yourself for what's to come."

Mina

Karen had me on pins and needles. I mean, her dad had doing great, and then he was lying on his deathbed. That just goes to show how the tables will turn on your ass before you know what done hit you.

I spent all day on Sunday ducking Chilae's calls. What the hell had I gotten myself into? I don't know what the hell I was hiding from because Chilae knew right where to find me, but I had to get my head together.

I haven't prayed as much as I did that day in ages. I knew what I was doing was wrong, but I'd already agreed to it. Chilae called me at least thirty times, and by nightfall he was at my door, trying to kick it in. To keep my neighbors from being in my business, I jumped up to open the door before the cops were called and a crowd gathered outside. That's how much noise he was making.

"Chilae, you can get the hell off my damn door like that. What's all the kicking and banging for?" I answered the door with tons of attitude to try and throw him off but it didn't work.

"Bitch, I been calling you all day. Why you ain't returned my calls?"

"Chilae, Karen's dad is in the hospital and . . ."

"Mina, I ain't got time right now for dumb shit. It don't take but a minute to pick up the gotdamn phone. You know what we gotta do tomorrow."

"Look nigga, just state ya purpose for being here. I know what I gotta do," I came back to let him know I wasn't scared all like that. Shit, he asked me to do him a favor, not the other way around.

"You know we have to go over the procedure on what you gotta do, and I had to drop off the money. Don't go getting stupid on me now."

"Nigga, just say what you gonna say."

Chilae looked like he was ready to murder my ass up in there, and I returned the same look. When dudes think they got you shook, they start treating you like shit, and I'd be damned if that how it was going down. He went on to explain that I had to be at the Greyhound station by six on the dot to get to Maryland. The bus would be arriving in Maryland at 8:15 when I would be picked up by Candy, Omar's girlfriend. That shit threw me for a loop for like four seconds because I didn't know Omar had a girlfriend. I guess my plans to get with him while I was down the way was a no go.

Candy would take me to the spot were I would meet up with Omar and Cee-Lo, and she would come back to get me when it was time to go. I had to count out fifteen bricks of coke, and it would be put in a black duffle bag. I didn't have to do nothing but give them the book bag with the money in it, and by the time I got down the stairs, Candy would be outside waiting for me.

Chilae opened the oversized backpack and I saw that it was loaded with large text books on the inside. When he pulled them out, he began to flip through the pages, and by the time

I got to page ten, the middle was cut out of the pages all the way except about ten pages in the back. Piles of money were stacked neatly inside. Omar would put the coke in the books in place of the money and I would bring them back the same way.

"Now, this is where you got to pay attention. Being stupid could have you in the pen, and that's exactly where your ass would be if you're caught," Chilae said before continuing.

I'm thinking to myself that he had to have been playing. *Let me get locked up for getting caught with his shit and the entire operation will be a rap. Fuck with me.*

Candy would drop me off at the bus station at twelve o'clock. The bus pulled off at 12:10 in the morning. Omar had a hook up with the night guy that does the search, so when the bus pulled up I had to be the first in line, and I was supposed to sit in the back by the window. The bus would be getting back to Philly at 2:30, and he would be there to pick me up.

"Now, did you get everything I just told you?"

"Yeah, I got chu. It sounds easy."

"That's my girl. Bring daddy back his shit, and you'll be rewarded."

"Cool, so let me get some sleep and I'll holla at you tomorrow," I said, feigning fatigue knowing damn well my ass wouldn't be getting an ounce of sleep tonight.

I would be getting five thousand dollars when I got back. I would just keep that in mind the entire trip. I already had my pocketbook ready with my iPod and a book to read to keep me occupied for the two hour trip, and my outfit was already laid out. I chose a simple pair of dress slacks and a button down shirt accented with a pair of loafers. I didn't want to be too dressed up, but I still had to represent when I went down there. Folks always know when you ain't from their part of the world.

"Oh, Mina, one more thing before I go. Do not discuss

business over your cell phone, or any phone for that matter. The jakes are always listening."

"No problem," I replied, anxious for him to leave. I needed tomorrow to get here as quickly as possible, and I wanted to try and get some rest.

Chilae just sat there and stared at me, and there I was thinking he was done talking. It was so quiet you could hear a mouse piss on cotton up in there. I felt awkward, and really didn't know if I should be asking him questions or something at this point. Just as I was fixing to say something to him, he called me over.

"Mina, come here, let me look at you," he said in a husky voice like he was about to fuck me or something.

Sex was the last thing on my mind, but I went over to see what he wanted.

"Turn around and take your clothes off. I want to see you undress."

"What?" I responded in shock. I know this dude wasn't trying to get it and we had business to take care of.

"Take ya clothes off." He already had his dick out, as small as it was, and I had to hold my damn laugh in front of this dude. Damn, I really didn't feel like the bullshit right now.

"Chilae, come on with all that. This is business, and I need to go to bed. I gotta get up early in the morning."

"Oh, it's just business, huh? You telling me you don't want all this dick in you?" he replied while stroking his dick like that shit was down to his knees. It was so small that it got lost in the palm of his hand, but he acted like he didn't notice it.

"No, it ain't that, but my period is about to come on and my stomach is already starting to cramp up."

"Is that so? Well let me put it in your ass."

"Chilae, I'm just not in the mood. I got you, though. Soon as my period goes off it's on. Plus, I'm nervous about tomorrow, so I really can't even think about nothing else." This dude was really trying to get it. *Man, if he don't go 'head with that shit. Right now it's about the money.*

"Well, I guess I can't get no head either because your throat hurt too, right?" he said sarcastically while stuffing his privates back into his pants. I mean, his dick sat on top of his balls all snug and cozy and shit. No hang time was evident. How did he not get it?

"Yeah, I guess so. But once I get back, we'll politic, okay?"

"Just make sure I see you Tuesday. I already got your money put to the side."

"Okay, I'll see you then."

Chilae finally left, and I had to lean against the door to breathe. I had a big day ahead of me, and I just wanted it to hurry up and get here. I ran some more hot water into the lukewarm bath I had drawn earlier and soaked my bones until the wee hours of the morning. I kept running the scenario through my head on what I was supposed to do, and if everything worked out right I'd be five gees richer within the next two days. Surprisingly, once I finally got into the bed I was out like a light, and had all kinds of energy when I woke up.

When I got to work, I put the book bag in my locker and secured it with a padlock. It amazed me how fast my day went, and throughout the day I opened my locker to check and make sure it was till there. Doing the same thing I did the other day, I worked through my lunch break and made sure I got extra work done to satisfy my supervisor for allowing me to roll out early again. Just as Chilae told me, I was down at 9th and Filbert by quarter to six waiting in line to board the bus.

I already had my ticket in my hand and my backpack on my back. I could see that the guard wasn't searching every single bag, so hopefully he'd skip me. Since that whole 9/11 incident, everyone had been extra cautious. My heart beat faster as the line moved closer, and I was damn near about to faint. There was one more person in front of me, and the guard didn't even bother to check him, but when my ass walked up he was all in my damn face.

"Ticket please," he said angrily like he hated his job. Why do customer service if you not a people person?

I handed him my ticket and he examined it like the shit was written in Spanish or something. I was starting to get antsy and impatient, and he was definitely starting to piss me off.

"What business you have in Maryland, young lady?" the rent-a-cop asked. I looked at him like he done lost his mind before I answered.

"What business is that of yours? Does harassment go with buying a ticket?"

He looked shocked for a second that I came back at him like that. Hell, it ain't like I had a damn bomb strapped to my chest or some shit. Some people just overdo their damn job, I swear.

"No it doesn't, but I've asked everyone the same question."

"No you didn't. Did you forget that I was standing in line all this time? I didn't hear you ask anyone about their travel reasons. I'm not trying to miss my bus, so what else do you want to know?"

"Just get on the damn bus."

I rolled my eyes at him and walked to the bus, giving the driver my ticket. After I found a seat toward the back, which was a miracle because that's where everyone seemed to migrate to, I got comfortable and waited for the bus to pull off. It was a straight ride from there to Maryland, so I pulled out my iPod and chilled.

Halfway through, I must have fallen asleep because when I heard the bus driver welcoming us to the Baltimore Transportation Center, I was damn near the last off the bus. When I got off the bus, I didn't know who to look for, and I thought to call Chilae and ask. He said we couldn't discuss business over the phone, but what was I supposed to do?

Just as the last person was clearing out of the station and I had been standing there for ten minutes, my cell phone rang. A 443 number popped up, and I assumed it was someone from down there because the number Omar gave me to contact him had the same area code. When I answered the phone, it was Candy telling me to come outside. She was in a red Expedition.

Her truck was the only one in the street, so I didn't hesitate to walk over to it and hop in. A cloud of weed smoke rushed toward me when I opened the door. I was surprised that she could see out of the dark tinted windows with all the smoke that was inside, but she pulled off like it wasn't nothing.

She didn't say a word to me, she just hauled ass through the streets, barely stopping at stop signs. She held the blunt that she was smoking toward me in a gesture for me to smoke, but I passed on it. I ain't see her roll that el and I didn't know what they puffing on in those parts. I been done fucked around and took a hit and ended up like how Smokey was on Friday, running down the street in my damn drawers. She didn't seem to care; she just took another hit off of it and blew the smoke in my direction. I had to stay focused this time out, so I didn't need anything clouding my judgment.

Candy wasn't as cute as I thought she would be. She had a body like a brick house, but her face left a lot to be desired. She wasn't butt ugly, but she wasn't cute by any means. She had a flat pie face with wide spread eyes like the singer Brandy. Her skin was in immediate need of rescue from Proactive, and her nose was huge. She must have had some bomb-ass head or the pussy was fire, because there was no way Omar was with her based on looks.

I found myself studying her like she was a bug under a microscope, and had to divert my attention elsewhere before she thought I had a problem with her. I was too far away from home to be getting into some shit. I took in the scenery instead, and twenty minutes later we pulled up to some off-

brand projects. She stopped the jeep in front of a row of build-
ings and turned the music down.

"Go to apartment C. Omar and Cee-Lo waiting on you."

To my surprise, this chick had gold fronts, and that just
blew me out of the water. I know some dudes from the Dirty
South do that, but Maryland ain't that far down south for that
nonsense. I just got my shit and got out of the car. I wasn't
even good and on the curb before she pulled off, never mind
she didn't tell me what building to go into. I just assumed
since we were parked in front of 1907 that was where I should
be so I chose that door to walk into.

The building was just like the ones in Bartram Village where
I lived. There was a pissy elevator that wasn't working, so I took
the stairs. There were two apartments on each floor, but none
of them had letters on the floor. I stood in the hallway looking
around stupidly until I saw a capital letter C written with a yellow crayon on top of the door on my left. Taking a chance, I
knocked on the door and was greeted by Omar. For the first
time, I breathed a sigh of relief and walked into his apartment.
Half my job was already done.

Chilae

"Yo Karen, I need you do something for me, ma. It's crucial to business."

Mina should have been in Maryland handling that business for me, so I wanted to get some other shit done. I saw business being back on the rise sooner than expected, and I needed to get me a hideaway quick. Not that many people knew where I rested my head at night, but one person was still too many, and people start to talk in desperate situations. I needed me a spot where not even my crew or family could find me if some shit went down.

An hour later, Karen was at my house looking sexy as usual. For Karen to be white, she really had her shit together. I was starting to rise to the occasion quickly and man would I have loved to smash her ass real quick. I had to keep my mind focused, but once she got me the new spot it would be on.

"Chilae, please let this be important. I was on the way to the hospital to see my dad before my class later tonight."

"Damn, girl, you still in school?"

"Chilae, why did you call me over here?"

"Wow, short tempered today, huh? I called because I need

me a hideaway. Somewhere no one would know to find me except you and Mina. Shanna can't even know about the spot."

I thought for a second she was going to black on me because every time I called her I needed something, but to my surprise, she looked as if she was really contemplating what I said. I didn't even want the spot in my name, just in case the law started to get particular.

"Well, I do have this spot over in Dover that no one knows about. I go over there every so often when I need to clear my head. It's a hot spot, but I only have a bed in there. I never got the chance to furnish it."

"Oh, that's not a problem, ma. I'll do all that for you. When can we go see it?" I asked anxiously, happy that it was possible. Shit was going too smooth, so I was definitely looking for something to go wrong. I'd be lying if I said I wasn't worried about Mina, but I knew she would be able to pull it off.

Shanna was upset because I didn't ask her, but she be on some cute shit, and when it came to business, I needed someone that had some fear in them. All I needed was to have Shanna making a run for me, and someone looked at her the wrong way. She been done dropped my shit and started a damn fight, forgetting the damn mission. Mina, on the other hand, was too scared to get caught, so I knew she'd walk a straight line all the way through.

I guess Shanna thought she was doing something by hooking up with nutt-ass Jarrell, but he was actually doing me a favor by keeping her occupied. I didn't need her in the way right now, and as long as I acted like I gave a fuck, he'd hold on to her. That would give me time to set some shit up on his ass. Shanna had the bomb-ass pussy and she'd have him whipped in no time, the same way she used to have me. By the time he came around, my ass would be long gone and I'd be running shit again. Yeah, shit was definitely looking up.

"What are you doing tomorrow? We can take a ride over there, and maybe stop by the casino. Dover Downs is right near there," Karen said on her way out the door. Normally she stuck around for awhile, but today didn't seem to be one of those days.

"Tomorrow is not good. Mina will be back from Maryland in the morning, and I need to meet her at the Greyhound station. What about Friday? That way we can shop down there on Saturday and get some furniture up in there. Whatever you want, I'm buying."

"Friday it is. See you then."

That was the best news I heard all day. I was on my way out the door to see what the streets were talking about when my cell phone rang. The number had a Maryland area code, so I figured it had to have been Omar or Cee-Lo. Either things were going good or Mina had fucked up.

"Make it quick, the streets are watching," I spoke into the phone. That meant that there was a possible bug on my line, and it took the law at least thirty seconds to start recording.

"The eagle has landed," the voice said on the other line. Omar was in business mode as usual, so I made it quick.

"Cool. Make it happen."

Ending the call, I went on to see if money was being made. By the time I got down to 52nd Street, I pulled up just in time to see Brenda being escorted out of her house by the cops. I didn't see the whips of any of the crew, so I kept on riding by like I was just passing that way. When I got up on them, I made eye contact with Brenda through the cop car, and she looked scared. I winked at her to let her know I saw her, and I would be expecting her call. What the hell happened since the other day? She had been running that spot for years, so someone must have opened their mouth to the law.

I jetted down to Siegel Street to see Sonny about what was going on. Pine Street was his spot to look over, so I needed him to tell me what the fuck went down. Now was not the time to be losing money when we were just starting to get back on track.

When I pulled up on 21st Street, I could see Sonny, Dave,

and Choppa's rides parked out front. I circled around the block and found me a spot close to the corner. I took a second to calm down because I was ready to bust up in there swinging on everybody. It seemed like every time I tried to get back on track something kept me from it. We had mad money and product in that house. A hit like that would have us messed up for a minute.

As I got closer to the door, I could hear the fellas inside laughing and busting it up like we didn't just miss out on a couple millions dollars and shit. That just fueled my anger and I ran up into the house like a madman.

"Damn, nigga, who chasing you?" Sonny sat back, surprised to see me.

Their entire conversation came to an end. I was beyond pissed and needed immediate answers.

"Who's chasing me? Nigga, what the fuck happened up Pine Street? Why did I just ride by my shit getting raided by the fuckin' cops?" I was pissed, and those dudes were looking at me like I was speaking another fucking language. If I didin't get answers soon, someone would be dying tonight.

"Nigga, calm down. Brenda got a tip that the law had been checking the spot so we moved everything out. The only thing they found in there was a dime bag of weed and a couple of hundred dollars that Brenda had stashed in her pocketbook," Choppa said while taking a puff off his Dutch.

I was still pissed because shit like that I needed to know. What if shit didn't go down smooth? That would have been an el that would have took us all under. That shit would have been a slap in the face because I knew Jarrell was sitting back waiting for me to fuck up so he could move in. I took a second so that I could calm down. Shit like this was unheard of and almost unbelievable. I needed to hear the whole story.

"Run that by me again. Brenda knew shit was going down and she stayed? For what? I would've rolled out of there with y'all."

Dave went on to explain that Brenda had started getting high, and instead of giving her money most of the time, they paid her half and half so that she could still fit the bills and get high at the same time. All of this shit was going on without me knowing, which made me wonder what else they were keeping from me.

When Brenda first started getting high we should've moved that shit from up out of there. Were these dudes trying to take over and I was just now getting hip to the shit? I thought me and Karen may be going to see about the house sooner than Friday because I was losing control of shit, and not even my right hand man Sonny could be trusted at this point.

"My question is, why am I just now hearing this shit? Huh? Why am just now knowing some shady shit that is going on in my business? We have monthly meetings and this was never bought up. Y'all niggas tryna run game on me or something? Is it like that now?"

"Yo Chi, it ain't nothing like that, dawg. All I was trying to do . . ."

"All you were trying to do is what? Take my shit behind my back? Y'all niggas still hungry?" I went off on Sonny because I was hurt. Me and him came from hustling nickel bags to running a dynasty, and he gonna slight me like this?

When he suggested that we bring on Dave and Choppa, I was hesitant because young boys always got some shit they trying to prove. For over three years we had been running the operation with minor glitches here and there. We did take a fall once after Dave and Choppa saw fit to rob a couple of Jarrell's houses because they had beef with some of the guys from Divine Land. I thought it was ridiculous considering Trenton was so far away.

It was known that Jarrell had some Philly shit going on, but it was up north, and we weren't even making noise up there since we had Southwest, South Philly, and West Philly on lock. There were enough junkies out there for everyone to eat, and since we were only moving weight, we really didn't have to deal with any addicts. That's why I couldn't understand what the issue was. The crazy thing was, when it came time to bust guns and wreck shit, Dave and Choppa were right there on the front line with us like real soldiers showing their loyalty on more than one occasion. It was a toss up, but I knew what I had to do.

"Chi, on the real, nigga, you need to calm down. We did what we thought was in the best interest for the business. Ain't nobody trying to slight you, man. We figured since you had shit going on with getting Mina to do the drop and all that we would handle it. But do keep in mind that you didn't put me in the position I'm in if you didn't think I could handle it, partner," Sonny came back as if he was offended.

That was a good sign, because when a nigga think you stealing and you ain't, he will definitely act on. Even still, I'd be keeping my eyes open for snakes because they run close to you too.

I didn't even bother to say anything else to them. I just got up and rolled out. Sonny and Dave were still trying to talk to me, but Choppa had a sneaky-ass look on his face like he wasn't saying something. I hit Karen back to let her know there would be a change of plans. We'd be getting Mina from the train station in the morning and heading up to Dover, Delaware. I had to make moves before it was too late.

Mina

I was expecting Cee and Omar's spot to be decked out. I'm from the projects, so I know the outside of someone's crib don't mean shit. It's what's on the inside that counts. They had a basic bachelor's crib that could have only been used for business because there was no way they were entertaining up in there. Then again, those dudes had major gravy, so a bitch will sit up in some dust for a couple dollars and a chance to ride shotgun in that nigga's whip.

It wasn't a nasty mess, but it was plain as hell. They had a large dining room table propped next to a wall, and a big-ass television next to another. There were two reclining chairs placed in front of it with an end table in the middle of them. I saw a PlayStation 2 sitting on top of a cable box on the floor in front of that, and two controls rested neatly on the top. The kitchen looked neat from my viewpoint, and it smelled like a lemon candle had been previously burning.

As soon as I took a seat, Omar picked up the phone and was telling someone about an eagle. That had to have been the code word to let Chilae know I arrived safely. I took a seat in one of the reclining chairs, but as soon as I went to lean back, Omar told me to go watch television in the room and to lock the door behind me. He would knock three times when he was ready for me to come out.

Now I'm thinking to myself that I had to be at the bus station by twelve, but I was sure that they knew I had to keep a schedule. I grabbed the backpack that I was carrying and went into the room. Chilae didn't tell me to do that, but there wouldn't be any money exchanged until I saw the product. I wanted to call and ask Chilae what I should be doing, but I knew that they would be filling the books with bricks and all I had to do was bring them back home.

The room was on another level when I walked in there. It didn't even look like it belonged in this apartment. The blood red carpet was so soft my feet sunk two inches into it when I stepped inside. The California king sized sleigh bed looked to be made of a heavy cherry wood, and it was draped in red satin sheets and fluffy pillows covered in red and black pillow cases to match.

I didn't even want to sit down because the room looked straight out of a Bed Bath & Beyond catalog. There were red and black satin curtains that bowed out to show the black mini-blinds hanging from the two windows in the room. The dresser was made from the same wood as the sleigh bed, and there was a beautiful cabinet that housed a television and cable box.

My nosey ass was all in the drawers, and there was nothing but girl shit inside the drawers and closets. This must have been Candy's spot, and they were using it for a drug spot. She had a sharp-ass shoe collection too, and since we appeared to wear the same size, I tried on a few pair before placing them neatly back into the boxes and turning on the television. My favorite episode of *Martin* was playing on TV One, and I sat back on the bed and got comfortable.

I must have dozed off for a second, because the three knocks on the door startled me and when I looked at the clock on the nightstand, it read 11:09pm. I jumped up and answered the door, and Cee told me to come into the living room with the money.

Whereas the living room was bare before, now the closet door was open and a safe was open inside of that. There was also a section of the kitchen floor missing and a door was opened in there, revealing packs of drugs of all kinds. I forgot protocol and went and looked inside. There were packs of coke, weed, ecstasy pills, and crack already in the vial. I couldn't believe the shit I was seeing, and when I walked over to give him the backpack, there were so many stacks of green bills in the safe, it was ridiculous.

I finally took a seat at the other end of the table and watched Omar count out the money from the books I was carrying. Every time Omar took out money, Cee-Lo put two packs in its place. I was supposed to have fifteen packs if I remembered correctly, but I only had five books. Once the money was taken out of the books, Omar put the books back in the bag, then pulled out three smaller hardcover text books and put them in the sides. There were fifteen packs altogether once he was done. He didn't say the money was fucked up, so I assumed everything was okay.

"Thanks for coming through, ma. Candy is outside waiting for you. I hope the next time you come you can stay a little while. We need to recap the night we had before," Omar said before kissing me on my forehead and walking me to the top of the step.

I heard some people out front, and when I got outside, there was a bunch of dudes sitting on the stoop. Omar didn't even bother to walk me down, so I slid by them as quickly as possible and hopped into the jeep with Candy. She didn't say anything to me; she just turned the music up louder, the same as she did earlier, and screeched off down the street toward the bus station.

I felt even more self-conscious than I did before, because now I actually had the product on me. I didn't have to go through all of the checkpoints and shit like I did when I came down there from Philly. I saw Candy whisper something to the guard and hand him an envelope. Seconds later, he called for everyone going to Philly and the line moved swiftly. I took the last seat in the back, and once the bus was filled, we were on the move to Philly.

I was wide awake and alert during this ride, thanks to my quick nap back at Omar's crib. The bus driver was smoking on the road, pushing the bus to Philly at top speed. In no time, we were halfway through Delaware, and he made a stop at the bus station there. The wait was longer than usual, and it looked like there was commotion outside on the bus platform.

Chilae told me he would be meeting me at the bus station, so timing was critical. We were already there ten minutes too long. Just as I was going to call Chilae to let him know there was a problem, this big burly police officer got on the bus shining his flash light in everyone's face. The dog he had with him was barking up a damn storm, and for the first time that night, I really started to get scared.

I was sitting there with a backpack full of drugs worth millions, and once again I could hear the clink of the bars and all that. The cop started making his way down the aisle, and just when I thought it would be over, the dog started going crazy about halfway through. Next thing I know, the dog started attacking this guy sitting in a window seat. We didn't know what to think, but I was just glad that they stopped where they did,

The police were quick with evacuating him from the bus, and pretty soon we were back on the road. I didn't realize how close we were to Philly because not even a half hour later we pulled up and I was jumping into Chilae's car.

I was surprised to see Karen in the car with him, but that was none of my business. I just wanted to get home and get in my bed. Chilae handed me an envelope once I gave him the bag, and I counted out fifty crisp one hundred dollar bills. That was the most money I made in a few hours, and I was looking forward to making a lot more.

Karen

I went on to see my daddy at the hospital and he was doing a lot better. It was still hard for him to talk, but he did get out that my mom was up there crying and wanted him back home. That was all bullshit in my eyes, because she was just out for the damn money. We all were, of course, but I ain't marrying anyone and having a child as a means to hold him down. Any man with me will be there because he wants to be.

I let my dad know that school was going well, and that I didn't have that much time to go. The doctor came in and gave me an update, and halfway through, my dad fell back to sleep. He looked so peaceful. The doctor told me he was doing better, but they would be keeping him for another couple of days just to make sure he didn't go through another relapse. They would be continuing the chemo a little longer just to make sure the cancer was completely gone.

I kissed my dad on the cheek before I left and ran up out of there before I ran into my mother again. On the way down, I got a call from Chilae asking me to meet him at his house. He was a little upset, but I had to at least go to class to turn in my paper. I told the teacher what was going on with my father and let him know that I would be back in class at the end of the week.

When I called Chilae back, he was more upset than he was earlier, and it took everything in me not to curse him out. I let him vent while I drove back across town. When I got to his spot, he was already outside. I parked my jeep behind his and got out, taking the passenger seat in his. He explained to me what happened with Brenda and his boys and how he was ready to murder everybody.

"Chilae, first of all, calm down. Now tell me what happened again."

Apparently, some dumb shit went on at Brenda's house and the team made moves behind his back without telling him. As he talked I looked in the back of his truck and it was filled with trash bags. He explained that some had coke and some had cash, but he took everything from Sonny's house and he wanted to take it to Delaware.

"Okay, follow me, but we ain't got that much time. It's already nine o'clock, and Mina will be getting back here around 2:30. You need to be there when she gets in. I have a safe in the bedroom closet that you can put everything in."

"Okay, ma. Let's make it happen."

Just as I was getting out of his jeep, his cell phone rang. I waited to see if it was Mina thinking something went wrong, but it was Sonny going off on the other end of the phone. Chilae put the call on speaker so that I could hear what was said.

"Yo Sonny, what's the problem, man?" Chilae spoke into the phone nonchalantly like he didn't have a care in the world.

"Yo, we been robbed, nigga. Everything that I brought over from Pine Street is gone, man."

Chilae looked at me with an amused expression on his face. Obviously he was trying to teach Sonny a lesson about doing shit behind his back, and I had to applaud the tactic that he used. When you are in business together, you let your partner know what's going down at all times. People could have died unnecessarily behind that type of shit.

"How the hell that happen, Sonny? See, this the shit I'm talking about. That's why we supposed to communicate man," Chilae said, getting all hyped like he didn't take the money himself.

"I know, man. I know. I knew I shouldn't have listened to Choppa, man. I knew I should've told you what was up, man. Now look at us."

"Run that by me again. You letting bottom niggas make decisions for you now? Nigga, is you smoking the product or something? You know how much money and shit we had? What Mina bringing back ain't gonna be enough to fix this shit, man," Chilae responded.

He was still playing the role, but he was visibly upset by what Sonny just told him. I was just as shocked as him because I didn't know that the business had taken a turn for the worse like this. Sonny was definitely slipping on his game.

"Look, man, I know I fucked up. Just tell me what I need to do and I'll fix it, man. Just tell me what to do."

Sonny sounded like he was about to end it all. A mess up, if this truly was one, of this caliber always ended in death. I mouthed for Chilae to play along with it until we all got a chance to sit down and talk. Someone would definitely have to pay. That's the only way lessons are learned.

"Listen, gather everyone from off the blocks and houses. We will be meeting in the morning at six on the dot. Don't discuss nothing until I get there."

"Okay, man, not a problem. That'll give me time to spread the word. Yo, man, I'm really sorry for this shit, man. I know I fucked up."

"Yeah, man, you did, but what can we do about it right now? I'll see you in the morning."

Chilae ended the call and looked at me like he was at a loss.

We both knew what had to be done. Chilae would have to make an example out of someone and sadly it would have to be Choppa. There was something about him I didn't like anyway, and I told Chilae he looked like trouble from day one.

"Yo, follow behind me. We can be there in about an hour. That will give us time to put the shit up and be back to get Mina from the bus station. You need to take her right back up to Delaware tonight to make the drop, and she needs to know that's where she'll be doing the drops for now on."

"I feel you on that, ma. Okay, let's make it happen."

I hopped in my truck and we made a mad dash for I-495 south headed toward Dover, Delaware. I was shocked that Chilae was slipping like this, but when you have too many niggas wanting to be the chief, there were never enough braves left. I'm certain that once Choppa was taken care of, his soldiers would straighten up. An example had to be made; it's as simple as that.

I pushed thoughts of my dad out of my head because now wasn't the time to crumble. I knew if nothing else, I had to at least try to get along with my mother for my dad's sake. I didn't want him to die with a heavy heart knowing we couldn't make amends. I would at least try to be cordial when he was around. He didn't need the added stress of us bickering at each other.

The road was empty so we made it up to my house in record time. I had a nice little mini-mansion in a secluded, wooded area away from everyone else in town. It was close enough to the city to shop, but far enough away to have peace of mind. I was so deep into the woods that you had to get off of the main road and take a dirt road through the trees to get there.

No one knew I was out there except for the man that sold me the property five years ago and my daddy, but he probably couldn't remember how to get here. I knew I would have to show Chilae in the daytime because the woods looked way different at night.

When we pulled up to the garage, the light sensor came on •

and with the push of a button, my garage door opened up. I pulled up into one spot and Chilae pulled right up next to me. The garage door automatically closed behind us, and I propped the door open that connected to the kitchen so that we could move everything in. He had about thirty trash bags in the back of his car filled with money and coke. In just under an hour, we had everything inside.

I cracked open the safe and took the few hundred dollars and the diamonds I had inside and placed them on the bed. In neat rows, I stacked up bricks of coke and stacks of cash until the safe was full. We then went downstairs and put the rest of it in the safe I had in the basement. Just counting off the top of my head, I estimated over two million in cash and drugs, so I know Chilae was heated when he rode passed Brenda's house.

"So, what we gonna do about Brenda?" I asked Chilae, knowing he would just leave her in the clink. She did let us use her spot, so I at least wanted to get her moving back on the right track.

"I'm still waiting for her to call. Why, you gonna get her out? From what I hear, she was smoking our shit anyway."

"Yeah, Chilae, I'm getting her out because the one thing about a crackhead is they will do anything under pressure. We don't need her blowing up our spot. I'll talk to her about rehab or something."

"Whatever you wanna do, Karen. Now let's go. Mina should be pulling in soon."

"Okay, let's ride, but I'm riding with you. I know I'll need to show you how to get back up here, and we need to wait until after the meeting when it's daylight. Mina needs to get some rest, too. She has work in the morning. We'll bring her up here over the weekend."

After shutting off all the lights, I waited for Chilae to pull out before I set the alarm and got into his vehicle. I showed him the way out, and, once we were back on 95, it was smooth sailing from there on out. His "crew" had no idea that a lot of the decisions Chilae made was after he talked to me. We both knew that if the guys knew that a chick was running the spot, it would be a free for all on the streets. I let Chilae run wild because I didn't want to be the one to occupy him, but I knew I would have to run a tighter ship from then on.

We pulled up just in time to see Mina walking through the Greyhound bus station. When she saw Chilae, she ran and hopped into the vehicle, surprised to see me sitting in the passenger seat. We chatted like everything was normal while I checked the bag to make sure everything was there. I wouldn't be able to check the quality of the product until later on. We would show Mina how to do down the line, but now we had business to take care of.

Chilae

After dropping Mina off at her crib, me and Karen made another trip back up to Dover to put what we just got into the safe. Both of them were filled to capacity. The product was on point as usual, and I was a very happy customer once again. We had enough coke in our other two safe houses to keep business running until the middle of next week. I put the codes to the safes in my phone as if it was a phone number so that I could handle business even if Karen wasn't around.

Karen drove her car back and I followed her out because I was still lost. Just as she said, her room was the only room in the crib that was decked out, so I knew I would be spending some chips come the weekend. Once we got into Philly, Karen went to see about her father and I went to meet my crew at Sonny's house. I pulled up on 21st Street to see the block locked with vehicles parked on the pavement and everything.

Reaching under the seat, I pulled out my .45 with the silencer and tucked it in my coat. I felt bad for Choppa's mom because he would be nonexistent after today. Hey, that's the business. What could I do? Soldiers that stepped out of line were dealt with. It's as simple as that. I really wanted to get at

Sonny, but Choppa just had a big-ass mouth, and I couldn't wait to shut his ass up. He was a little too cocky with his shit to just be a line man, and I knew I had to dead that nigga before he did me.

I could hear the commotion on the inside as I walked up to the house like there was a party going on. As I got closer, it sounded like they were in there pointing the finger at each other, but when I walked in the house, all conversation stopped. Everyone looked like they were about to shit on themselves, and you could cut the tension in the room with a knife. The one thing I didn't want was fear because a scared nigga would clap back. I just wanted respect, and I saw I would have to get it the hard way.

Choppa was sitting in the middle of the room, right where I needed him to be. Sonny couldn't even make eye contact because of the guilt, and I knew there was other shit that he hadn't told me. I would have to take care of him soon too, but until I found someone worthy to take his place, he would have to do. I stood in the middle of the floor and slowly looked around at everyone that was in attendance. The only people that weren't there were Jamal, Brian, and Scott because as a rule there were always someone to watch the safe houses at all times. No safe house was supposed to be left empty, just in case some shit popped off.

"So, fellas, how is the business treating y'all?" I asked the room, not singling out anyone in particular.

I heard collective murmurs of everyone saying that they were cool, and that the money was right. They all certainly looked as if they were eating because there was ice glistening all over the place, and everyone was dressed in the best. Even the lookout boys was flossy.

"Everything is good, Chi. What's up with you?" Sonny asked like he didn't know the reason for this meeting. I swear I hate a bitch nigga, and I couldn't wait to be rid of his ass for good.

I gave him a disgusted-ass look and continued on with what I was saying. He was standing there with shifty-ass eyes like he was hoping no one put his ass on blast. I was ready to open his chest up right there, but I refrained from cutting up at the moment.

I took the time to search the room to see who could be a possible prospect. It was time for me to start training someone else to keep shit on straight when I wasn't around. I couldn't be everywhere at once, so I needed someone I could trust at some point to keep money right.

"Well, it seems as if some of us can't be trusted. Apparently, Sonny thinks we got robbed earlier. This after he saw fit to take directions from one of his workers and move my product without consulting me first. You all know what that means, right?"

No one offered an answer because they all knew that it would end in death. Someone was going to die tonight, and we all knew it. I started dismissing the crew a few at a time, relief showing on the faces of the guys that got to leave. As they were leaving out, I talked about the importance of loyalty, and I could see that the majority of them were really down for me.

Within an hour everyone was out except for me, Sonny, Dave, and Choppa. Choppa was still sitting in the middle of floor with a silly-ass smirk on his face like he had nothing to worry about. I offered to refill his drink, but he refused, telling me that he was cool.

"So, Sonny, tell me how it got to be that Choppa started making decisions?" I went behind Sonny's bar to pour myself a drink while I waited for him to answer. I was giving him a chance once again to come clean, but of course, he took the nut way out. It was cool because that would make it so much easier for me to smoke his ass down the line.

"What had happened was," Sonny began stuttering over his words.

I went behind the bar and started shining up my .45 because

Choppa had to go. I just wanted to give him a chance to speak his piece before he was gone. I mean, I am a fair man, you know. The decision I was about to make would definitely serve as a lesson for Sonny. Every nigga out here was expendable until proven otherwise.

"Look, Brenda was bringing unnecessary attention to the spot, so we moved the shit before the law rolled up in there. I thought Sonny made a god decision on that," Choppa said all cocky like he was in charge.

"Is that right?"

"Yeah, that's right. Would you had rather us left the shit in there and had the cops take it all, or for us to do what we did and move it out before they came?"

"I would have rather y'all came to me with the situation when it first became a problem," I said without raising my voice. This dude was really puffing his damn chest out at me like he had something to prove. That was too bad because he would have made a good lieutenant one day.

"Well, Chilae. That's what you brought Sonny on for, right? To make decisions when you're not around?"

"Exactly, so the decision he's about to make will be all his."

The three of them looked at me like I was speaking in Chinese. Sonny had the shakes because he knew how it was going down. He'd been there before. I had the same problem with Ray, and I had to dead him. That's how Sonny got his position.

"Yo, what is this nigga talking about, Sonny? What did he mean by that?"

For the first time that morning, Choppa's face registered fear. Someone had to go, and it was now up to Sonny who it would be. I handed Sonny the .45 and took a seat behind the bar with my nine millimeter in plain view just in case the tables turned. It wouldn't be nothing for him to turn and pull the trigger on me, so I had to be prepared.

Sonny looked at the heat he was holding like he wasn't sure how it worked. I let him make it up in his mind what he would do. The last time we were in this position, he was under my right hand man and some shady shit had gone down. It was up to Sonny at the time who would be next in line. He either had to kill himself or off my lieutenant. Sonny was now my right hand man, so you know the outcome of that. There are no second chances, so we had to make it happen.

"Choppa, I'm sorry it had to end this way."

Just as Choppa went to lunge from his seat, Sonny put one right between his eyes. His body hit the floor with a solid thud, and unlike in the movies, only a little blood trickled from the bullet wound to his head. Dave and Sonny began moving the furniture from the area rug so that they could lay his body in a sheet. A friend of mine worked at a meat grinding plant where they disposed of all of the parts of the animals that they couldn't sell to us to eat. I spoke to him yesterday about my troubles, so he would be expecting a body later on. No one would ever find Choppa.

I took the heat from Sonny's shaking hands and stepped over Choppa's dead body. Dave would be able to handle it from here, and I would be talking to him about stepping up his position. He was obviously the one with the heart. Soon after that we would be getting rid of Sonny, so I had to keep my eyes on the team.

I hopped into my jeep, and after making my rounds to be sure everyone was on post and doing what they were supposed to do, I headed home to get some much needed rest. I didn't predict too much of that happening for a long time.

Shanna

I had to find a way to get back at Jarrell. Since he saw fit to play me like he did, I had to dig in his pockets. It took about a week of ignoring his calls, but I finally picked up the phone Friday morning. I figured a week was long enough for him to be begging and pleading on my answering machine. He was right on time, because I saw this cute Fendi bag that I just had to have. It only cost about twelve hundred. That's nothing for a man who was probably sitting on millions.

I was fresh to death in a cute little pair of Akademiks jeans with the Valero jacket to match, and an Akademiks baby tee underneath. The bottom of my pants were tucked into calf-length boots the color of baker's chocolate. Jaydah had just touched up my weave yesterday, so I was killing them. I finished up with a light touch of MAC Lipglass, and when Jarrell beeped his horn, I was down the steps in no time.

He was sitting in a shiny new 2006 BMW. Probably some shit that some silly ass chick done put in her name for him. I got into the passenger seat and threw on my D&G shades. I was ready to spend this dude's money. He had a lot of making up to do. On the way down he had on that new CD by Robin

Thicke, and my favorite song, "Lost Without You," was playing. If ever I got a man that was truly mine, I hoped we felt like
this about each other. It surprised me that he was even listening to a white boy R&B singer. Let me find out he had a sensitive side.

The trip up I- 295 was a smooth one considering it was a
Friday afternoon. Forty-five minutes later, we pulled up to the
Quaker Bridge Mall and luckily found a spot right by the entrance. He would bring me all the way the hell up to Trenton,
but money spent the same everywhere, so I could care less.

Once we got into the mall, our first stop was at the Champs
footwear store where this dude bought like five pairs of Timberland boots and a corny ass Pittsburgh Steelers jersey. I did
get a pair of cream and chocolate Pumas, and we were off to
other stores in the mall. I planned on tearing the mall up, and
he would be dropping my ass off at the end of the night. Fuck
him and his crazy-ass dogs.

We went into one store after the next, and I made sure that
for everything he purchased, I matched it. I was truly enjoying
myself, and I could honestly say that I'd been on shopping
sprees before, but Chilae had never flossed me like this. On
our way out of Carol's Daughter, I bumped into the bitch that
I had to whip up on when me and Chilae was at the mall. She
looked me up and down like she wanted to bring some noise,
and I was hoping I wouldn't have to cut a fool in front of Jarrell so soon.

She looked like she was going to say something to me, but
when she saw Jarrell her whole facial expression changed. I
held my tongue and my temper to see what he would do, but it
appeared that he knew her as well.

"Lord, look what the cat done drug to the mall. Killa, what
you doing up in here?" she walked over to him and gave him a
tight embrace, rolling her eyes and frowning her face at me
from over his shoulder. I was two seconds off her ass as it was,
and it was killing me not to jump on her damn neck.

"You know how I do, ma. I'm just out shoppin' with my baby. You know, spending some of my hard earned money."

A smiled briefly spread across my face as I listened to the conversation. He let that bitch know that we were together, but for all I know she could have just been a bug-a-boo that he was trying to get rid of. She didn't act like what he said phased her one bit, the same way she was when I wilded out on her ass over Chilae. She looked like she was going to say some smart shit, but changed her mind at the last second.

"Okay, pa. Well, I don't want to keep you and your boo from shopping. Tell Big Keith to get at me."

She strutted away looking like an overworked whore, and Jarrell kissed me on my lips before we moved on. I figured she was a damn groupie. She probably done fucked every dude from both sides, and was still trying to get money out of 'em. Real get money chicks know how to keep eatin'.

We made a stop in True Religion, Doll House, Forever 21, and Seven, where I racked up a couple thousand dollars before we left the mall. I knew I'd be stripping and doing lap dances later on tonight, but after looking at all the shit I had in the trunk, it was worth it.

When we got back down the way, Chilae was parked in front of my building. I knew that was going to be a problem with me getting out of Jarrell's car, and I hoped that Jarrell or Chilae would just leave peacefully.

The look on Jarrell's face said he was ready to get things clapping, and I tried to divert his attention from the obvious. Chilae didn't get out of his car, and I saw someone else sitting next to him, so I know he saw us. I leaned over to give Jarrell a kiss, but he was so focused on Chilae that I had to tap him on his shoulder twice before he acknowledged my presence.

"Call me later, okay? I want to model some of these clothes for you, big daddy."

"Aiight, shawty, I'll do that."

He got out and helped me get all of my bags out of the car with a steady eye on Chilae and whoever was in there with him. Normally I would have made him carry my shit upstairs, but the situation was already tense, so I just struggled with the bags myself. When I got up on the stoop I turned back around and waved to him before going inside. I could see Dave sitting inside the car with Chilae, but I didn't acknowledge either one of them although they were staring right at me.

Something was telling me that shit was going to pop off, but I didn't think it would be so soon. As soon as I put my key in the door, I hard ten gunshots back to back and a car screech off from the block. I dropped everything on the hallway floor and ran back downstairs, my body shaking like a leaf. I could see people scattering like roaches when the light is turned on and I immediately thought the worst. My heart began to beat faster and I was hoping Chilae wasn't shot. I didn't want Jarrell shot either, but Chilae had a place in my heart that would never go away.

When I got outside I saw a crowd standing around someone on the ground and my heart dropped more. I could hear some-one screaming and crying and as I pushed my way through the crowd my heart felt heavier in my chest. I was pushing people to the side with as much strength as I could muster up because I felt weak.

It seemed like it took forever, but by the time I got to the inside of the circle, my body just hit the ground. Stephanie, one of my neighbors who lived in the building, was on her knees screaming at the top of her lungs. She was holding her three-year-old child up to her chest with her hands pressed against her back, trying to stop the blood flow.

Shortly after, I heard the sirens coming, and I chose that moment to make my exit. I could hear people in the crowd saying that it was my fault they were shooting outside, and I needed my ass whipped. I swear I felt like shit, but how was I supposed to know that Chilae would be out there when I arrived? I went up to my apartment and locked myself inside, falling apart at the seams.

It sounded like the ambulance was right out front, and, when I looked outside, I saw police cars, camera crew from all the local news stations, and it seemed like the entire projects was on my block watching the scene. I turned on Fox 29 and the news was being shot live. I listened as people told what happened, and apparently Jarrell was the one that started the shooting. Chilae never got a shot off, and once the coast was clear, they pulled out the other way.

I picked up the phone and called Karen. She answered on the first ring, and at the sound of her voice, I broke into fresh tears. She said she was watching the news and her and Mina were on their way. I don't know what the hell I just got myself into, but I knew for sure that it wasn't good.

Karen

At the same time Shanna was calling me, I was watching the spectacle that was going on in her neighborhood on the news. All I could think was "What the hell did she get herself into?" No names were mentioned, but I was almost certain that the shooting had something to do with Chilae and Jarrell. The few people they interviewed said that it was her fault that a child had gotten shot. They didn't say whether the child survived, but when I saw Stephanie's sister on the news, I knew it wasn't looking good.

I kissed my dad on the forehead because I was going to see what happened, and when I got outside, a call from Shanna was coming through. My girl was hysterical, and it took me a while to calm her down even though she wouldn't let me hang up the phone.

By the time I got there, the crowd had dispersed, but there were still enough people outside for it to be a potential problem later on. I took the steps two at a time all the way up to the third floor, and when I got up there, Shanna looked a hot mess.

Her ponytail was lying on the floor in a heap of hairpins,

and her own hair was all over her head like she got swooped or something. Her eyes were bloodshot red, and she had the shakes like she was going through crack withdrawal or something. I closed the door, and went to give my friend a much needed hug. Shit didn't have to be this difficult, you dig? Why can't we all just get along?

"Shanna, what happened? Tell me from the beginning."

Shanna had to take a minute to get her head together, but the tears never stopped flowing. She told me how her and Jarrell had went shopping earlier and that she ran into the girl that she had a problem with before over Chilae. That made me wonder if the girl had told Chilae that she saw Jarrell and Shanna together. What reason did he have to be sitting outside Shanna's house? We already had the drugs moved to Dover, so why was he over here?

She said she felt that something was going to go down, and she was trying to get Jarrell to leave before some shit was said. By the time she got upstairs, she heard the gunshots, and when she came back down, Stephanie was holding her daughter and neither Chilae nor Jarrell was in sight.

"Girl, I feel like shit. Why the hell they gotta go through this?" Shanna said between tears.

I didn't have an answer for her, and I really felt bad that she got herself caught up in this mess.

"Listen, get your head together. None of this is your fault. You didn't know they were going to act a fool in broad daylight. Get some clothes. We gonna hide out for a few days."

I know Chilae told me that he didn't want Shanna to know where the hideout was at, but I had to take her somewhere. I wanted her to be somewhere where she could have peace. I knew me and her were going to have to have a long talk, though. She couldn't keep living her life like this. My first thought was to take her to my other spot in Center City, but I had shit to do, and would be better able to watch her if she were with me.

While she was in the back, Mina came busting through the door like someone was chasing her. The look on her face said that she had heard everything. I just shook my head and updated her on what I knew. Mina was just as shocked as I was.

When the bedroom door opene,d Shanna had her Louis Vuitton luggage all packed, and she looked a lot better than she did earlier. Mina gave her a hug, and Shanna damn near fell apart again. I was glad that Mina showed up because I wanted to show her where the hideout was anyway.

Just as we were on our way out the door, a news flash came across the television. We stopped to hear the latest update, but I'm thinking maybe we should have gone on out the door. The news reporter that was outside earlier was giving an update outside of the Children's Hospital of Philadelphia. Stephanie's daughter, little three-year-old Neveah Lucky, didn't make it. She passed away moments ago, and it was like a madhouse outside of the hospital.

All of us looked at each other, and the next thing we knew, Shanna had passed out and hit the floor. Mina ran and got a cold rag, and I waved a paper fan over her face until she came to.

"Shanna, come on and get it together, sweetie. We gotta get up out of here."

Mina and I had to practically carry Shanna down the steps, and when we got outside there was definitely a crowd. A few of Stephanie's family members ran up on Shanna like they were going to snatch the life out of her. It was apparent that they had heard the news also, and was ready to fuck Shanna up. I thought for a second I was gonna have to pull out the guns, but when they saw me and Mina weren't playing, they got up out the way and we moved on. They thought I was taking them to my spot in Center City, but when I hopped on I-95 and turned the music up, they knew to just sit back and enjoy the ride.

When we pulled up to the spot, there was a truck parked in

my garage that I didn't recognize. I was pissed thinking that Chilae bought someone up here, and then I had to check myself because Shanna wasn't supposed to know where we were making it happen. When we got fully inside of the house, Chilae was sitting at the kitchen counter with a chicken platter in his face.

Shanna was the last to come in and when he saw her he damn near spit his food out. She still looked like she was previously in a war zone, and he looked like he just saw death pass before him. I sat my bag on the counter and got something to drink. I was actually glad he came through here because I needed to know what part he played in that little girl's death earlier.

"Karen, what is she doing here?" Chilae asked without acknowledging Mina or Shanna.

I was sure he was referring to Shanna since we already discussed that Mina should know where the spot was. I looked at him like I didn't know what he was talking about and chose not to answer his question.

"What happened back at Shanna's house? A child died, Chilae," Mina said, getting a glass of water also.

He looked at me like I just said something bad about his mother and he crumbled right in front of us. I had a million questions to ask him, and furthermore, we would have to tell Shanna some of what was going on. She knew about the drugs and Mina, but we had to come up with another reason as to why I had this house all the way in east bumble fuck and why he had keys to it.

Shanna ran over to Chilae, and they embraced on some old Bobby and Whitney shit that made me almost lose my damn lunch. Mina and I just looked at each other and decided to let it be what it was. We had to get a plan together. That's what it all boiled down to.

"Carmen told me that she saw Shanna at the mall with Jarrell, and I wanted to let her know she should be watching her back when she's out with him because his baby mom has been known to slice bitches. She carries a surgical blade that she stole from the hospital when she used to work there."

"So, you mean to tell me that you were kissing up on some bitch that was cool with someone that will kill my ass? Chilae, you are so fuckin stupid," Shanna screamed out, shedding fresh tears. She struggled out of Chilae's grip and went and cried on Mina's shoulder. At least we knew that he still cared about the girl.

"Shanna, if I knew that shit I wouldn't have fucked her, okay?"

"You fucked her? Chilae, I hate you!"

"Shanna, fall back, because I know Jarrell done got the ass. At least I cared enough to come and tell you to watch your damn back. That's the only reason why I was out there in the first damn place."

"Who let off the shots, Chilae? That's all that matters now."

I jumped into the middle of their argument because I knew if nothing was said, they'd be arguing all night. Someone was definitely going to fry for this, and I just needed all of us to be on point just in case the law came asking questions.

"As soon as Shanna went in the building, I decided to go on home and I would get back with her later on. I only got down to the corner. I wasn't even looking for no beef with Jarrell. Not in broad daylight in front of all those people. When I went to turn the corner, I stopped because a little girl ran into the street chasing a ball," Chilae said to us with what looked to be tears in his eyes.

I wasn't even trying to see that shit; I just wanted to know what part he played in this senseless murder.

"By the time I looked up, Jarrell had pulled over to the side of the car and let off shots before he hauled ass around the corner. My first instinct was to chase his ass, but I knew the law would be pulling up soon, so we jetted the other way. I dropped Dave of at the spot then I jetted out here to get my head together. It wasn't until I turned on the television that I knew the little girl got hit. I didn't know until y'all got here that she died."

"So we need a plan," Mina said.

"What am I supposed to do? If I stop seeing Jarrell, he's going to know something is up," Shanna said in a scared voice, and she had every right to be afraid. She was dealing with a damn lunatic.

"You're not going to stop seeing him. If he sees that you stayed with him through this, he'll start to trust you, believe me. Your mission now is to find out as much as you can about how he's running his shit. Me and my boys need to take care of his ass for good."

"That's the smartest thing you said all day, Chilae," I said, giving Chilae his props briefly before addressing Shanna again. She played a major part in this and could not crack under pressure.

"Shanna, you need to get your head together. Hiding out will only make you look suspicious, and you weren't the one that pulled the trigger. You know the law will be asking you questions, so you know what to do. After all, you were upstairs when the shooting took place, so you didn't witness anything. Just do what you do best, and don't let them see you sweat."

We all decided that it was best that we stay overnight and go back to the city in the morning. Chilae ran out and got two air beds for Shanna and Mina, and I just sat back and laughed, wondering who he would decide to sleep with later on. I was cool with him staying in the guest room with Shanna. That was the most likely choice since she didn't know that Chilae was fucking all three of us, but how would Mina take it?

Shanna couldn't know that this was the hideout either, so we had to get shit in order. I knew I wasn't going to have time to talk to Chilae tonight, but I sent him a text message letting him know not to go home until after we talked. I would take Shanna and Mina back in the morning, and then me and Chilae would map out everything. Jarrell had to go down, as sad as it was, because I had mad love for him. He was making shit difficult in maintaining my funds, so I didn't really have a choice.

There were so many thoughts going through my head, and it was giving me a headache. We could not go back to that shit that went down in 2004, or there would be no bouncing back. I laid my head on the pillow with intentions on talking to Mina, but before I knew it, I was fast asleep. Bad dreams had me tossing and turning all night, and life had to get better, some way, somehow.

Chilae

Shit had definitely taken a turn for the worst. That nigga had the balls to bust at me in broad daylight, and here I am trying to keep shit peaceful. I wasn't even mad that he had scooped my girl because Shanna knew what needed to be done. I'm sure she was collecting info on his ass just in case we had to dead that dude later on, but when I found out who his baby mom was, I had to let her know what the real was. Shanna can hold her own, but surprisingly, there are people out there crazier than she thinks she is.

Something was telling me I should've just left, but I didn't want to get caught up later and forget to tell her. Now I was caught up in some dumb shit just as business was getting ready to be worthwhile again. I figured I had enough drama with that Choppa situation, but it seemed like bad news always comes in threes.

I was surprised to see her ass walk in the door, and even more surprised that she showed me love. Shanna and I have done the make up to break up so many times, it was ridiculous. I got a little tense to see Mina there also. I knew Karen wouldn't ever say shit, but Mina was a bit emotional and might start running her damn mouth.

Karen suggested that I go get a couple of beds for the overnight stay, and I was happy to just leave the house. Shanna wanted to come with me, but I really wanted to take Mina so we could talk about her trip and how her next one was going to go. I knew what was best for me, though, so I took Shanna along.

I didn't really say nothing on the ride over to the local Target because I was still a little pissed that out of all the dudes, she chose to get back at me with Jarrell. What could have easily been a simple vacation from each other would eventually turn into either me or Jarrell being murdered, and I'd be damned if my body would be put in the ground so soon. I still had a lot of living to do.

"Shanna, you know what you gotta do, right?" I asked her once we were on the highway. Shanna wasn't a dumb broad, but I just needed to know that she had her head on somewhat straight.

"Chilae, I got you. No matter who I'm with, you know my heart is yours."

"This ain't about no love shit, Shanna. I need you to be on some Inspector Gadget type shit when you around this dude. I need updates and shit. You can't stop seeing him now. You are the only eyes we have on that side, and it's time for you to step the game way up."

She looked a little hurt that I gave it to her raw, but that's how it was going to have to be for now on. Shit, take one for the team. I needed her to stick in there long enough for me to make a move on his shit, then I didn't care what she did. Ain't no way I'm taking her back after that nigga been tapping on that ass all that time. Don't no nigga want no used pussy.

"Chilae, I said I got you. Trust me on this."

I was quiet the rest of the ride, and once we pulled up at

Target, I let Shanna go in and get the air beds while I waited in the lot. Karen sent me a text message saying she wanted to talk. We definitely had to get up to speed with each other because starting today shit would be crazy.

What's funny is I had three chicks that I'd been dicking down, and I knew I would be stuck with Shanna's ass tonight. I wanted to lay up with Karen, but that would be a death wish within itself. Hell, if I had it my way, we'd all be in the same bed getting that shit on, but they wouldn't go for that. Mina probably would, but Shanna been done went wild up in there.

Deciding to call Karen back before Shanna came back out, I hit her up on her cell phone as opposed to calling the crib. She answered on the third ring, and I could hear her and Mina laughing about something before she said hello.

"Yo, you got ten minutes, what did you need to say?"

"I can't even get into that right now, but we all need to get shit straight before we roll out tomorrow. Get a couple of pizzas and we'll sit around and talk. Everyone needs to know their purpose."

"Aiight, I'll dip in the Pizza Hut down the road. Call the order in so I can just run in and get it."

"Already done."

So many things were running through my head, and I had to take a second to close my eyes and get my mind right. Karen was right. The best thing to do was to put it out there so that we could move forward. This shit had to run smooth. There was no room for error at this point.

I must have dozed off because when I heard the car door open, I pulled my gat from the side of the door and had it in Shanna's face. Man, she almost caught it because I briefly forgot where the hell I was at.

"Nigga, get that gun out my damn face. Have you lost your mind?" Shanna said, jumping back and dropping the bags on the ground.

I was in a zone for a second and almost pulled the trigger.

"Damn, my bad Shanna. I was slippin'."

"Yeah, nigga, you was. Why would you fall asleep in a damn parking lot?"

"Just get in the damn car."

She had some more smart shit to say, but I ain't care. I just pulled off out the lot and raced down the street to the Pizza Hut to pick up the food. She bitched about having to go in there and get the shit, but oh fucking well. That shit was for them; I already ate.

When we pulled back up to the crib, I found Mina and Karen at the table playing cards and chillin'. This was not the time to be falling back, and I was getting more upset by the second. While they attacked the pizza boxes like vultures, I went and set up the beds in the other rooms. I was already pissed about being reduced to a damn air bed when I could have been lying back on Karen's pillow top. By the time I got into the kitchen, half of the first pie was gone and Karen was already breaking down some shit for them.

"So, Shanna, you got to keep shit with Jarrell like it's normal. Answer his calls when he shoots one to you, and if he want you up there, go. Mina, you already know how to get down."

"Mina, you and I will talk more at a later date, but so far so good for your first run. You'll be going back out again on Friday afternoon after work and coming back Saturday afternoon. Is your license straight?"

"Yeah, I'm good, why?"

"You'll need it in the long run."

They talked for a while longer and I just sat back and listened to what they had to say. Shanna seemed to be scared of Jarrell a little, but she would certainly get over it. There's no room for fear in this business. Mina seemed like she calmed down a lot also, and just as we were about to call it a night, Shanna's phone rang with Jarrell on the other end.

It got quiet as hell for a second, and I was wondering what

the hell the hold up was. We already discussed what to do, and she seemed stuck on stupid. By the third ring, I was ready to answer it myself.

"Bitch, what is you waiting on? Answer the damn phone."

She picked up and the entire conversation had me sick. I couldn't really hear what he was saying but judging by her response, he must have been asking her about her well being. She laughed and giggled into the phone, playing the part too damn well if you ask me. That's exactly why her ass would be a has-been once it was all done and over with.

I could hear him trying to give her his side of the story, and of course he put that shit all on me like I came at him first. As hard as it was for me to bite my tongue, I did it. I ended up walking into the living room to keep from hearing what was said, and by the time I came back, she was making plans to hook up with him on Thursday. When she hung up the phone, she looked relieved, and I just got pissed all over again.

"Shanna, stay focused. You know what you gotta do," I said to her in a calm voice even though I was ready to scream.

While they cleaned up the kitchen, I went and put some clean linen on the bed that me and Shanna would share, and I made myself as comfortable as possible in the jeans and wife beater I had on. I didn't want her to get any ideas that something was popping off because on that note, it was a done deal. From here on out it was game time, and I wanted to be the one to win.

Mina

A lot done changed over the next couple of months. My runs down to Maryland for Chilae went from once a week to three times a week just like he said. After all of that mess with Shanna and Jarrell, Chilae didn't want to take any chances with me on the bus, so we went shopping for a vehicle. I thought he was going to get someone to drive me up and back, but to my surprise, he put everything in my name and I was even able to pick out the car I wanted. I ended up driving off the lot in a navy blue 2006 Nissan Altima that was fully loaded. He got rims put on it and everything. Of course, Shanna liked to hit the roof when she found out I was rollin'.

I was able to stack my cash up, and for the first time since Black Ron been gone, I had no worries. Although I remember his last words to me like he said them yesterday, it had been way too long since he has passed for me to still be reminiscing. I had money to make and new niggas to get it from. Things with Omar started changing too, and instead of me going down there and coming right back, Chilae okayed it for me to stay overnight as long as I was back in time the next day. I would only stay the night when I went down on a Friday because I still had my job and I had to be to work at eight in the morning.

It was funny at first because Omar was trying to act like he wasn't really interested in me, but on the sly, I could see him eyeballing me on the sidelines. My gear changed a lot too, being that we were now in warmer weather. For it to be June, it was warm like it should've been August, but I was cool with it. The hotter it was, the less clothes I had to put on.

I came down on a Friday night and as bad as I wanted to shake my ass somewhere, I was stuck up in the house with Omar. Cee-Lo and Candy went to the club, which confused the hell out of me because I thought her ugly ass belonged to Omar. I wouldn't be surprised if both of them were hitting that ass, but they had that all to themselves. As usual, I was sitting in the damn room waiting for him to knock on the door three times. I figured since I would be there all night, I might as well get comfortable.

I stopped at Wendy's on the way over, so after I ate my food, I laid back on the bed to watch television. I took the liberty of taking off everything but my thong. If Candy came back there I would just get dressed, but she had an overnight bag with her just as she did the last time I stayed the night.

I must have been more tired than I thought, because I wasn't even in the bed for a good half hour before I fell asleep. At around three in the morning I heard the knock on the door, but what reason did I have to get up now? We already discussed that I would be there until the morning and usually when I woke up the bedroom door was already open.

Omar knocked on the door at least nine times, and it was truly starting to work my nerves. I got up out the bed with just my thong on not bothering to cover my breasts. When I opened the door, Omar stepped back like he was surprised to see me damn near naked. I was not in the mood for small talk at three o'clock in the morning, and my face showed it.

"What's up, Omar? Something wrong?" I asked, faking concern so that I could get back in the bed. It was a little chilly in the apartment, and my nipples were hard from the cool air.

He looked at me like he lost his thought and I was getting annoyed. I turned and went to get back in the bed. Shit, he can tell me what he wants from the doorway. I bent over to pick up the pillow from the floor and when I stood back up, I bumped into Omar. I looked back to see what the problem was, but I couldn't see much in the room with the lights out.

He began feeling all over me and kissing me on my shoulders. My body stiffened because I didn't know if Candy was going to pop up unexpectedly and I didn't want to get caught fucking in her bed. I pushed him back a little and got in the bed under the covers. All the times I came down there and he never tried anything. He would look and comment on my outfits, but he wouldn't do anything. That's what made me think he was seeing Candy. But even when Candy was gone and it was just me and him in the house, he still didn't make a move.

I closed my eyes and tried to fake like I was sleep, but my clit was jumping against my thong, and I was ready to give him some. I could feel him standing next to the bed looking down at me, and I laid on my back purposely just in case he decided to make a move. I was getting goosebumps from the anticipation, and just when I decided to make a move, he walked away.

I thought he was leaving the room, and I mentally prepared to masturbate because there was no way I was going to be able to go to sleep that frustrated. Instead, he closed the door and came and stood at the end of the bed. I laid completely still like I was still sleeping and I tried not to respond as he slowly pulled the covers down off my body.

When the air hit my skin my nipples were like rock hard pebbles once again and I got wet, soaking my thong in the process. He pulled the cover down until I was completely exposed and he just stood there looking at me.

I didn't say anything and neither did he. His hands were warm on my skin as they moved from my pedicured feet and up my thighs. He knelt down in the bed and rested his body in between my legs, pressing his face into my cloth-covered pussy. I spread my legs a little wider to accommodate his shoulders and rested my feet on his back.

He pulled my thong to the side and spread my lips with his thumb and forefinger. With his other hand he pushed three fingers in me and his mouth took hold of my clit shortly after. He was doing the damn thing to me, and I was moaning like crazy while fucking his fingers like it was a dick inside of me. I pulled my knees back to my chest to spread myself wider and bounced under his tongue until I came.

Omar sucked and licked my clit until my orgasm resided, but before I could reach my bag to pull out a condom, he was pushing his stiffness into me. At that point it was no turning back, and I enjoyed the feeling I was getting from his stroke. Skin to skin felt so good and it'd been a while since I had it that way. The only other person I let hit raw was Chilae and he wasn't nearly that big.

Omar had me under his spell for at least two hours, and when I woke up in the morning I was completely sore. I noticed that he had a little cough while we were having sex, and that shit had me looking at him sideways. Do not cough while we fuckin'. That shit made me think a nigga had some shit to hide, and I ain't play those games. I thought he was going to act like shit ain't go down, but to my surprise, we went and had breakfast and talked a little before I hopped on the expressway, and I was smiling all the way down I-95.

On the way down, I noticed this car following me. At first I figured they were just going my way, but when I slowed down or switched lanes, so did the car. I started to panic a little, but I kept my head and watched the car periodically without trying to appear that I knew they were following me. I wanted to call someone and ask what to do, but I played it cool and pulled over at the Chesapeake House rest stop right before I was to enter Delaware.

I took my time in the bathroom, hoping that once I got out, the guy in that car would be gone. I didn't see him anywhere in sight, but I took an extra few minutes in line getting something to snack on and a drink before heading back to my car. I didn't see him when I got back out to my car, but there was a business card stuck in my windshield. I picked up the card and there was a picture of a pair of eyes staring back at me. No words or anything. I stuck the card in my back pocket to show Karen when I got back and hopped in my car.

I was on the expressway for about a half hour, making sure not to go over the speed limit and all that. I didn't see him for a while and thought he had gone about his business, but when I looked up the next time, I saw the car again. I started to panic and almost hit the guardrail because the car had crossed over the line.

I kept my composure as best as I could, and kept my car at a steady pace. He followed two car lengths behind and it wasn't until I saw the sign that said "Welcome to Delaware" did I see him get off the exit. That was definitely a Maryland nigga on my heels, and I would be mentioning it to Chilae when I got back. I wasn't made for the clink, and I wasn't trying to be visiting no one's jail in any state anytime soon.

When I pulled up on the block, it was just after 11AM, and Chilae's jeep was parked outside of Shanna's house. I wanted to talk to her anyway, and I needed to see Chilae, so that just killed two birds with one stone. I called Karen to let her know I was back in town, and I ran upstairs to talk to my girl. That guy wasn't following me for no reason, so we had to come up with another plan.

Chilae

I thought that shit with Jarrell would never blow over. I mean, we were still at each other's throats, but the gunfire had slowed down since earlier in the year. I sent my boys to clap back at Jarrell's boys for that bullshit he pulled at Shanna's, and even though it wasn't my fault, I put a lot of money up for Stephanie's daughter's funeral. She was ready to bring it to Shanna, but I had to let her know what it was really hitting for. Shanna ain't have nothing to do with that, and besides all that, Shanna would've smoked her boots for real.

Shanna really felt bad though, and at the funeral, she fell out like they were her own family. She must have spent at least two straight months apologizing, and after our last talk, it finally sunk in that she wasn't to blame.

I was at Shanna's house getting an update on Jarrell since they had been kicking it real tight for a while. He came back afterward with a shopping spree and been keeping her pockets fat, which was cool with me because that meant I ain't have to give her ass shit. It was hilarious because even though she was with Jarrell, she kept trying to break me off, but I passed on the ass. I ain't want shit that nigga had, especially some left-over shit I passed to him. He blamed that entire incident on me, telling her I shot first, but Shanna knew me well enough to know I would have never did that shit in broad daylight. She says she was only with him right now for the team, but we would see what it was hitting for when the time came.

Mina pulled up right on time, but she looked distraught. I didn't really want to discuss business in front of Shanna, especially since she was still trying to figure out the connection me and Karen had. She didn't come right out and ask, but I knew it was still in the back of her mind to ask me why I was at Karen's place that night. She said she was a little mad at Karen for not telling her she had a spot over there all this time, but I hushed her ass right up. Even people who told everything still had secrets, so it wasn't nothing to be pissed about.

I received a call from Omar letting me know that everything was good, and that Mina should be in Philly within a couple of hours. That was why I came over Shanna's way. I hadn't really been in my apartment since that shit with Jarrell. I'd been basically hiding out in Dover. All of the furniture I had in that spot I put in the basement out in Dover. The only thing I kept together was my bedroom, just in case the law came busting up in there, I had some proof that I was staying there. The only thing I had in the safe was some jewels that were expendable, and a couple hundred dollars. All of the drugs and chips I had were moved with the furniture.

So, I didn't want to talk business in front of Shanna because really her only purpose was to get info on Jarrell. We bus'ed it up for a little while, then I pulled Mina to let her know we had to roll out. She drove behind me to the hideout, and when we got there, she spilled the beans on everything.

"The drop was cool, but on the way down, I noticed this car following behind me." She was still visibly shaken.

"How do you know he was following you? I mean, you were on the expressway. He could have just been going the same way," I came back, trying to put her at ease. The last thing I needed was for her to start trying to back out. It would be too much trying to find someone to replace her at that point. I was thinking that maybe she felt that way because she had our shit stashed in the spare tire in the trunk and maybe she was just getting paranoid.

"Yo, I thought the same thing but when I slowed down, so did this cat," she said, puffing the el like she was really stressed the fucked out.

"Mina, if you are slowing down and cars are behind you, naturally they will too, ma. That way there won't be a collision, you follow me?"

"Chilae, listen to what the fuck I'm saying to you, man. I was thinking the exact same thing, but when I switched lanes, that car was right behind me."

"Maybe he thought to go around you, and ain't have a chance to," I came back, trying to diffuse the situation. I knew where Mina was going with this, and a part of me didn't want to believe that the law was on her ass this soon.

"Chilae, I swear I'm about to kirk kick the shit outta you, man. When I pulled over to the rest stop, so did that nigga. I call myself going to the bathroom and giving that dude time to skate, but when I got out, this was on my car." She gave me a business card with a pair of eyes on it.

I didn't know the law was giving out calling cards, but someone was definitely watching her. I was still trying to act nonchalant to calm her down, but we definitely had an issue on our hands.

"Okay, Mina, just calm down. It could have been someone just digging you; that's all."

"Nigga, when someone is digging you they ain't following ya ass across the fuckin' country. When I got back in my car and got on the expressway, he was right the fuck back behind me, Chilae. He followed me until I got to Delaware, so I know some Maryland niggas is on my ass. I ain't tryna get locked up on some bullshit."

I took a seat at the kitchen table and put my head in my hands. There was definitely some shit going down in Maryland, and I knew I had to call Omar and Cee-Lo to put them down on what was going on. I did believe someone was watching her because she had been going down there all this time and nothing of this nature had ever went down. We were so careful though, so I was just wondering how the law would know to even keep a tail on her.

Karen needed to be there because Mina was falling apart and I needed her there to keep shit cool. Mina wanted out, I could tell, but I needed her to stick in there for a little while longer. Maryland ain't that far away, but I had a hookup at FedEx that was willing to work with me if her house could be the drop off. We may have to implement that sooner than later if I can't convince her to go back down.

"Mina, listen to me ma, okay? This is what we're going to do . . ."

I came up with some quick scheme bullshit until I spoke with Karen to convince her further. I told her that we would switch cars so that whoever was following her wouldn't know that she was down there. If me, her, and Karen rotated cars every week, that would throw them off guard at least a little bit. We also had to keep shit tight in Philly because you just never know who's watching you.

She seemed to calm down a little once I spit that idea at her, but I just wanted her to go and lay down while I made some calls. She chose Karen's room even though the guest rooms were now set up. Once she was relaxed and near sleep, I hopped on the horn and hit Karen up immediately. We all needed to get it together and figure out what our next move was. I didn't really even want to bother Karen because of the situation with her pops, but it was business. What could I do?

"Karen, we have a problem," I spoke into the phone when she finally answered. I didn't want to make the situation more than what it was because I really didn't know all of what was going on. No one knew Mina was our transporter, so who would know to look for her?

"What happened? Did Mina get locked up?" Karen said, nearly screaming into the phone. She knew the seriousness of this situation, and we could not have a repeat of 2004. We just couldn't afford it at this time.

"No, ma, she ain't locked up, but this ain't a conversation we need to be having on the wire. When can you get here?"

"Give me like two hours. My dad is being discharged today, and I want to make sure he's straight before I make any moves."

"Cool, see you then."

After hanging up with Karen, I called Omar up to see what the deal was up there. I really couldn't get into too much on the phone because the law was always listening, but I had to at least put a bug in his ear so that he knew to keep an ear to the street. On some real rap, he had a lot to lose too, and a part of me was thinking that maybe he knew some shit.

When he answered the phone, he sounded like he was asleep, so I just briefed him on what I knew and he gave me his word that he would look into it. Karen said she wouldn't be getting there for another hour and a half at least, so I just sat back and let the shit bounce around in my mind a little while.

Mina genuinely seemed distraught, and I really needed this shit to work out. The last thing I need was for her to skitzin' and shit because she thinks the law is on her ass. I went upstairs to check on her, hoping maybe she at least fell asleep. Being scared takes a lot of energy out of you, and the way she was acting, I knew she had to be exhausted.

When I walked into the room, Mina was laying on her stomach in the bed in nothing but a thong and a wife beater. Her clothes were folded neatly in the chair next to the dresser, and her shoes were stuck under it. Her ass looked pillow soft from my view, and was a perfectly round bubble. My dick got hard instantly and I looked at my watch to see if I had enough time to crawl up in that before Karen pulled through.

I still had a little over an hour, so I crept over to the bed, leaving my Timbs at the door. Her breathing was real light, and her ass jiggled just a little from her moving her legs around. I was already stroking my dick through the opening in my boxers, and I was ready to put that smack down on the ass immediately.

I knelt down on the end of the bed and moved her thong to the side, exposing her pussy from the back. There wasn't a hair in sight, and I could see some of her juices on her lips. I stuck one finger in her, and then two, causing her ass to rise up a little. She opened her eyes and looked back at me with lust all in her fuckin' eyes.

She didn't protest, so I continued with my exploration, pulling her hips up in the doggy style position before I continued. She reached back and spread her ass cheeks, giving me easy access to all she had to offer. I wasted no time sliding up in that ass, and she was bouncing all that ass back on me like a pro. I wondered briefly how in hell Omar passed up on this, because there was no way in hell it would've been me.

"Whose pussy is this, girl?' I asked her while smacking her on the ass, the jiggle of her butt cheeks almost making me cum prematurely.

"It's your pussy. Take it, baby. It's yours."

"It's mine, huh? What's my name, baby? Say it, what's my name?" I said, getting really into it. I was pounding her ass like a power drill and it was about to be a major explosion. Her pussy was tightening around my dick, and if she bounced back once more, it would be curtains.

"Omar, baby. Take it, it's yours."

I paused in my stroke for a second because I wasn't sure if I heard her ass right. *Did she just fuckin' call me another nigga's name?* I was fixing to punish her ass for that shit, and just when

I went to ask her to clarify, the alarm on the house went off, and I could hear Karen calling out to see if anyone was there.

I pushed back off her to get dressed, and she looked a little guilty when she rolled over to put Karen's bathrobe on. I was ready to smack her ass up, but I refrained. Instead, I went down to holler at Karen so that we could make sense of what was going on. So she was still fucking Omar, huh? Cool, I see what kind of game we playing here.

Mina came down a few minutes later and I put that issue to the side to discuss the situation at hand, but we would definitely be discussing the shit later. Her fucking Omar was not an option. So what she ain't mine? That was bad for business, and I didn't need Omar thinking shit was sweet. Before the night was out, we would be talking. Believe it.

Karen

"So tell me again what happened."

We'd only been doing the transporting for a couple of months, and it was too early for glitches. I wondered briefly if Shanna had slipped up and said something to Jarrell about the operation. She'd been hating on Mina since she found out that Chilae picked her instead, and I wouldn't be surprised if during a dick down she said something.

"This guy in a red car was following me. I wasn't sure at first if he really was, but when I slowed down and switched lanes he was on me. He even got off at the same rest stop as me, and when I came out, this card was on my windshield."

She gave me a business card that had a pair of eyes on it. The average person would have brushed it off, but I knew that meant someone had their eyes on her. I wanted to pull her out of it and lay low, but the product was selling just as fast as she was getting it, so we needed her to go down there.

"Maybe we can get Omar to double up on this next run so that we can lay low for a second. We don't need any mistakes," I suggested, trying to come up with a quick solution so that

Mina wouldn't get caught out there. This wasn't the same as before. She was my friend.

"Yeah, that sounds like a good idea. She can drive my jeep down so that she'll feel better. Do you think one of us should go with her?" Chilae said with a concerned look on his face.

This was the first time in a while that I'd seen him acting a little scared. It was about damn time.

"No, we don't want to switch shit up at the last second. That could've just been a coincidence with that car, but if it's not, we don't want to bring attention to whoever it is that we know they on us. We'll just be playing it extra safe for a while."

"So do we have enough to last us until maybe Wednesday? I need to chill for a second and get my head together," Mina said, finally taking a seat at the table. She looked like she was ready to call it quits, but we needed her to hang in there.

I was thinking about making a run myself, but I had to be around for my dad. He was cool now, but it seemed like every time we thought he was out of the woods, he'd relapse. It would kill me if I were away and something happened.

"Let me talk to Omar first. Instead of going out on Mondays like you've been doing, Wednesday will be better. Don't try to disappear on us, Mina. We need you right now."

"Chilae, get off her back. Me and you both know how this could go down, so she has a right to be scared."

"I know, but she can't duck out now. All I'm saying is just be around when it's time to go."

"I will be. I just need a few days to chill, damn. Why don't you make yourself useful and run my money so I can go home?" Mina came back with way more attitude than I was expecting.

Chilae was being an asshole, but I think this had something more to do with her being in my bathrobe than her getting paid. I know they were fucking in my bed, and I would definitely be saying something to both they asses later. That's what I have guest rooms for.

"You just make sure you handle your business and bring your ass right back. You ain't got time to be fucking around with Omar," Chilae said, getting in her face. This dude was really losing his damn mind.

"Chilae, fall back. Mina, I'll see you around the way. Go home and get some sleep. We'll talk some time tomorrow. I'll give you your money before you go."

Shanna

"So you like shopping and all that, huh? Well this is what I need you to do for me . . ."

Jarrell had been talking my head off for the past couple of hours. He wanted me to help him get back at some dudes he had beef with, but I was not the one to be out there bustin' guns and all that. If he wanted me to do something easy like move some weight back and forth like Mina was doing for Chilae then it could be done, but I ain't no killer, so it wasn't going down.

"So, all I got to do is what?"

Jarrell explained to me that he had a supply of powder that I would use to put into these niggas drinks at the club. He knew the bartender, so all I had to do was order the drink for myself, slip in the powder, then have the bartender pass it on to the victim. They would think the drink was from me, so they wouldn't have a problem sipping it. The drug was powerful enough to make them pass out, but it wouldn't kill the person. That's when Jarrell or someone from his crew would take the person out the club and to the spot where they would be handled. By the time they woke up, they would already be tied to a chair and beaten half to death.

I was nervous as hell because I ain't want none of that to come back on me, but Chilae said it was best that I acted like me and Jarrell was on the straight and narrow to get the information I needed for his crew. My thing is, I ain't want to be the one Jarrell came to kill at the end of any given day.

He said he wanted to show me something, and since I was his girl we shouldn't have any secrets from each other. We were riding out to New York, but he wouldn't tell me what part. All I knew was it was way up there, and the area was rural to say the least. A couple of hours later we pulled up to this sugar warehouse, and that just confused me even more.

I kept my mouth shut, walking a few steps behind him into the operating plant. There were machines everywhere, and workers were scrambling around packing bags of Domino sugar into boxes to be shipped. We walked through the factory and met up with this fat white guy in an office way at the end of this long hallway.

I took a seat in the office and pretended like I was looking through a *Vibe* magazine while they talked. Come to find out what I thought was sugar was really Jarrell's cocaine supply and they had it packed in Domino sugar bags so that they wouldn't have a problem having it delivered throughout the state. I couldn't believe what I was hearing. I thought Chilae was moving work on a major scale, but it was nothing like this.

Jarrell had me working in one of his convenience stores that he had over in Jersey. He had it all set up, and it looked like he was running a legitimate business, but a lot of the guys that came through there did business in the back. Regular everyday customers came through to buy goods, but the big money was made in the back of the store.

I was also responsible for ordering supplies for the store to keep it running, and I had to be careful that what I ordered was from certain places. A mix up could kill tons of people.

When I ordered "sugar" for the stores, I made sure that when the shipment came in it was taken right to the back. That way an unsuspecting customer wouldn't accidentally buy a bag of coke thinking it was what the label on the bag intended.

The company also supplied their little sugar packets to franchise stores like Dunkin Donuts and McDonald's, so it was critical that things went where they were supposed to go. Some of Jarrell's product was put inside of domino sugar packs as well. That way, if one of them were stopped by the cops or whatever it would look like they had a bunch of sugar in their pockets, the cop wouldn't know what the contents of the packet really was.

So they were having this meeting and the guy pushes a few buttons on the desk phone that slides an entire wall back. I'm still sitting there acting like I'm paying them no mind, but I did look up to see that behind that wall was a vault that was huge like the ones kept inside of banks.

"Shanna, come here for a second I need you to hold something for me," Jarrell hollered from inside the vault.

I went over to see what he wanted. When I got inside, there were so many stacks of money he could afford to buy an entire continent. Also on the shelves were stacks of gold bars, and the drawers were filled with diamonds that he traded with the Columbians.

I was amazed at all of that, but I was more amazed at the man they had tied to a chair sitting in the middle of the floor. He looked like he had been dragged down ten blocks, and beaten with metal bats. I didn't know what all of that was about, but I recognized him from the club the other day. He was the first guy I had sent a drink to, and I saw Grub and Mike escort him out of the bar. I knew they were setting up these guys, but I refused to let them tell me why.

Jarrell was walking circles around dude and asking him questions about some money and drugs that were missing. I didn't think he would be able to talk because he was so badly beaten. Apparently this dude had been skimming off the top, but if the amount of drugs they produced in this warehouse were any indication of how much cash was being made, this dude was eating.

He mumbled something to Jarrell, but before he could finish his thought good, Jarrell smacked him across the face with one of the gold bars he had on the shelf. This dude was spitting out blood and teeth and shit, and I had to put my hand over my mouth to keep my food in. For the first time since we started, I was second-guessing telling Chilae anything. That could easily be me or him sitting in that chair.

"Hold this bag open, Shanna. This is how I do niggas that steal from me," Jarrell said, handing me a clear storage bag.

The man was sweating profusely and his eyes looked like they were going to pop out of his head. I was shaking like a damn leaf, and was tongue tied. I felt bad for the brother, but I guess when you're a thief that's how it all goes down. Jarrell pulled out a knife about a foot long and in one swift movement he slammed the knife down on dude's hand. His fingers hit the floor looking like little bloody sausages and he screamed at the top of his lungs.

"Pick those up and seal the bag. I'll be sending those to his mother."

I looked at Jarrell like he was crazy, and he returned the look, letting me know he really was. Using the bag, I scooped up the bloody flesh from the floor and sealed the bag. Then I passed it to Jarrell's partner. I wanted to tell someone else this shit, but I was scared to death. The most I would be able to do was give Chilae a warning to back off. But he wouldn't. Since I didn't want to be the one sitting in the chair the next time, I decided to keep my mouth shut.

One of the guys who was working on the floor came and cleaned up the blood, and we all left the vault, leaving the man tied to the chair inside. I sat in the car while Jarrell finished up business, and we were off back to Trenton. I didn't say a word on the ride back, and Jarrell didn't try to comfort me because he seemed like he was lost in his own thoughts.

When we pulled up to the house, he let me out and I went inside. After that first night, whenever I was over, he kept he dogs locked up. I went straight to the bedroom and stripped naked, waiting for Jarrell to get back. I had to work in the store in the morning, so I would be spending the night, but I couldn't wait to get back down the way. I had to tell someone what was going on, and as much as I wasn't feeling her right now, Mina was the only one I could trust. I still couldn't believe Chilae picked her over me, but compared to the shit I just saw, what she was doing for Chilae was a cakewalk.

Mina

I went back down to Maryland a couple of times, switching up cars and all that. I didn't feel like anyone was following me, so I started to relax again. Omar and me were really getting in deep with each other, and when I stayed the night, he slept in the bed with me. We talked on more than a few occasions. He made me aware that the apartment belonged to Cee-Lo and Candy, and that when I came through, they stayed at his crib across town. No one knew where it was at but them three, so that's why I stayed there with him.

As usual, when I woke up in the morning, the car was already packed. I just had to get in and go home. Omar had really put it on me the night before, so I was feeling a little sore and tired, but I knew I had to get back to Philly, so I didn't have time to be hanging around.

Once I got on I-95, I set my cruise control at seventy miles per hour and set back for the ride. I was doing good, listening to the music, and thinking about what I would be buying with the money I would get when I noticed that damn red car again. I sat up and put my foot on the break to release the cruise control, choosing to drive manually. The windows in the car were tinted halfway down so I couldn't see if the driver was male or female, but just as before when I switched lanes, so did that car.

I was starting to panic, so when I saw the next rest stop coming up, I decided to get off like I did before to see if I was really being followed. Just like before, the car followed me over and got off. I parked my car near the front of the building and hopped out, trotting up to the restrooms.

I rinsed my face with cold water and wiped my hands with paper towel, pacing back and forth in front of the sinks trying to think what I should do next. I thought to call Karen, but remembered that my cell phone was in my pocketbook, which I left in the car. I couldn't stay in the bathroom forever, so I just walked out there to see what would happen.

I stood in line and got a soda so that it wouldn't appear obvious that I knew someone was following me. By the time I got outside, twenty minutes had passed and I didn't see any sign of the car that was tailing me. I got in my car, and backed out of the space, moving quickly toward I-95. I knew enough to know that cops couldn't go past their jurisdiction so if I could at least make it to Delaware that car would turn off.

Back on I-95, I wasn't even driving for a good minute before that car was right on my heels. He flashed his lights at me to pull over, and I started to ignore him, but I didn't want to get charged for running from the law. He didn't have the typical lights on top of the roof like regular police cars. His lights were more like that of an undercover car. I pulled over on the shoulder shortly after, getting my information together and making sure my seat belt was on. The person in the car took his time getting out, and I was getting impatient. It ain't like I was speeding or something, so I was good. As long as they ain't check the trunk.

After about ten minutes he got out of the car and was walking toward me, like ten other cop cars pulled up and boxed my car in. I knew then that they had me, but I decided to play it off like I didn't know what was going on until the very end. My cell phone was ringing in my pocketbook, but I'd be damned if I reached for it and some trigger-happy cop been done killed me and shit.

"License, insurance, and registration please," the male cop spoke into the window while shining a damn flashlight inside. Hell, it was daytime. What was the flash light for?

"What did I do, officer?" I asked while reaching for my pocketbook. I already had everything set aside, but I wanted to see who called so I would know who to hit up first if some shit went down.

I reached through the open window and gave him the items he asked for and when he walked away I called Karen back. I was nervous as hell, and although I didn't want to say much over the phone, I had to let her know what was going on before the cop came back to the car.

"Hey girl, what's up? Did everything go good?" Karen asked in a chipper tone. Money was looking real good right now, so she had reason to be happy.

"Yeah girl, everything is good. The block is hot but I should be home shortly."

"The law is on you? What's happening now?" Karen said starting to panic. This drop was one of our biggest, and our last shipment went fast, so we had to re-up sooner than we thought.

"Girl, they got me going in circles, but I'll hit you back. They swarming down on me," I said to her in code, trying to let her know that I was surrounded and the cops were on me hard. The cop was coming back to the car, so I ended the call and turned the phone off. I just hoped Karen picked up on the hints I was giving her. They had me surrounded, and there was no way out.

"Miss, I'm going to have to ask you to step out of the car. There is a warrant for your arrest."

"A warrant? What did I do?" I asked, knowing that was just

an excuse to get me out of my car. My driving record was clean. They was getting me for this transporting shit.

"We'll explain it to you down at the station, ma'am. I just need you to get out of the car. I have to handcuff you for our own safety, but they will be removed once we get to the station."

I grabbed my pocketbook out off the seat, and the cop was nice enough to handcuff me the front way. I was escorted to another police car, and we sat and waited until a tow truck came to move my car from the road. I was relived because I thought they were going to leave my shit there.

It was a quick ride to the station, and to my surprise, instead of them putting me in a holding cell, I was sat in a room with a table and a chair on both sides. They took my pocketbook and locked it up during the fingerprinting process, and I was informed that if I were to be released, I would get it back.

I sat there for almost two hours before someone came in and talked to me. There was a woman and a man detective from the crimes unit that wanted to talk to me. The woman was calm and nice about it, but the man had a damn attitude problem.

"Miss Pierce, do you know why you're here?" the female detective questioned me while sifting through one of many file folders that were in front of her.

"I was informed that there was a warrant for my arrest, but it wasn't further explained," I replied, careful to not volunteer any information. They would have to tell me what the deal was before I agreed to any charges.

"You are here, Miss Pierce, because you have been transporting drugs to Philadelphia for the past couple of months."

My face didn't register any reaction, and I kept my mouth shut. I didn't know whether to admit to it or not, but I wasn't made for the clink, and I didn't know if they would lock me up right then or not. The female detective finally looked at me before she laid down pictures of Omar, Cee-Lo, Chilae,

Candy, and me in front of me. There were photos of me taking bags out of my trunk, and pictures of us in Candy's apartment of Omar putting the coke in my bag and putting the bag back in my trunk. All this time I had been going there and Candy's apartment had been bugged.

She pulled out pictures of me and Omar in the bedroom, and pictures of my license plate as well as of Karen and Chilae's car. They had pictures of Chilae doing business on the streets of Philly and they had shots of Karen's spot that was supposed to be "well hidden." I knew then that there was no turning back.

"So what do I have to do?" I asked the detective. I never said that that was me in the photos, but I didn't deny it either. I was about to do some major time, and I was falling apart slowly.

"Well, Mina, can I call you that?" the female detective asked.

I nodded my head for her to continue, but I swear I was barely breathing.

"If you work with us, I will make sure you walk away with little to no time at all. We want Aaron, Kevin, and Thomas, and we think you can help us."

"Aaron, Kevin and Thomas? I don't know anyone by those names. This is Chilae, and Cee-Lo and this is Omar," I said to her, pointing at their pictures respectively. All this time I was thinking these dudes were someone else and they had been using fake names. I kind of figured Cee-Lo was a nickname, but the others had me fooled. That shit had me looking at Karen sideways too, because she had to have known.

"I understand that you may know them by those names, but these are killers you are dealing with. This one right here," she said pointing to Cee-Lo's picture. "This one is HIV positive as well, so he needs to be off the street as soon as possible."

I sat back in the chair, nearly losing my mind. Karen had sex with him, and she couldn't have possibly known that nigga had the blicka. Although we used protection, you can never be too careful. And in the back of my mind I believe that Omar may have hit Candy a time or two as well. My coochie had been acting crazy lately too, so I was definitely wondering what the hell was going on.

They gave me so much information at one time that I couldn't stop the tears from falling. Everything that I worked for was going down the drain. This was my biggest fear from day one, and I guess I was getting payback for that shit I did to Black Ron and that guy from Atlanta. I couldn't go to jail, though. So what was I to do?

"So what do you want me to do?"

"I want you to help us get these guys. They are all danger-ous men, and we need your help."

"Okay, just tell me what needs to be done."

I knew I was going out like a nut, but I didn't give a fuck. The whole shit was a damn lie as far as I was concerned. I mean, fake names? Who does that? What else they lied about? Karen hurt me the most, and I was just hoping that she didn't know half the shit I just found out. Maybe she was fooled just as I was.

The guy detective finally said something to me after all this time. I was wondering if he was mute or something. They had an entire system down packed, and all I had to do was cooper-ate. I negotiated with them that if I helped them Karen and I had to be set free, and they agreed putting it on paper for all of us to sign. I explained that Karen was my friend and that we all hung around Chilae, but she was a college student taking care of her sick father so she didn't have anything to do with it. The catch was, if they didn't get all three guys, I had to do ten years. I knew at that moment that I would make sure all of those niggas were caught if it killed me.

The female detective gave me small bugs and cameras to set up around the house once I got there. There were also bugs set up in my car and cell phone so that conversations could be recorded. I felt so bad for Karen, but I would have to find a way to talk to her about it without fucking myself up.

We talked over what I had to do, and I was released from the station an hour later. My car was brought around looking the same as I left it, but I knew it would never be the same after this. All of the drugs and money that was in the trunk and spare tire was still there the way I left it. An unmarked car followed me to the crib in Delaware. I called Karen from the car at the station to let her know I was on my way to the spot.

She asked me a million questions of course, but I gave her some fake ass story about a mistaken identity thing that cops had me held up for. I told her they thought I was someone else that they were looking for in Maryland, and that everything was safe the way I left it. I laughed out loud telling her I did end up getting a speeding ticket from it, but everything was still on track and I would meet her there.

No one had made it to the crib yet, so I took that time to set up the bugs and cameras around the house while the detective that followed me set up shit outside. He was long gone by the time Karen got there, and Chilae pulled up a while later. He counted out the coke to make sure everything was there, and once he put in the safe, I broke down everything that happened.

Chilae

"So what did they say to you?" I asked Mina for the tenth time that night. She gave me and Karen this story about some Maryland cops thinking she was someone else and some other bullshit. I mean, if they were following her around and all that, why wouldn't they check the car? Every dime and ounce of coke was there, and it didn't look searched through, but I just couldn't leave it at that. Some shit had gone down, I just wasn't sure of what exactly.

"I told you everything that was said. They thought I was some other bitch, but once they got shit right in the system, I was let go. We didn't even make it off the expressway. They just had me standing outside of the car the entire time."

I looked at her through squinted eyes, trying to see if I saw a flicker of a lie bouncing around on her face. If the law has a reason to suspect that you into some shit, they ain't just gonna have you on the side of no damn road. At the same time, stranger things have happened, so maybe she was keeping it real with me. I just couldn't let it be left at that, though.

"I understand all that, Mina, but why did you turn your

phone off? You knew we would be trying to get at you. Your phone was off for a whole hour."

"Because I didn't want to give the cops a reason to look in the car, dumbass. Look, Chilae, I don't need this shit. Run the rest of the shit yourself. I'm out the fuckin' game," Mina said, slamming her glass on the countertop and storming out of the room.

Karen looked at me and rolled her eyes, but I wasn't sorry or remorseful. This was not the time to be caught up on some lying-ass mistaken identity bullshit. We were too close to making shit happen, and a fuck up was not in the plan. If some shit went down, this was the time for Mina to give us a heads up.

I thought to go in there and apologize to her, but fuck it. If she was telling the truth, then she had no need to be upset. Karen would smooth it over. I left the fucking house because I was ready to snap up in there. Speeding through traffic, I got to Philly in no time, and went to go talk to my boys. The block was hot, so it was time to tighten shit up.

Karen

I waited for a while after Chilae left before I went in to talk with Mina. I needed her to tell me what was really good now that Chilae was gone. I trusted Mina whole-heartedly and I had no reason not to, so I needed her to tell me exactly what had happened. I'll admit that her story sounded a little suspect, but at the same time, none of us was there to see it, and the girl was probably just scared.

When I got upstairs, she was in the room sitting on the ledge looking outside. She had her bag packed and on the bed. I guess she got all the stuff together that she had been leaving there for the past couple of months. I tapped on the door to get her attention, but she didn't turn around to acknowledge me. Walking over to the window, I took a seat next to her on the ledge so that we could talk.

"Mina, can we talk? I know Chilae can be an ass sometimes, but you are making good money from this," I began, hoping the mention of her cash flow would keep her in the game.

"Fuck the game, Karen. I'm tired of constantly having to prove myself to him."

"I know, but this will all be over soon. Chilae is about to . . ."

"Let's go get something to eat. We can talk outside," Mina said, cutting me off. She jumped up from the window and reached for her bag off the bed, taking the steps two at a time all the way down. She sat her bag in the chair and walked toward the back where the cars were parked telling me that we would ride in my car.

I just went with the flow, hoping to talk with her more in the car. Once we pulled off from the house I asked her what she wanted to eat. We ended up at the Pizza Hut down the road, but before I could get out of the car, Mina grabbed my arm.

"Now, Karen, I'm about to be straight up with you about something, but I need you to do the same for me. This is not the time for bullshit," she said while her eyes watered up. I knew this had to be serious, so I closed the door back and let her talk.

"Just tell me what's going on. It'll be between me and you," I needed her to trust me, but I was hoping that she wouldn't lay anything on me too heavy.

"Karen, what I'm about to tell you is some serious shit, and I swear if you repeat it I'll have to kill you."

I chuckled a little bit at the comment, but Mina looked dead damn serious. All of this shit was about to come to a head, and I knew my run in the drug game would soon be over. I wished Shanna was there, but I knew at this point we couldn't involve anyone else. She would have to pull up from Jarrell soon, too.

"You can trust me, Mina. Just tell me what happened."

She began by telling me that she got pulled over because the cops knew she was transporting for Chilae for the past few months. They had pictures of everyone except me, because I was back and forth between school and taking care of my dad. She got scared and copped a plea to help the cops get Chilae, Omar, and Cee-Lo if they kept me and her out of it.

I was speechless to say the least, but I continued to listen to her talk. She told me that the cops told her that the guys were using fake names, and she was hurt that I hadn't told her what was real from the beginning. I didn't even offer an apology, because I knew I was wrong for that.

"Listen, Karen, they bugged the house. That's why I had us drive in your car because they got all my shit on lock. So we definitely have to be careful with phone conversations and business around the crib. These folks ain't playing', and they will be swooping in real fucking soon."

I put my head against the staring wheel and closed my eyes. I had too much at stake to get caught up, and I had no choice but to let Chilae go down by himself for this one. We was back to that same 2004 shit, and I don't think this was a situation that my dad could get me out of this time. I had to go back home and think, but I knew we couldn't talk there, so whatever I didn't say now would have to wait until we got back in Philly.

"Okay, what we need to do is let Chilae handle as much of this situation at the crib as possible. He'll just think you're falling back because of the argument, and I'll just keep playing with the school and daddy thing until it all blows over. I knew I shouldn't have brought his ass out here. Now I got to find another spot."

"Yeah, well I need to start getting my cash straight because I'll be damned if I'm dead broke after all this, so we need to get that straight now. I need a hundred thousand to put to the side for right now. We'll talk later on about my payments, and for the record, I think they should be doubled since the jakes is on my ass."

I looked at Mina like she had lost her mind, but I knew she was right. She was the one sacrificing the most, and since Chilae didn't really know what the hell was going on, he wouldn't miss the money. I'd figure it all out before I spoke with him again.

"Mina, just give me a minute to get shit straight. For right now we'll just lay low until shit calms down and Chilae ain't on edge as much. I'll talk the payment situation over with him, and I'm sure he'll agree. The hundred grand will come out of my pocket. We'll talk by the end of the week."

She agreed, and we turned back around, not even bothering to order something to eat. Mina slept in the guest bedroom next to mine, but I'm sure she was doing the same exact thing I was doing: looking up at the ceiling in the dark wondering how to get out of this shit smoothly.

Shanna

"You can just sit the cases over by the back door. I'll have them moved later," I said to the cute delivery guy that brought in the shipment.

He brought in four cases of coke encased in Domino sugar bags, but I wasn't allowed in the back room under any circumstances, so I just had him put them to the side. One of the guys would be there soon to take the shipment to the back. I remembered his face from the factory that night, but I didn't acknowledge him. I didn't want no parts of any of that shit. As far as I was concerned, I was just running a convenience store.

A few customers came through while I was talking to one of the customers that came in all the time. I moved them out quickly so that we could finish our conversation. Apparently she knew Black Ron's wife that had showed up at the funeral, and word had it that she walked away with tons of cash, and her and Ms. Rita had been fighting about that shit since he passed. I rung up a few more customers not paying attention really, and when I saw Big Keith come up, I ended the conversation I was having and began restocking the store.

Jarrell's number one rule was he didn't want me to get to know anyone because if some shit went down, he didn't want me to have any connections over that way. That way I could go back to Philly and no one would know who I was. I was cool with that, but when you see the same people all the time, you're bound to spark up a conversation at some point.

In the middle of me putting more cans of corn on the shelf, Big Keith came storming out the back, snatching me up by my neck and slamming my body against the wall. I was speechless, partly because he was cutting off my air supply and partly because I didn't know what his anger was about.

"Shanna, what happened to the shipment?" he asked in a calm voice. He looked me dead in my eyes, which were beginning to roll toward the back of my head.

"I'm only going to ask you one more time, bitch. What happened to the shipment?"

I was grabbing at his hands for him to let me go, and I felt like at any moment I would pass the fuck out. He let me go and I dropped to the floor, coughing and spitting trying to catch my damn breath. He stood over me with his fist balled up, looking like he had fire dancing behind his eyes. I sputtered on the floor for a few more seconds before I could answer him back.

"Yo, what the fuck is wrong with you? The shit was dropped at the door like it always has been. Where the hell else would it be?"

"Bitch, don't pop fly. I ain't never liked your ass. I swear, I don't know why my brother is fucking with you."

"What the fuck that got to do with the shipment being dropped? It was by the damn door," I screamed at him, still looking up from the floor. I hated this nigga, and tried my best to stay far away from him at all times. Big Keith was indeed a big mu'fucka standing at six feet four inches and weighing in easily at about three hundred and twenty pounds. Dudes at the club called him "house" because he was about as big as one.

"There are three bags missing, Shanna. You give my brotha's shit to that punk Philly nigga?" he asked, cocking his fist back like he was going to put it through my damn skull. He was a big-ass nigga, so I knew for sure a fist that size would cause some damage.

"Keith, the shit was just delivered not even five minutes ago. And I haven't seen Chilae in months. Why would I do that when Jarrell is taking care of me like he do?"

Just when he was about to answer, Jarrell stormed into the store pissed like someone just killed his first-born. He started knocking shit off the shelves and acting like a damn fool. Me and Keith was sitting back trying to stay out the way not knowing what the fuck happened, but neither of us wanted to ask what was wrong. Finally, after about five minutes of tearing the store up, Jarrell just broke out laughing like a damn maniac. I'm still on the damn floor, mind you, but I'd be there the rest of the night before I moved an inch in front of those crazy niggas.

"Turn the TV on, yo. You are never going to believe this shit," Jarrell finally said as he took a seat. I scrambled up from the floor mostly to get away from Big Keith, and I turned the television on. I kept it on Fox so that I could watch the news. I needed to know what was going on in the world.

Turning the television up so that we could hear it, there was a news flash from the University of Pennsylvania that was off the chain. Apparently people had been dropping dead at work and on the street from overdoses of cocaine since last night. The newscaster was saying that a drug shipment must have gotten mixed up with Domino sugar shipments to local stores such as Dunkin Donuts, McDonalds and Starbucks. Customers were stirring in multiple packets of what they thought was sugar, and the overdose was killing them on the spot.

I looked over at Jarrell, finally understanding his reason for going off. I also thought that the shipment that was dropped earlier may have been actual sugar also. Big Keith must have read my mind because he ran to the back of the store and started cutting open the bags to test the product.

Someone fucked up big time, and I was so glad that it wasn't on me. Shortly after Big Keith came back in with a satisfied look on his face. Somehow the tables had turned. He did say three bags were missing, and I was hoping that we got our shipment fucked up too because if not, I just sold three customers five-pound bags of coke for $2.99.

"Tell me something good, BK. I can't stand no more bad," Jarrell said, finally coming from behind the counter, reaching for a Mountain Dew out of the icebox. He still hadn't said anything to me yet, but I knew it was coming.

"It's all coke, but three bags are missing. I was just talking to Shanna about that just before you came in," Big Keith said, shooting a dirty look my way.

Jarrell turned around and looked at me, and I dropped my head to my chest like an obedient child. I just hoped to walk away alive from this. I didn't want to end up locked in a vault like that other dude.

"Shanna, can you explain that?" Jarrell asked in a calm voice. I knew that meant trouble, and I'd had rather him be pissed. At least that way I knew what he was thinking.

"As I was trying to explain to Keith earlier, when the drop was made I told him to put it by the door like you instructed me to because there was no one in the back to receive it. A few customers came in, and then Keith showed up."

"Who was that chickenhead you was chatting with earlier? I watched you from outside for like ten minutes," Keith came back, looking like he was ready to choke me up again.

"She was a customer, Keith. We were just chatting about the weather."

"For ten minutes, bitch? Didn't Killa tell you don't be getting all friendly and shit with the customers?"

I didn't bother to answer; I just put my head back down waiting for the repercussions. I could feel both of their eyes on me, and I just wanted to die at that moment. I fucked up this time. That's for damn sure.

"Shanna, play the tape back," Jarrell said to me in a low voice. I pushed the rewind button on the DVD recorder, and after about a few minutes I pushed that play button.

We watched the day progress on the television, and all the transactions I made. It showed customers coming in and out, and the shipment being dropped off. I was surely talking to one of the customers for a good ten minutes, and I also rang up three different people with bags from the shipment. They must have just scooped it up because it was sitting there, not thinking to grab a bag off the shelf. The tape showed the altercation with Big Keith and I, and Jarrell wilding out and tearing up the damn store.

"Yo Keith, you know those people?" Jarrell asked, referring to the three customers who purchased the bags.

"Yeah, they all live up in Divine Land. I can easily go and get the shit back," he replied looking at me like he wanted to bash my head in.

"Go get the shit," he said to Keith.

Keith took one last look at me before he left the store. Jarrell stood and looked at me for a long time, and I just knew I was about to catch a beat down. I braced myself for what I knew would come and flinched a little waiting for the impact.

"Shanna, straighten the store up for me, love. We'll talk later on, okay? Close the store when you done. We'll close early for the day."

I nodded my head and began to put the store back in proper order. It took me a little over an hour to clean up broken glass and perishable items, and I took the time to restock the shelves so that I wouldn't have to do it tomorrow. Hopping in Jarrell's car that he let me borrow while I was down there, I went to the crib and soaked in the Jacuzzi. When it rains it pours, and right now it was just drizzling. I knew for sure the storm was approaching soon. I was just waiting to hear the thunder.

Mina

Okay, so I didn't tell Karen the entire story, but how the hell do you bust out and tell your friend that she may be a possible HIV candidate if you not totally sure yourself? I mean, the cops could have been just saying that shit to scare me, but at the same time why would they lie? Cee-Lo and Candy was looking suspect the last time I saw them. When we got back to the crib, I didn't even bother to stay. I just got my shit and left. Hopefully she wouldn't discuss business in the crib, since I put her down on the bug situation. That may have compromised my shit, but she was my friend so it was only right.

In the back of my head I couldn't help but worry about the entire situation. The drugs were one thing, but my life was in another lane all together. I made an emergency appointment at my doctor's office so that I could get my situation checked out. I just needed to know. Thinking back to that night after we left the club, I know we both used condoms, but the head jobs was raw game, and bodily fluid is the same no matter how you flip it. Depending on the outcome, we would also have to explain this to Shanna and Chilae, so I had to definitely be sure before I spread the word.

I tossed and turned all night, trying to think happy fucking thoughts, but it wasn't happening. My biggest question was if Omar was hitting Candy too. It dawned on me that I didn't know shit about this dude, and I let him hit raw. What the hell was I thinking? I wanted to call and ask him what was really good, but that shit would seem suspect for me to just bust out and be like, "Yo, Omar, ya boy got that hot shit or what?"

The very next day I was down at the Woodland Avenue Medical Center talking with my doctor about my coochie situation. I'd been going to her since I was like ten years old, so we had a close enough relationship for me to just break it down to her like she was one of my girls.

"So tell me what's worrying you Mina," Dr. Sally spoke to me while looking through my chart.

I hadn't been back since my yearly check up a couple of months earlier, and usually when there is something wrong the office will call, and if they don't then you good.

"Well, I was recently informed that a guy that one of my friends slept with is allegedly HIV positive," I began in a nervous whisper, batting back tears from the corners of my eyes. I ain't even want to speak that shit into existence.

"Okay, I'm confused. If it's your friend's dude, why are you nervous? Are y'all sharing men?" she asked while writing notes in my chart. I was a little embarrassed to answer honestly, so I chose another route.

"No, we don't share men, but I think that her boyfriend may be sharing a girl with his friend. You follow me?"

"Okay, so your girlfriend's boyfriend has a friend that has a girl that they may be sharing?" she asked recapping what I just said for better understanding.

"Yeah, that's what I'm saying."

"Were you guys using protection?" she asked me while looking me in my eyes.

I felt horrible, and sensed that she would know if I was lying, so I just kept it real.

"We did the first time few times, but the last time we slipped up and went raw. Shortly after I heard the news, so I came to see what it was hittin' for. I need to know."

She looked at me for a second longer before she made more notes in her chart. I wanted to ask her the results of the vaginal test she took the last time I was here, but I was scared to find out. She was writing for what seemed like ages, and I felt worse as the minutes ticked by.

"Okay, Mina. This is what we'll do. First, your pap came back testing positive for bacterial vaginosis. You can get that without being sexually active. It's just an imbalance in your hormones, sort of like what happens when a yeast infection goes untreated for too long . . ."

She continued to break down the situation, and what the procedure would be for the HIV testing. I would have to sign a consent form because HIV tests aren't done unless they are asked for. They also offered the quick test where your mouth was swabbed with a Q-tip, and you got the results in twenty minutes. I passed on that, needing time to get up the courage to come back for the results.

"So, I'll have your blood drawn, and in two weeks you can come back for the results. If you aren't back in two weeks, we can mail the results to you. Just think positive, and keep in mind that people with HIV are living longer nowadays due to new medications that are developed. Don't go in thinking you have it, but if you do it's not the end of the world."

"Okay, I understand. And thanks for your time. I really appreciate it."

"No problem, just go over to the lab and get your blood drawn, and we'll take it from there. If you have any further concerns before your results come back, feel free to call or come back in, okay?"

"Okay. Thanks for your time, Dr. Sally. I really appreciate it."

Once the doctor left, I gathered up the pamphlets that she gave me on living with HIV, and other STD's. I can't believe I put myself in a situation like this. I was like a walking zombie on my way to the lab to get my blood drawn. Normally I tense up and all that when getting stuck with a needle, but on this day I felt numb, and just wanted it over with.

On the way out I saw this girl standing behind the appointment desk, and she looked vaguely familiar. When I got closer I realized that it was that girl that claimed she was pregnant by Black Ron when he died. I did not feel like this shit today, and I hoped that since we were not in the right place to be rehashing that shit she would just let me be. Better yet, I hoped she wouldn't recognize me.

I walked past the desk like I didn't recognize her, but I heard the bitch saying some slick shit that made me turn around. My mind was telling me to just ignore the shit and keep it moving, but my fist was ready to be all up in this chick's mouth. Against my better judgment I turned around and looked at her. She had her face all balled up like she smelled shit or something, and the girl next to her was looking at me all crazy as well.

"You got something you want to say to me?" I asked while walking toward her. I didn't want to fuck her up the first time, she forced me into it. But this time it could go down.

"I don't remember saying anything to her? Do you?" she asked her co-worker as if I was hard of hearing.

Instead of responding, I turned and kept walking. Today was just not the day for her shit. She was still talking slick, but I decided to let it slide. Hopping into my car when I got outside, I went toward home with so much on my mind. What would I do if my tests came back positive?

I was so caught up in my thoughts that I paid no attention

to all the females sitting on the stoop in front of my building. I just figured they were one of my neighbor's peoples or something. I grabbed my pocketbook and hit the alarm once I got out, my head still in a daze.

When I got to the steps, there were three chicks sitting there and none of the bitches would move. I said excuse me three times before stepping on the middle bitches fingers. Fuck I said excuse me, what more did they want?

"Bitch, I know you saw my hand there," she said, jumping up off the step and blocking my way so that I couldn't get by.

"Bitch, I know you heard me say excuse me," I came back, throwing my car keys in my pocketbook, preparing to fuck someone up. I didn't want to lose my keys in the process, just in case some shit went down.

Next thing I know all the girls on the steps stand up, and at the same moment the bitch from the clinic pulls up. *Damn, where are my girls when I need them?*

Instead of waiting for her to get up close, I hit the first bitch across the head with my pocketbook and just started swinging. Hell I might go down, but I was taking somebody with me. And I would definitely be getting these bitches back one by one.

Karen

There was no way I was getting caught up in this Chilae shit . . . not again. Although Mina gave me the heads up, something was telling me that they weren't going to wait long to come end this shit. They have been obviously watching us for a while, and I called one of my dad's friends from the FBI to tell me what was going on.

He confirmed what I knew to be true. They had been watching us closely since before Mina started running for us, and they knew about Chilae getting rid of one of his people. Hell, I didn't even know that. We talked for a good while, and he warned me to stay away from the house. They had footage of Chilae in the house breaking the coke down and everything. They also had shit from sales that was made by Chilae to under-cover cops that had come to buy weight, and that bitch they had over in West Philly told everything when they didn't come scoop her up out of jail.

I wanted to talk to the agents that were on Mina in Mary-land, but he told me that they were outside of his jurisdiction, and what Philly wanted Chilae for had nothing to do with what they wanted. It was just a matter of who got him first, although they were working together. I didn't know that Mina had copped a plea to get off, and she included me in it also. I felt bad because I had to let Chilae go down by himself.

After I left there, I went up to the hospital to check on my dad. I graduated from school in three weeks, and I was hoping after all this time he would be home. Over the last few months he was in and out of the hospital, and every time I thought he would get better it got worse.

When I pulled up in the parking garage, I lucked up on a space right by the door. I was happy today because my daddy was feeling better and the doctor said he would be going home. I stopped at the cafeteria on the way up so that I would be able to stay in his room until it was time to go. On the way up, a code blue was announced over the loudspeaker. Doctors and nurses were running down the hall when I got off the elevator. I felt bad for that poor family because that could have been me.

As I got closer to his room I saw my mother leaning against the wall crying with one of the nurses holding her up. I dropped my food and ran down the hall, and all I remember seeing was one of the doctors trying to get my dad to breathe. It seemed like the world was going in slow motion at that point, and I couldn't breathe my damn self. *He was fine this morning. What happened since then?*

My mother tried to come over and hold me. I broke away from her, not wanting her to touch me. Several of the nurses were trying to pull me out of the room, but I just needed to know that my daddy was breathing. All of the sound in the room was gone, and all I saw was the line on the monitor go from an up and down motion to a flat line. I could see the doctor pumping his chest, and trying to get a heartbeat, but that damn line stayed flat.

"Time of death is 4:15," the doctor said right before the room went black and I passed out.

When I woke up, I was in a hospital bed and my mother was

standing over me holding a cool rag on my forehead and wiping tears from her eyes. I didn't even want to ask if my dad had made it. From the look on her face, I already knew the answer. And although she was shedding tears, her eyes said something altogether different.

I brushed her hand away from my face and tried to sit up, but it felt like my head weighed a ton. It felt like someone had hit me on the head with a bat, and all I wanted to do was leave.

"Honey, he's gone. I'm so sorry . . ." my mom cried on the side of the bed while trying to hug me. I drew up as much strength as I could and pushed her back so hard she fell on the floor against the wall.

"Don't act like you care. You wanted him to die," I cried out not being able to deal with the fact that my father wasn't here anymore. Pushing the button for the nurse repeatedly, I wanted so badly for the floor to swallow my mother up right in front of me. Why couldn't she have been the one to go?

"Can I help you?" the nurse asked, while shutting off the call light beside my bed.

"Yes, I want her to be escorted out of here right now. The only visitors allowed in are my girls Mina and Shanna."

"You picking those niggers over me, your own mother? What have I done for you to hate me so much?" she screamed from her place on the floor. I wished I had the energy at that moment to whip her ass. The black nurse that had come in the room was clearly offended, and it showed on her face.

"You had me, and that I could have done without. Please, get her out of my room."

"Gladly," the nurse responded, calling security from my room phone. I hated that she had to witness such prejudice, but we can't pick who we're related to, and all I could do is apologize.

Once my mother was finally gone I called Shanna, but she didn't answer the phone. After leaving her a message, I hit

Mina up, and she was yelling into the phone like she was a crazy person.

"Mina, slow down. Stop yelling and tell me what happened."

"That bitch had me jumped," she continued to scream into the phone. I was puzzled as to which bitch she was referring too. I just hoped it wasn't Shanna's crazy ass. "That bitch I had to fuck up when Ron died. She works at the clinic, and she got me jumped."

"What were you doing at the clinic? You knocked?" I asked her, trying to make sense of the situation.

"No, bitch, I'm not. But that bitch will never be as soon as I get my hands on her. Where the fuck is Shanna? I need y'all to come now."

"Mina, I can't come now."

"Why the fuck not?" she asked sounding even more vexed than when the call began.

"I'm in the hospital, Mina."

"You're in the hospital? Oh my goodness, what happened? What's wrong?"

I couldn't even speak the words at first. She said hello three times thinking I had hung up the phone. My tears flowed effortlessly, and my chest felt so heavy. I couldn't speak at first, and I didn't know if I ever wanted to again. I was still in shock.

"Karen, are you there? Tell me what's wrong, sweetie. What happened?"

"Mina," I began in a low voice that was barely audible. My heart was aching at the thought of speaking the words out loud.

"Just take your time. Tell me what's wrong."

"My father died."

Shanna

Jarrell came in the door around nine, and I had to reheat the meal I had prepared for him. He had the snaps earlier, so I was hoping he was in a better mood by now. I didn't want to call and ask him if Big Keith was able to get the coke back, but I'm sure he'll let me know one way or the other.

He ate in silence, and after I fixed him a second plate I hopped in the shower to refresh myself from earlier. I put on a sexy little negligee for him, and straightened up the bed so that I could lay on top of the covers.

It took a little while for Jarrell to come upstairs, but when he did make it up I was hoping he would have stayed where he was. He had the grizzly on when he walked up in the room with one of his mean-ass dogs by his side. He hadn't brought the dogs around me in a while.

He was quiet, not really saying much about the outcome of what happened earlier, and I didn't know what was going to happen to me. Jarrell was definitely unpredictable, so I didn't want to think the best or assume the worst. All I could do was wait and see.

I moved back on the bed until my back was touching the

headboard, wrapping my arms around my legs that were pulled up to my chest. That damn dog was half on the bed, half off, drooling and shit all over the damn comforter. He just stood at the bottom of the bed and looked at me, and I looked back refusing to be the first to speak.

"Today's your lucky day, boo," Jarrell said with a sinister smile on his face.

"Big Keith was able to get the packages back?" I asked with a hopeful tone, knowing I wasn't quiet ready to die.

"Yeah, he got there just in time. Two of the packages weren't yet opened, and one woman had made Kool Aid for her kids right before he got there, but everything worked out."

"That's good to hear. Sorry about the mix-up."

"Don't worry about it. It wasn't your fault," he said in the same tone, removing his clothes and climbing up on the bed next to me. The dog was now all the way on the bed and drooling on my feet, but I was scared to move.

He laid his body on the side of me, and I turned my body a little to face him, not wanting to move my feet that the damn dog was now drooling on. He took my nipples into his mouth, and as good as it felt, I couldn't concentrate with that damn dog breathing on me.

I spread my legs, still keeping an eye on the dog at the edge of the bed. Jarrell roughly fingered my pussy and painfully pulled on my clit, but I was scared to flinch. The dog looked ready to attack, and I had to get out of there in one piece. Pulling my body around to the side he threw my legs over his shoulders and being eating me out. My face was mere inches from the dog's, and I just knew I was going to be sick. Between the smell of the dog's breath, and the drool that was threatening to land on my outstretched arm, I couldn't take it anymore.

"Jarrell, why are you doing this?" I replied while keeping an eye on the mutt that was moving up farther towards e on the bed.

"Ain't no fun if the homies can't get none, right?" he laughed, his finger now pressing against my clit. I didn't know what he was referring to, but my guess was he was talking about Chilae.

"Jarrell, come on. You can't be serious. What did I do to deserve this?" I asked with tears starting to stream down my face. I'd rather him beat my ass than take me through this kind of torture, and despite my best efforts, my body was beginning to tense up from a fast-approaching orgasm.

"Ma, I'm just rewarding you for a job well done. I ain't doing a good job?" he asked, making the dog move back off me and lay on his back at the end of the bed.

"Get up and bend that ass over."

I looked at Jarrell to see if I could plead, but his face said he wasn't trying to hear nothing I had to say. I got up, and turned around so that my feet hung off the side of the bed. I put my ass high up in the air the way he liked it, hoping it would be over soon.

"Shanna, don't act like you don't know what it's hittin' for," Jarrell said pointing toward the dog. I looked back at him like he was crazy not understanding what he meant by that.

"Jarrell, please don't do this. I'm sorry for whatever I did. I can't take it back there," I was pleading for dear like because I knew what he was about to do. Anal sex is not my thing, and I'd do anything else besides that.

"Of course you can. This is how you get down, right? I can do whatever I want as long as I'm paying, right?"

"Jarrell, I'm not . . ."

"Bitch, get your ass up there and make it happen," Jarrell said, pulling out a loaded 9 millimeter from his pants that was dropped by the bed on the floor. I hesitated to move, but when he cocked the gun, I got into position and prepared for the worst.

I swear the damn dog must have been ready as soon as I put my ass up and my head down. She got next to my face on the bed and started growling. I wouldn't dare move even though I want to jet up out of there. Jarrell climbed on the bed behind me, pulling my ass up, and pushing my head forward. My tears ran like a faucet on high as I closed my eyes. I couldn't believe he was making me do this shit.

He ran up in me raw, and it hurt like hell because my pussy was bone dry from this experience. He fucked me rough and hard, not giving a damn that I was completely humiliated.

The dog was breathing hard and whining and shit, and Jarrell had all of his weight against my back so I couldn't move. I just wanted it to be over. After another minute or so Jarrell got off of me, and slid back into his clothes. The dog hopped off the bed, stopping to look back at me at the door before going on about its business.

At this point I had definitely hit rock fuckin' bottom. Man, it ain't get no lower than that. On the low I wiped my mouth off on the comforter so that Jarrell wouldn't see me, because I honestly didn't know what move to make next.

"Get up and get ya shit on. You gots to go."

I didn't even argue. I simply slid off the side of the bed in search of the jeans I had on earlier. I went to go to the bathroom that was connected to the bedroom to wash my face and mouth out but he stopped me dead in my tracks.

"Yo, ma, whatever you got to handle you can do that when you get home. It's time to roll. That's my last time telling you."

I didn't even bother to argue. I got dressed in record time, and we were on our way out the house. When we got out to the driveway the other dog was barking and gritting on me and shit like she knew I had fucked her man or something. At that point I didn't even care. I just got in the back seat like Jarrell instructed me, and kept quiet during the ride home.

"Bitch, I'll slow the car down. You better jump the fuck out as fast as you can. I'll roll the window down for you."

When we approached my block, he rolled the window

down and slowed the car down to about five miles per hour. I spent most of the block squeezing my body through the window, and by the time he got to my door, I used what strength I had left to slide down the side and roll out the way, so as not to get ran over in the process.

There were people outside and everything, but I didn't even care. I laid on the ground for a few minutes before I got up and slowly walked to my building. Was it worth it in the end? That was one of many thoughts that ran through my head while I climbed the steps to my third floor apartment. I wanted to call Shanna and Mina but I was too embarrassed, and too damn tired.

I didn't even bother to shower; I just got into the bed and pulled the covers up. I didn't have any more tears left, and my pride was gone. At the moment I wanted the earth to just open up and swallow me up, but if it were that easy, it would've happened a long time ago.

Chilae

Had I known the jakes were going to swarm down on me so soon, I would have been better prepared. It's been about three weeks since Mina broke the news about her fake ass mistaken identity situation, but I knew it was more to that than she let on, so I had to making moves early.

I began by stashing money around my mother's house, and I took some money down to the Delaware spot because I knew the jakes wouldn't know to look for me there. I had a floor safe put in Karen's basement that she knew nothing about, so I knew for sure as long as she didn't get rid of that house and I got locked up I could come back for my loot.

I've talked to Karen a couple of times, but I've been totally avoiding Mina all together. She hasn't been back down south since that incident because Karen felt it best that she lay low for a while and try to get back on track to a normal life, and I agreed. We paid her fifteen grand for the last run, but the way she shopped she'd be ready to get back on the grind sooner than she thought. Candy been making the runs down lately. We figured if we brought the shit the other way, we'd have less chance of getting caught. The law was looking for us to bring drugs from Maryland. They wasn't expecting Maryland to bring the drugs to us.

I met up with Dave to see what the streets were hitting for before I hollered at Sonny. I knew my days on the streets were numbered, so I was grooming Dave to run shop. Sonny would just get walked over, and that I wasn't trying to have. I might as well hand the streets my shit personally in that case.

He gave me the lowdown, telling me that the law had came around questioning everybody about who I was and all that, and I wasn't the least bit surprised when he said that Sonny looked like he was going to crack soon. Some niggas just ain't made like the soldiers that rolled back in the day. At that point I didn't even want to look at anyone. Instead, I went to my apartment to see if anyone had stopped there and if my shit was still intact.

When I walked in the door, piles of mail sat on the floor from me not being there for the past few weeks. Everything was in my momma's name, so I just took out the utilities and put the rest of it to the side. Checking the wall safe in my bedroom, everything was still there.

I went to sit on the side of the bed when I heard a knock on the door. I wasn't sure I heard it at first, but when the knock came again I stepped lightly to the door to see who it was. Who knew I had come here? When I looked out the peephole my man Red was on the other side. Everyone was suspect now days, so I started not to open the door, but he saw my car parked on the side street, I'm sure. He knew if I wasn't home, I was in the vicinity. Red was cool, but any man will dime you out if the price is right. At that moment, I felt like the world was against me.

I crept back over to the window, and I didn't see any cop cars outside, and everything on the street looked normal. He knocked again and started calling my name out. I ran to open the door real quick because I didn't want anyone to hear him. Snatching him in by the collar, I slammed the door shut, and threw him against the wall.

"Nigga, what is you calling me out for, and what is you doing here?" I asked him all paranoid, my eyes darting back and forth like I was high off something.

"Man, I saw your ride parked on the side so I just stopped up. Damn, it's a dice game popping in the hall two doors down and I came to see if you wanted to loose a couple hundred," he replied while choking a little from the hold I had on his neck.

I let him go after staring him in the eyes to see if he was lying, but he just had a scared ass look on his face. I went and looked out the window once more just to be sure this shit wasn't a set up. Seeing that the coast was clear, I led him to the bedroom so that we could talk. I didn't want anyone walking by in the hallway hearing what we were saying.

"Yo, Chilae, you cool, man? You acting like the law is on you or something, man," Red said while taking a seat on the bed. I didn't remember inviting this nigga to sit down, but I let it slide.

"Naw, ain't nothing like that. I thought you was my baby mom or something, she been on my ass all week." I looked at him suspiciously wondering why he really stopped by, but I was just trying to get in and get out so I chanced it by opening the wall safe I kept behind my mother's picture in my room.

Pretending like I wasn't paying Red any mind, I counted out the couple of stacks I had inside, while gauging his reaction from the sidelines. He tried to act like he ain't notice my cash and jewels up in there, but i could see his mind ticking a mile a minute. I just hoped I wouldn't have to kill his ass.

"So you going to Butta's party next weekend?" he asked making small talk.

I started to answer, but I heard a noise in the hallway. I was pissed because I couldn't see the front of the building from the window in my room.

"I heard that jawn was gonna be the bomb . . ."

"Nigga, shut the fuck up, I can't hear."

"What you listening for, man? I was just saying . . ."

I took the opportunity to smack him in his damn mouth. I hate a chatting ass nigga. Listening closely for noises in the hallway, it just sounded like people were walking down the steps from the third floor. Relaxing a little I turned back around, and this nigga was holding his mouth like a little bitch. I went to tell him to raise up when my front door was knocked off the damn hinges.

I didn't know rather to run or not as about a million niggas from the S.W.A.T. ran up into my shit like black roaches. I couldn't even bust at these cats because my shit was in my jeep. It seemed like everything was going in slow motion as they threw me and Red on the floor. I could hear was this nigga crying about not having nothing to do with it.

I didn't even bother to put up a fight because all I had here was a couple dollars and some jewels. I made sure all the work we had was distributed and what wasn't was down in Delaware. Those dudes had nothing on me.

"You have the right to remain silent. Anything you say can be used against you in the court of law. You have the right to an attorney . . ."

When we got outside, there was a crowd of people standing around wondering what happened. The news got around fast because all the news stations were outside taking pictures and trying to ask me questions. I didn't even bother to try and hide my face.

Fuck it. Let the world know that these niggas is wrong for having me handcuffed like this.

I could see my jeep sitting on top of a police department repo truck, but I still wasn't worried. Both of the guns I had stashed in there were registered to me, and I ain't have no bodies on them, so I was cool.

Moments later we pulled up to the station, and I just found me a comfortable spot in the cell they put me in and waited. I had one phone call. The question is who did I call? Karen or Dave?

Epilogue

Mina

Istayed in the house for about a week after that bullshit went down. I still can't believe those bitches jumped me. It was cool, though. I'd be getting their asses back one by one. I just couldn't let anyone see me with this black eye.

I spoke to Shanna the other day, and by the time she finished telling me all the shit that went down with Jarrell and how he treated her, we were both on the phone in tears. All this on some get money shit, and for what? At the end, we were right back where we started. Do I regret it? Nope, because you gotta learn how to play the game before it plays you.

I got a call two days ago from Karen telling me that Chilae got locked up. That shit had me shocked because I didn't think it all would go down that quickly. I wondered briefly if they had raided the Delaware spot because its mad money stashed up in there, and he can't spend that shit from jail, so I might as well make use of it. I was just glad that the car he got for me was in my name, because when the law starts rounding up shit they comes and takes every damn thing, and I need my whip.

The detectives from Maryland must have kept their word because no one questioned me or Karen about the situation to my knowledge, and I wasn't going to find out why. Karen ain't been the same since her father passed, and she had her hands full running the company so we caught up when we could. She graduates in two weeks so I'm excited for her.

I ran down to check my mail and saw that I had a letter from the health clinic. I hadn't been outside to go back and check on my results from that HIV test that I took, and if they called I didn't know because I didn't bother to answer my home phone or check my messages. Everyone that I needed to talk to called my cell phone.

When I got back upstairs Karen and Shanna were just pulling up. I took a seat on my couch, leaving the door open for them. When they walked in, Karen was holding what looked like a flyer in her hand, and both of their faces held looks of confusion.

"What's wrong with y'all?" I asked them out of curiosity. They were too quiet for my liking.

"The question is what's wrong with you?" Shanna replied, neither of them taking a seat.

"Umm, I'm good. Why you ask?"

Instead of answering, Karen gave me the piece of paper in her hand. I was expecting to see a party flyer or something, but what I saw almost made my heart stop. On the paper was a photo of me smiling on the top, and under it read "this girl is HIV positive." It was a bunch of other shit on the page, but that line was all I could see. It was funny that they brought that paper up at the same time I got a letter from the health center, and that made me wonder how true it was.

"Those papers are all over the damn projects, stuck up on poles, and at the damn store sitting in stacks and shit. Is it real, Mina?" Karen asked with tears in her eyes.

I didn't say anything. I just jumped up and got the letter from the health center that I just pulled from the mailbox.

Ripping the letter open, the page from Quest Diagnostics was on top of two other pages. As I read down the page to find where my tests results were, my hands started to shake and my eyes teared up. As I read the lines that sealed my fate, my heart started beating faster and faster.

"What does it say?" Shanna asked, trying to read the letter over my shoulders.

It was like I had lost my voice. The words started to blur then everything went black. I could hear Shanna and Karen asking me if I was okay, but I was speechless. My worst fear had come true. I was HIV positive, and since we were all screwing around with the same people, that meant it was possible that Karen and Shanna had it, too. I couldn't say a word if I wanted to. I just gave Karen the paper and fell back on the couch.

Karen and Shanna burst into tears, but this was only the beginning. Now me and Karen would have to tell Shanna that we were both fucking Chilae, and that they both had to be tested. All of this just to die early. I swear if I had this time to do it all again I would, but it was too late for all that now. Damn, life sucks.

SNEAK PREVIEW OF

My Little Secret

Coming in September 2008

Ask Yourself

Ask yourself a question . . . have you ever had a session of love making, do you want me? Have you ever been to heaven?
—Raheem DeVaughn

February 9th, 2007

She feels like melted chocolate on my fingertips. The same color from the top of her head to the very tips of her feet. Her nipples are two shades darker than the rest of her, and they make her skin the perfect backdrop against her round breasts. Firm and sweet like two ripe peaches dipped in baker's chocolate. They are a little more than a handful and greatly appreciated. Touching her makes me feel like I've finally found peace on earth, and there is no feeling in the world greater than that.

Right now her eyes are closed and her bottom lip is tightly tucked between her teeth. From my view point between her wide spread legs I can see the beginnings of yet another orgasm playing across her angelic face. These are the moments that make it all worthwhile. Her perfectly arched eyebrows go into a deep frown, and her eyelids flutter slightly. When her head falls back I know she's about to explode.

I move up on my knees so that we are pelvis to pelvis. Both of us are dripping wet from the humidity and the situation. Her legs are up on my shoulders, and her hands are cupping my breasts. I can't tell where her skin begins or where mine ends. As I look down at her, and watch her face go through way too many emotions I smile a little bit. She always did love the dick, and since we've been together she's never had to go without it. Especially since the one I have never goes down.

I'm pushing her tool into her soft folds inch by inch as if it were really apart of me, and her body is alive. I say "her tool" because it belongs to her, and I just enjoy using it on her. Her hip length dreads seem to wrap us in a cocoon of coconut oil and sweat, body heat and moisture, soft moans and tear drops, pleasure and pain until we seemingly burst into an inferno of hot like fire ecstasy. Our chocolate skin is searing to the touch and we melt into each other becoming one. I can't tell where hers begins . . . I can't tell where mine ends.

She smiles . . . her eyes are still closed and she's still shaking from the intensity. I take this opportunity to taste her lips, and to lick the salty sweetness from the side of her neck. My hands begin to explore, and my tongue encircles her dark nipples. She arches her back when my full lips close around her nipple and I began to suck softly as if she's feeding me life from within her soul.

Her hands find there way to my head and become tangled in my soft locks, identical to hers but not as long. I push into her deep, and grind softly against her clit in search of her "j-spot" because it belongs to me, Jada. She speaks my name so soft that I barely heard her. I know she wants me to take what she so willingly gave me, and I want to hear her beg for it.

I start to pull back slowly, and I can feel her body tightening up trying to keep me from moving. One of many soft moans is heard over the low hum of the clock radio that sits next to our bed. I hear slight snatches of Raheem DeVaughn singing about being in heaven, and I'm almost certain he wrote that song for me and my lady.

I open her lips up so that I can have full view of her sensitive pearl. Her body quakes with anticipation from the feel of my warm breath touching it, my mouth just mere inches away. I blow cool air on her stiff clit causing her to tense up briefly, her hands taking hold of my head trying to pull me closer. At this point my mouth is so close to her all I would have to do is twitch my lips to make contact, but I don't . . . I want her to beg for it.

My index finger is making small circles against my own clit, my honey sticky between my legs. The ultimate pleasure is giving pleasure, and I've experienced that on both accounts. My baby can't wait anymore, and her soft pants are turning into low moans. I stick my tongue out, and her clit gladly kisses me back.

Her body responds by releasing a syrupy sweet slickness that I lap up until it's all gone, fucking her with my tongue the way she likes it. I hold her legs up and out to intensify her orgasm because I know she can't handle it that way.

"Does your husband do you like this?" I ask between licks. Before she could answer I wrap my full lips around her clit and suck her into my mouth, swirling my tongue around her hardened bud causing her body to shake.

Snatching a second toy from the side of the bed, I take one hand to part her lips, and I ease her favorite toy (The Rabbit) inside of her. Wishing that the strap-on I was wearing was a real dick so that I could feel her pulsate, I turn the toy on low at first wanting her to receive the ultimate pleasure. In the dark room the glow in the dark toy is lit brightly, the light disappearing inside of her when I push it all the way in.

The head of the curved toy turns in a slow circle while the pearl beads jump around on the inside hitting up against her smooth walls during insertion. When I push the toy in she pushes her pelvis up to receive it, my mouth latched on to her clit like a vice. She moans louder, and I kick the toy up a notch to medium, much to her delight. Removing my mouth from her clit I rotate between flicking my wet tongue across it to heat it, and blowing my breath on it to cool it bringing her to yet another screaming orgasm, followed by strings of *"I love You"* and *"Please Don't Stop."*

Torturing her body slowly, I continue to stimulate her clit while pushing her toy in and out of her on a constant rhythm. When she lifts her legs to her chest I take the opportunity to let the ears on the rabbit toy that we are using do it's job on her clit while my tongue find it's way to her chocolate ass. I bite one cheek at a time replacing it with wet kisses, afterwards sliding my tongue in between to taste her there. Her body squirming underneath me let's me know I've hit the jackpot, and I fuck her with my tongue there also.

She's moaning telling me in a loud whisper that she can't take it anymore. That's my clue to turn the toy up high. The buzzing from the toy matches that of the radio, and with her moans and my pants mixed in we sound like a well-rehearsed orchestra singing a symphony of passion. I allow her to buck against my face while I keep up with the rhythm of the toy, her juice oozing out the sides and forming a puddle under her ass. I'm loving it.

She moans and shakes until the feeling in the pit of her stomach resides and she is able to breath at a normal rate. My lips taste salty/sweet from kissing her body while she tries to get her head together, rubbing the sides of my body up and down in a lazy motion.

Valentine's Day is fast approaching and I have a wonderful evening planned for the two of us. She already promised me that her husband wouldn't be an issue because he'll be out of town that weekend, and besides all that they haven't cele-brated cupid's day since the year after they were married so I didn't even think twice about it. After seven years it should be over for them anyway.

"It's your turn now," she says to me in a husky lust filled voice, and I can't wait for her to take control.

The ultimate pleasure is giving pleasure . . . and man does it feel good both ways. She starts by rubbing her oil-slicked hands over the front of my body, taking extra time around my sensitive nipples before bringing her hands down across my flat stomach. I've since then removed the strap-on dildo, and am completely naked under her hands.

I can still feel her sweat on my skin, and I can still taste her on my lips. Closing my eyes I enjoy the sensual massage that I'm being treated to. After two years of us making love it's still good and gets better every time.

She likes to take her time covering every inch of my body, and I enjoy letting her. She skips past my love box, and starts at my feet massaging my legs from the toes up. When she gets to my pleasure point her fingertips graze the smooth hairless skin there quickly teasing me before she heads back down, and does the same thing with my other limb. My legs are spread apart and lying flat on the bed with her in between relaxing my body with ease. A cool breeze from the cracked window blows across the room every so often caressing my erect nipples making them harder than before until her hands warm them back up again.

She knows when I can't take anymore any she rubs and caresses me until I am begging her to kiss my lips. I can see her smile through half closed eyelids, and she does what I requested. Dipping her head down between my legs she kisses my lips just as I asked, using her tongue to part them so that she could taste my clit. My body goes into mini-convulsions on contact and I am fighting a battle to not cum that I never win.

"Valentine's Day belongs to us right?" I ask her again between moans. I need her to be here. V-Day is for lovers, and her and her husband haven't been that in ages. I deserve it . . . I deserve her. I just don't want this to be a repeat of Christmas or New Years eve.

"Yes, it's yours," she says between kisses on my thigh, and sticking her tongue inside of me. Two of her fingers have found there way inside of my tight walls, and my pelvic area automatically bounces up and down on her hand as my orgasm approaches.

"Tell me you love me," I say to her as my breathing becomes raspy. I fire is spreading across my legs and working its way up to the pit of my stomach. I need her to tell me before I explode.

"I love you," she says and at the moment she places her tongue in my slit I release my honey all over her tongue.

It feels like I am on the Tea Cup ride at the amusement park as my orgasm jerks my body uncontrollably and it feels like the room is spinning. She is sucking and slurping my clit while the weight of her body holds the bottom half of me captive. I'm practically screaming and begging her to stop and just when I think I'm about to check out of here she lets my clit go.

I take a few more minutes to get my head together, allowing her to pull me into her and rub my back. It's moment s like this that makes it all worthwhile. We lay like that for a while longer listening to each other breath, and much to my dismay she slides my head from where it was resting on her arm and gets up out of the bed.

I don't say a word. I just lie on the bed and watch her get dressed. I swear everything she does is so graceful, like there's a rhythm riding behind it. Pretty soon she is dressed and standing beside the bed looking down at me. She smiles and I smile back, not worried because she promised me our lover's day, and that's only a week away.

"So, Valentine's Day belongs to me, right?" I ask her again just to be certain.

"Yes, it belongs to you."

We kiss one last time, and I can still taste my honey on her lips. She already knows the routine, locking the bottom lock behind her. Just thinking about her makes me so horny, and I pick up her favorite toy to finish the job. Five more days, and it'll be on again.

About the Author

Anna J is a writer from Philly who also walks the run way in her spare time as a full-figured model. Co-author of Stories To Excite You: Menage Quad, Anna put her writing skills to the test in this hot collaboration that was released during the fall of 2004.

Her debut novel, an *Essence* magazine best selling novel, **My Woman His Wife** is high on the charts and a god read for those that enjoy a steamy love affair with a little bit of drama to boot. The contuation of the drama can be found in **The Aftermath,** Anna J's second novel under Q-Boro Books where Monica is still off the chain, and drama is still a main factor.

If your Anna J cravings still aren't satisfied, you can also find other hot stories of hers in *Fetish: A Compilation of Erotic Stories, Morning Noon and Night: Can't Get Enough, Sexin' and Flexin': Erotic Short Stories,* and *Fantasy: Erotic Short Stories* in bookstores nationwide.

Anna J. was born and raised in Philly, where she still resides and is at work on her next novel, *My Little Secret.*

LOOK FOR MORE HOT TITLES FROM

Q-BORO
BOOKS

DARK KARMA - JUNE 2007
$14.95
ISBN 1-933967-12-9

What if the criminal was forced to live the horror that they caused? The drug dealer finds himself in the body of the drug addict and he suffers through the withdrawals, living on the street, the beatings, the rapes and the hunger. The thief steals the rent money and becomes the victim that finds herself living on the street and running for her life and the murderer becomes the victim's father and he deals with the death of a son and a grieving mother.

GET MONEY CHICKS - SEPTEMBER 2007
$14.95
ISBN 1-933967-17-X

For Mina, Shanna, and Karen, using what they had to get what they wanted was always an option. Best friends since day one, they always had a thing for the hottest gear, luxurious lifestyles, and the ballers who made it all possible. All of this changes for Mina when a tragedy makes her open her eyes to the way she's living. Peer pressure and loyalty to her girls collide with her own morality, sending Mina into a no-win situation.

AFTER-HOURS GIRLS - AUGUST 2007
$14.95
ISBN 1-933967-16-1

Take part in this tale of two best friends, Lisa and Tosha, as they stalk the nightclubs and after-hours joints of Detroit searching for excitement, money, and temporary companionship. These two divas stand tall until the unforgivable Motown streets catch up to them. One must fall. You, the reader, decide which.

THE LAST CHANCE - OCTOBER 2007
$14.95
ISBN 1-933967-22-6

Running their L.A. casino has been rewarding for Luke Chance and his three brothers. But recently it seems like everyone is trying to get a piece of the pie. An impending hostile takeover of their casino could leave them penniless and possibly dead. That is, until their sister Keilah Chance comes home for a short visit. Keilah is not only beautiful, but she also can be ruthless. Will the Chance family be able to protect their family dynasty?

Traci must find a way to complete her journey out of her first and only failed

LOOK FOR MORE HOT TITLES FROM

Q-BORO
B O O K S

LOOK FOR MORE HOT TITLES FROM

Q-BORO
B O O K S

OBSESSION 101
$6.99
ISBN 0977733548

After a horrendous trauma. Rashawn Ams is left pregnant and flees town to give birth to her son and repair her life after confiding in her psychiatrist. After her return to her life, her town, and her classroom, she finds herself the target of an intrusive secret admirer who has plans for her.

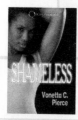

SHAMELESS- OCTOBER 2006
$6.99
ISBN 0977733513

Kyle is sexy, single, and smart; Jasmyn is a hot and sassy drama queen. These two complete opposites find love - or something real close to it - while away at college. Jasmyn is busy wreaking havoc on every man she meets. Kyle, on the other hand, is trying to walk the line between his faith and all the guilty pleasures being thrown his way. When the partying college days end and Jasmyn tests HIV positive, reality sets in.

MISSED OPPORTUNITIES - MARCH 2007
$14.95
ISBN 1933967013

Missed Opportunities illustrates how true-to-life characters must face the consequences of their poor choices. Was each decision worth the opportune cost? LaTonya Y. Williams delivers yet another account of love, lies, and deceit all wrapped up into one powerful novel.

ONE DEAD PREACHER - MARCH 2007
$14.95
ISBN 1933967021

Smooth operator and security CEO David Price sets out to protect the sexy, smart, and saucy Sugar Owens from her husband, who happens to be a powerful religious leader. Sugar isn't as sweet as she appears, however, and in a twisted turn of events, the preacher man turns up dead and Price becomes the prime suspect.

LOOK FOR

Attention Writers:

Writers looking to get their books published can view our submission guidelines by visiting our website at: *www.QBOROBOOKS.com*

What we're looking for: Contemporary fiction in the tradition of Darrien Lee, Carl Weber, Anna J., Zane, Mary B. Morrison, Noire, Lolita Files, etc; groundbreaking mainstream contemporary fiction.

We prefer email submissions to: candace@qborobooks.com in MS Word, PDF, or rtf format only. However, if you wish to send the submission via snail mail, you can send it to:

Q-BORO BOOKS Acquisitions Department
165-41A Baisley Blvd., Suite 4. Mall #1
Jamaica, New York 11434

*** By submitting your work to Q-Boro Books, you agree to hold Q-Boro books harmless and not liable for publishing similar works as yours that we may already be considering or may consider in the future. ***

1. Submissions will not be returned.
2. Do not contact us for status updates. If we are interested in receiving your full manuscript, we will contact you via email or telephone.
3. Do not submit if the entire manuscript is not complete.

Due to the heavy volume of submissions, if these requirements are not followed, we will not be able to process your submission.